CW01496769

GREEN SPECULATIONS

GREEN SPECULATIONS

SCIENCE FICTION AND TRANSFORMATIVE ENVIRONMENTALISM

ERIC C. OTTO

 THE OHIO STATE UNIVERSITY PRESS • COLUMBUS

Library of Congress Cataloging-in-Publication Data
Otto, Eric C., 1976–
   Green speculations : science fiction and transformative environmentalism / Eric C. Otto.
      p. cm.
   Includes bibliographical references and index.
   ISBN 978-0-8142-1203-5 (cloth : alk. paper)—ISBN 978-0-8142-9305-8 (cd-rom)
   1. Science fiction—History and criticism. 2. Ecofiction—History and criticism.
   3. Ecology in literature. 4. Environmentalism in literature. 5. Ecofeminism in literature.
   I. Title.
   PN3433.6.O88 2012
   809.3'8762—dc23
                              201201828

Cover design by Thao Thai
Text design by Juliet Williams
Type set in Adobe Sabon
Printed by Thomson-Shore, Inc.

♾ The paper used in this publication meets the minimum requirements of the American
National Standard for Information Sciences—Permanence of Paper for Printed Library
Materials. ANSI Z39.48-1992.

9   8   7   6   5   4   3   2   1

FOR TRICIA AND BEATRICE

CONTENTS

ACKNOWLEDGMENTS   ix

INTRODUCTION   1

CHAPTER ONE   The Subversive Subject of Ecology   19

CHAPTER TWO   Ecotopia, Ecodystopia, and the Visions of Deep Ecology   45

CHAPTER THREE   Ecofeminist Theories of Liberation   74

CHAPTER FOUR   Ecosocialist Critique   100

AFTERWORD   122

NOTES   127

BIBLIOGRAPHY   134

INDEX   143

ACKNOWLEDGMENTS

I would like to thank everyone who helped me bring *Green Speculations* to fruition. This book went from idea to first draft under the enthusiastic guidance of Andy Gordon, and I received valuable input from Sid Dobrin, Bron Taylor, and Phil Wegner. As I revised the manuscript further, I was fortunate to get astute feedback from Keira Hambrick, Patrick Murphy, Tonia Payne, and Andrew Wilkinson. The two anonymous reviewers of the manuscript offered detailed insights that challenged me to think more deeply about my arguments and analyses, and they encouraged me to pursue lines of inquiry that I initially overlooked but that have added much to the final book. I am especially grateful for the attention that Rebecca Totaro and Jim Wohlpart of Florida Gulf Coast University gave to this project. Along with Peter Blaze Corcoran, Maria Roca, and Joe Wisdom, Rebecca and Jim have mentored me for many years and put me on the path that led to this book. Also at FGCU, Kim Jackson and Doug Harrison kindly offered me their feedback in the proposal stage of this project. At The Ohio State University Press, Sandy Crooms and Maggie Diehl have been wonderful to work with, and wonderfully patient and supportive. I would also like to thank copyeditor Kristen Ebert-Wagner, text designer Juliet Williams, and cover designer Thao Thai for being the best at what they do.

Parts of *Green Speculations* originally appeared in the following publications:

"The Mars Trilogy and the Leopoldian Land Ethic," from *Kim Stanley Robinson Maps the Unimaginable: Critical Essays* © 2009 Edited by William J. Burling. Series Editors Donald E. Palumbo and C. W. Sullivan III by permission of McFarland & Company, Inc., Box 611, Jefferson, NC 28640. www.mcfarlandpub.com.

"Science Fiction and Transformative Ecological Politics: Biocentric Wisdom in Three Early Works," from *The Everyday Fantastic: Essays on Science Fiction and Human Being* © 2008 *Edited by* Michael Berman by permission of Cambridge Scholars Publishing, 15 Angerton Gardens, Newcastle, NE5 2JA, UK. www.c-s-p.org.

"Kim Stanley Robinson's *Mars* Trilogy and the Leopoldian Land Ethic," from *Utopian Studies* 14.2 (2003): 118–35.

I thank McFarland & Company, Cambridge Scholars Publishing, and *Utopian Studies* for their permission to use this material.

My final words of appreciation go to those closest to me, those whose contributions to this book didn't come in the form of scholarly advice or editorial feedback, but instead as years of encouragement, companionship, laughter, and so much more: my grandparents, my parents, my siblings, and my wife and daughter. My parents, Sandy and Joe, have supported me in every way possible, and for this I cannot thank them enough. Most of all, my wife and best friend, Tricia, and my intelligent and beautiful daughter, Beatrice, have given me nothing but love as I have worked on this project. I am thrilled to dedicate *Green Speculations* to them.

G REEN *SPECULATIONS* attends to the intersections between transformative environmentalism and science fiction literature. Transformative environmentalism comprises a number of movements that have emerged since Rachel Carson's *Silent Spring* initiated modern environmentalism in 1962. These movements offer theories about the ideological origins of and solutions to environmental degradation. They interpret environmental problems not as "problems *of* the environment," to apply language from educator Noel Gough, "but, rather, [as] problems of modern scientific, industrial, and predominately Western society's transactions with the earth" ("Neuromancing" 5). Nor are transformative environmentalism's efforts directed toward "'end-of-the-pipe' outputs of environmentally destructive behavior," efforts that law professor Lisa Heinzerling notes characterize environmental policy today (1446). Informed by the life sciences, which remind us of our dependencies and effects upon nonhuman nature and ecosystemic processes, as well as by various schools of philosophical thought, transformative movements instead work to change the *inputs* of such destruction, "the individual attitudes, habits, and behavior that lead us all to want and demand things that necessitate environmental damage" (Heinzerling 1446).

1

And no doubt, the environment is damaged. Writing in a 2009 issue of *Nature* with twenty-eight colleagues representing a range of scientific disciplines, global sustainability expert Johan Rockström points to "Earth-system processes and associated thresholds which, if crossed, could generate unacceptable environmental change" (472). Rockström and his colleagues determine that the thresholds or boundaries for carbon dioxide emissions, species extinction, and nitrogen pollution have already been crossed, threatening the global environmental stability of the last ten thousand years. Recent measurements of atmospheric carbon dioxide show the level of the greenhouse gas to be eleven percent higher than science indicates is the highest acceptable amount to avoid sea-level rise, more widespread drought, and other climatic consequences. The rate of species loss is currently at one hundred to one thousand times "what could be considered natural," a rate that science tells us is leading to drastic and extensive ecological damage (Rockström 474). The agricultural use of nitrogen—which along with the use of other "nutrient-associated pollutants" such as phosphorus and sulfur "has emerged as one of the most important drivers of ecosystem change in terrestrial, freshwater, and coastal ecosystems"—now exceeds safe levels by almost two hundred fifty percent (Duraiappah et al. 8). In addition to these crises, others on the horizon include the effects of phosphorus pollution and ocean acidification, as well as the ecosystemic alterations brought on by excessive freshwater and land use.

That science fiction offers an important literary contribution to discussions of such environmental degradations and their sources has been previously recognized. I would like to insert this book into a family of commentary that collectively seeks to locate within the genre those texts and generic characteristics most valuable for environmentalist thinking. Gough, for example, highlights the merits of science fiction as environmental literature against critics who undervalue its environmentalist commitments or who find the genre's conventional tropes (e.g., "the assumption that virtually all problems are amenable to technical solutions") to outweigh these commitments ("Playing" 409). He calls science fiction "an environmental literature par excellence" for its frequent attention to the ways in which environments, or "externalities," affect its characters, in contrast to realist fictions that put such externalities in the background to favor character-driven action ("Playing" 411). Another advocate of the genre, Ursula K. Heise writes in a 1999 letter to *Publications of the Modern Language Association of America*, "science fiction is one of the genres that have most persistently and most daringly engaged environmental questions and their challenge to our vision of the future" (1097). Supporting this assertion in her recent book *Sense of Place and Sense of Planet,* Heise highlights several works of science fiction (esp., John Brunner's *Stand on Zanzibar* [1968] and David Brin's *Earth* [1990]) in making the case for a shift in American environmentalism from its historical attraction to localism toward a globalism that would ground questions of local sense of place in a cosmopolitan ecological awareness.

Patrick D. Murphy, who consistently pursues new frontiers for ecocritical analysis, has been at the forefront of fleshing out science fiction's environmentalist potential. He finds in the genre "several varieties of nature and environmental engagement": there are science fiction novels that (1) "provide factual information about nature and human–nature interactions as well as provide thematically environmentalist extrapolations of conflict and crisis based on such information," (2) "provide analogous depictions of ecosystems and human interaction with such systems," and (3) "demonstrate the disastrous consequences of exploitive relationships between humans and other humans, humans and other sentient beings, and humans and ecosystems in which they are an exotic" (*Farther* 41). Moreover, in *The Cross, the Plow and the Skyline* political scientist Ernest J. Yanarella articulates the ways in which science fiction appropriates the Judeo-Christian apocalyptic tradition, the Jeffersonian pastoral tradition, and the technocentric, urban tradition to reflect on the viability of current sociopolitical formations as well as to imagine new ones. About science fiction Yanarella writes, "as critical political theory [science fiction] often issues in a powerful critique of existing social institutions, cultural norms, and prevailing structures of power. In the process, it opens up alternative ways of socially constructing the lived world and disclosing utopian possibilities latent in the present and emergent in that different possible future" (6). With this general observation and his subsequent and more specific political and ecocritical analyses of a range of science fiction texts, Yanarella attests to the value of the genre as a "surprisingly sophisticated intellectual guide" for addressing important sociopolitical and cultural questions, especially those of environment (304). Finally, Lawrence Buell notes in his 2005 study of environmental literary criticism, "For half a century science fiction has taken a keen, if not consistent interest in ecology, in planetary endangerment, in environmental ethics, in humankind's relation to the nonhuman world" (56). Buell sees as particularly important those science fiction works that defy the genre's technocentric hubris, works that suggest "we're probably stuck, whether we like it or not, with the world we've got" (e.g., Ursula K. Le Guin's *The Lathe of Heaven* [1971] and Karen Tei Yamashita's *Through the Arc of the Rain Forest* [1990]) (58).

Anticipating these more recent scholarly treatments of science fiction's environmentalist promise, Kim Stanley Robinson writes in his introduction to the 1994 anthology *Future Primitive*,

> the process of rethinking the future, of inventing a new consensus vision of what it might be . . . is happening all across contemporary culture, in a great variety of forms, with names like the environmental movement, green political parties, deep ecology, the land ethic, landscape restoration, sociobiology, sustainable agriculture, ecofeminism, social ecology, bioregionalism, animal liberation, steady-state economics. All these movements contain efforts to reimagine a sustainable human society. (10–11)

The range of groups expressing environmental concern today is indeed broad, comprising political parties, philosophers, natural scientists, and economists who are increasingly understanding, experiencing, and responding to anthropogenic environmental degradation and its costs. Adding to this range, Robinson declares, "Science fiction is part of this work" (11). Taking seriously Robinson's assertion, as well as the claims of the aforementioned scholars, *Green Speculations* highlights science fiction works that can be read as constituting a subgeneric category of science fiction—an *environmental science fiction*—and that share with transformative movements an interest in environmental degradation and its origins. Among these works are future histories, postapocalyptic fictions, utopias, and more. This book communicates the environmentalist possibilities of science fiction to students, teachers, and scholars of the genre, of environmental literature, of environmental studies, and of other (inter)disciplines interested in the value of aesthetic and imaginative representations of and for the planetary present and future. It is my effort to affirm environmental writer Christopher Cokinos's recent argument that "readers of environmental literature concerned with the future of the planet"—and I will add, with the present of the planet—"might do well to put down [the works of the naturalist John] Muir and pick up some science fiction" (par. 16).

Subsequent to an exploration in the second part of this introduction of key points of intersection between the literary strategies of science fiction and those of more conventional environmentalist discourse, the following chapters take up the issue of environmental science fiction's place as a body of literature that reflects, sometimes prefigures, and in its finest moments theorizes transformative environmentalism and its assorted

move from
past→future

targets of criticism. The representative texts I examine provide narrative accounts of environmental issues and various schools of environmental thought, in several cases doing so before such matters made it into the consciousness of a larger group of activists and scholars. They can thus serve environmentalism as educational instruments to inform readers about environmental issues and criticisms of anthropocentrism, techno-centric patriarchy, and growth-centered capitalism in transformative envi-ronmentalism's deep ecology, ecofeminist, and ecosocialist movements. But beyond this pedagogic quality, environmental science fiction some-times theorizes these criticisms of dominant Western ideology (again, even prefiguratively), creating transformative environmentalism in addi-tion to reflecting it. My first chapter addresses instances when (proto)envi-ronmental science fiction exhibits clear engagements with the idea that humans are "part of nature," which is expected given that Darwinian biology was the prevailing scientific paradigm of the late nineteenth and early twentieth centuries. It then examines Frank Herbert's *Dune* (1965) as a literary moment when this idea reaches its full maturity. Among other problems that *Dune* raises about part-of-nature thinking, the novel ques-tions whether underscoring the biological verdict that humans are part of nature—something that transformative environmentalism, following espe-cially Rachel Carson, frequently does—will have any sort of transforma-tive effect on human-centered colonialist cultures, for such cultures have interpreted this verdict to justify their oppression of indigenous peoples.

In chapter 2, I borrow language from utopian studies and the deep ecology movement to examine the value of ecotopia and ecodystopia for catalyzing sweeping changes to a number of modern trends that according to deep ecology are rooted in an entrenched anthropocentric value sys-tem. Representing ecotopian fiction, Ernest Callenbach's *Ecotopia* (1975) and Marge Piercy's *Woman on the Edge of Time* (1976) criticize human population and economic growth, monoculture agriculture, hyperindivid-ualism, and producer-driven consumer culture by measuring their effects against more deliberate and ecologically conscious manners of existence. As ecodystopias, Brunner's *Stand on Zanzibar* and *The Sheep Look Up* (1972) call for similar cultural analysis by using a literary strategy dif-ferent from that employed in the ecotopias; their dystopian obligation to envision nightmarish worlds enables them to assert a warning regarding what we do to the environment today *and* to think about the unintended consequences of deep ecological, ecotopian dreaming, such as encourag-ing a disproportionate focus on overpopulation as well as inciting physical ecoterror.

Tracing various genres of environmental feminism as they are represented and theorized in Sally Miller Gearhart's *The Wanderground* (1979), Le Guin's *Always Coming Home* (1985), and Joan Slonczewski's *A Door Into Ocean* (1986), chapter 3 engages ecofeminism as a rich critical discourse that offers a number of important perspectives on gender and human–nonhuman relationships. Gearhart's novel illustrates *cultural* ecofeminism, arguing that an innate woman–nature link must be embraced as a way of confronting the social and environmental problems of patriarchal culture. *Rational* feminists object to such essentialism. To say women are more connected to nature than men is to perpetuate dominant stereotypes of women that have been used to oppress them in cultures where nature is devalued. Le Guin and Slonczewski seem deeply aware of this issue, both asserting the artifactual nature of gender categories and their relative levels of socially constructed naturalness. But while *Always Coming Home* and *A Door Into Ocean* challenge the cultural ecofeminist stance about women and nonhuman nature, as *dialectical* ecofeminist texts they also declare the critical possibility of socially constructed "feminine" ways of knowing and being in the world.

Finally, chapter 4 briefly reaches back to several of the works examined in the previous chapters and highlights additional ones in the study of what I believe is the most powerful and urgent collective interest of environmental science fiction and the previously discussed schools of transformative thought: the capitalist mode of economic production. While George R. Stewart's *Earth Abides* (1949) and Herbert's *Dune*—both discussed in chapter 1—do not participate in the types of environmentalist appraisals of capitalism prevalent since their publications, their attention to the myth of human supremacy and the dynamics of consolidated political power, respectively, foreshadow such critiques. More openly critical of capital, Callenbach's imaginary Ecotopians practice a stable-state economy that counters the capitalist exploitation of nature, and the citizens of Piercy's Mattapoisett realize a rustic and healthy society that defies the capitalist myth of economic progress. Brunner's dystopian works highlight the dangers of capitalist supremacy, exposing the growth economy and its consumerist ethos, and the corrupt, masculine spaces of Gearhart's, Le Guin's, and Slonczewski's ecofeminist novels are likewise capitalist spaces. Further, although philosophies such as deep ecology and cultural ecofeminism locate the cause of environmental degradation not in patterns of economic production but instead in nonmaterial value systems, it can be argued that the environmental degradation they respond to in their unique ways is driven by the dominant economic paradigm. Ecosocialism takes on this paradigm, and chapter 4's specific analytical focus is on the nascent ecosocialist critique of capital's symbolic and material activities as presented in Frederik Pohl and C. M. Kornbluth's *The Space Merchants* (1952), the critique of capitalist imperialist expansion in Le Guin's *The Word for World Is Forest* (1972), and Kim Stanley Robinson's ecosocialist vision in the *Mars* trilogy (1993, 1994, 1996).

At the level of literary strategy the writing and reading of science fiction is guided by certain assumptions and tendencies that also guide the writing and reading of much environmental nonfiction, the mode of environmentalist discourse that dominates the canon of works that engage with issues of environmental degradation, community activism, wilderness defense, environmental ethics, inhabitation, and more.[1] First, both science fiction and environmental nonfiction often employ a rhetoric of *estrangement* and *extrapolation* that compels readers toward critical reflection on seemingly invisible everyday attitudes and habits. Lauded by the Formalist literary critic Viktor Shklovsky as *ostranenie,* estrangement in one sense is the creative effort to isolate our perceptions of objects from our prior knowledge of objects and thus to revivify these objects as having aesthetic value beyond our routine, practical experiences of them.[2] In this regard, estrangement-as-defamiliarization leads us to the poetic experience of real and imagined marvels that I review below as having also an ethical effect. But estrangement is a varied narrative strategy with other practiced applications in both environmental nonfiction and environmental science fiction.

For example, very early in his 1948 (proto)environmentalist treatise *Our Plundered Planet,* which has been called "one of the first—perhaps the very first—of what would later grow into a minor industry, namely, popular environmental books," conservationist Fairfield Osborn speculates about whether Earth's human civilization is existing as successfully as another human civilization living elsewhere in the universe (Jamison and Eyerman 64). Of course he cannot know the answer to this question; he promptly leaves behind "the difficulties of attempting to find specific clues regarding man's existence and future destiny from the perspective of the universe as a whole" and shifts instead to known science, to clues regarding humanity's viability from the evidence provided in then current scientific literature (Osborn 10). But Osborn's thought experiment is an estranging one that enables his subsequent appraisals of modern humanity.[3] By initially asking his questions about humanity from the distanced "perspective of the universe," rather than from our immediate perspective as embedded participants in the very things we need to evaluate, he invites a resituating of our point of view to compel more open and objective observation. Osborn invites us to consider ourselves as a faraway observer might consider us. This effort to estrange thus approaches the "cognitive estrangement" famously coined by Darko Suvin in his *Metamorphoses of Science Fiction,* in which whatever is made strange—in Osborn's case, our observational perspective—is made so to enable an appraisal of our actual world.

Suvin's basic argument, as Carl Freedman aptly sums it up, is that for fiction to estrange cognitively it must first create "an alternative fictional world that . . . [refuses] to take our mundane environment for granted" (16–17). To estrange in this sense is for the narrative to break the rules for what we understand as normal daily life by introducing "a strange newness," or a *"novum"* (Suvin, *Metamorphoses* 4). But in science fiction it is this estrangement in dialectical relationship with cognition that defines the genre and is indispensable to it. Cognition "enables the science-fictional text to account rationally for its imagined world and for the connections as well as disconnections of the latter to our own empirical world" (Freedman 17). Pure estrangement severs us entirely from our experienced reality and we are left in fantasy. Pure cognition, if not directed toward contemplating the presence of the *novum* in the narrative, severs us entirely from imagined possibility and we are left in a reality indistinguishable from our own. When estrangement and cognition interact, however, we are encouraged to assess the *novum* and consider its origins or conditions of existence. What is it? Why is it there? How did it come to be?

Rachel Carson's science-fiction-like effort to estrange her readers in the opening chapter of *Silent Spring,* "A Fable for Tomorrow," is one with a cognitive dimension. Although the dystopian imaginings in the chapter perhaps operated too much in 1962 within an apocalyptic master narrative to convince especially dismissive readers about *Silent Spring*'s legitimacy, it nonetheless represents a significant rhetorical move on Carson's part—one which, given the historical consequences of the book, must not have been excessively offensive.[4] Into a pastoral Anytown, USA, Carson introduces "a strange blight," the result of "Some evil spell" that kills everything in its path (2). But the evil spell is not the treachery of, say, mythological imps; nor does its resultant affliction presage a supernatural and inescapable doomsday event. Such fantasies would discourage the cognitive operation that for Carson ultimately connects the anomalous calamity, the *novum,* of her imagined town to everyday procedure in real towns across the country. Making the connection obvious she writes, "No witchcraft, no enemy action had silenced the rebirth of new life in this stricken world. The people had done it themselves" (3). To paraphrase science fiction scholarship on cognitive estrangement, in "A Fable for Tomorrow" the familiar state of affairs in the small-town American story is narratively interrupted to expose the danger of an otherwise unnoticed custom: the indiscriminate, seemingly obligatory use of insecticides.[5]

As these examples show, two founding writers of environmental nonfiction embraced one of science fiction's most effective and fundamental narrative strategies. Given Suvin's position as a Marxist scholar who therefore theorized cognitive estrangement within the critical tradition most attentive to science fiction's utopian subgenre, it is fitting that works of environmental utopian and dystopian science fiction—or ecotopian and ecodystopian fiction—employ cognitive estrangement prominently toward an environmentalist end. In Piercy's *Woman on the Edge of Time* the ecotopian future town of Mattapoisett exhibits some estranging characteristics, if viewed from the perspective of mainstream modern society: cooperative technological planning, organic public gardens, compostable diapers for infants. Every one of these estrangements in the author's imaginary ecotopian community provokes cognitive reflection on the viability of what they are replacing, because contemplating them requires us to recall our own society's models. Precisely by not embracing a cooperative technological planning that assures a more mindful, sustainable, and ethical use of technology, today's dominant ideology supports technological planning centralized in absentee corporate headquarters and realized in perpetually obsolete and disposable consumer objects, as well as in increasingly more powerful weapons of war. Precisely by not embracing organic methods and public ownership, prevailing ideology supports the private ownership of food that provides sustenance not to local communities but to people shopping in grocery stores hundreds or thousands of miles away from mechanized farms. Mattapoisett's ecotopian *nova* enable the critical interrogation of the social reality undergirded by dominant ideology.

The estrangements discussed so far (e.g., Carson's "strange blight," Mattapoisett's cooperative planning, organic gardens, etc.) are strange to us as readers who read within particular modern and Western social and historical contexts, and in our efforts to make sense of them we are lead toward critical scrutiny of these contexts. But as film scholar Simon Spiegel observes, often in science fiction the estrangement effect happens when something we fully comprehend as readers turns out to be strange for those in the fictional world of the narrative. Discussing this "*diegetic estrangement*," Spiegel cites the scene in the 1973 film *Soylent Green* when the protagonist, Detective Thorn, responds with "ecstatic joy" to the water running from the bathroom faucet of a luxury apartment (375). Running water is not a *novum* to an audience who uses such faucets every day; but we experience the working faucet as strange, because Thorn's reaction contradicts the normal response to running water that we expect. Contemplating the scene, we realize that the story must take place in world where water is scarce or its access tightly controlled. Another example of this type of estrangement takes place in Paolo Bacigalupi's "The Calorie Man" (2005). With its "megadonts," "IP men," and "Cheshires," the story is loaded with the kinds of strange *nova* that demand our comprehension and in every case encourage our reflection on the implications of genetic engineering. Suburbs and gas station signs, however, are not new to our experience, yet they are presented in the narrative as strange to its characters and setting. The implication of these diegetic estrangements, then, is that suburbs and gas stations are artifacts of a previous time, a time when oil flowed freely and its use structured the possibilities of economic and social life.

Soylent Green and "The Calorie Man" are ecodystopias; whatever the strategy of estrangement they exercise, they imagine future consequences of present-day activities, provoking critical reflection on these activities. The cognitive dimensions of ecodystopian estrangements often result from another strategic intersection between environmental nonfiction and environmental science fiction: extrapolation. In a 2008 interview by environmental journalist Michelle Nijhuis, Bacigalupi defines his role as a science fiction writer in contrast to the role of his interviewer:

> The speculative process, the process of going two or three steps down the road beyond what you can actually report, oftentimes [gives us] the information we really need to know. And it seems like scientists are inherently conservative, and science journalists are inherently conservative, because you don't want to be wrong. But that's where I can get involved as a science fiction writer. I don't have to be right, exactly, [but] I need to illustrate. I need to illustrate a feeling or experience so that people can say, "Does that seem like something we want to be going toward?"

Patrick D. Murphy makes a similar observation about extrapolation in science fiction that, like Bacigalupi's, can be read also as an observation about its use in environmental nonfiction: "extrapolation emphasizes that the present and the future are interconnected—what we do now will be reflected in the future, and, therefore, we have no alibi for avoiding addressing the results of our actions today" ("The Non-Alibi" 263). Extrapolation is one of environmentalism's favored critical strategies. Connecting the present *now* to a possible *then*, Osborn studied the practices of his contemporary society and projected these practices into the future. Carson did the same, as did the Club of Rome in its 1972 report *The Limits to Growth*, an influential scientific effort to model the long-term consequences of population and economic growth. Certainly, to "meet the needs of the present without compromising the ability of future generations to meet their own needs," sustainability movements require prefigurative, extrapolative thinking (World Commission 43).[6]

In *The Sheep Look Up* John Brunner shares the effort of environmental nonfiction to project from present trends an image of possible things to come, and the ensuing ecodystopia exhibits estrangements opposite those of Piercy's Mattapoisett: food scarcity, high population, contaminated beaches. The book's extrapolations lead to critical reflections on "our actions today." But we cannot stop at the idea that extrapolative narratives are valuable only because they imagine the future consequences of these actions. They are also valuable because they confront us with descriptions of the present, even if imaginatively rendered. To read extrapolative work as envisioning the possible future is to overlook the fact that the social and ecological discord referenced in such fiction and nonfiction is in many places already a reality, though perhaps not immediately apparent to certain readers. To read extrapolative work as instead descriptive is to recognize the fiction and nonfiction as representing this already existing though spatially distant reality. So while on the one hand Bacigalupi is right in raising the speculative question "'Does that seem like something we want to be going toward?'" it is also important to ask of science fiction and environmentalism's extrapolative moments "'Does that seem like something we should do something about right now?'" This spatial version of extrapolation could be called *global awareness,* and it is one of environmental science fiction's primary cultural functions.

Finally, in addition to estrangement and extrapolation, an attention to the *sense of wonder,* to the affective experience of the marvelous, is another intersecting convention between environmental science fiction and environmental nonfiction, though one that is not without complexities and complications. Writers of environmental nonfiction often underscore experiences of natural wonder as life-affirming, transformational experiences.

In her July 1956 *Woman's Home Companion* article, "Help Your Child to Wonder," for example, Carson reflects on her and her young nephew's "spine-tingling response" to "elemental things"—to the night, the ocean, the ghost crabs roaming the beach (25). She concludes, "Those who contemplate the beauty of the earth find reserves of strength that will endure as long as life lasts" (48). Similarly, Edward Abbey notes of Utah's Delicate Arch, its significance lies

> in the power of the odd and unexpected to startle the senses and surprise the mind out of their ruts of habit, to compel us into a reawakened awareness of the wonderful—that which is full of wonder.
>
> A weird, lovely, fantastic object out of nature like Delicate Arch has the curious ability to remind us—like rock and sunlight and wind and wilderness—that *out there* is a different world, older and greater and deeper by far than ours, a world which surrounds and sustains the little world of men as sea and sky surround and sustain a ship. The shock of the real. For a little while we are again able to see, as the child sees, a world of marvels. (45)

Environmental philosopher Kathleen Dean Moore believes that for us to experience wonder at the sight of crabs or geological features, to find in them strength or reawakening surprise, we must be receptive to the stories they tell, and thus be willing to listen and perceive without human egotism or possessiveness. Wonder thus leads to what might be called an *ethics of ecological difference,* analogous to feminist philosopher Luce Irigaray's "ethics of sexual difference," in which wonder is the quality that "beholds what it sees always as if for the first time, never taking hold of the other as its object. It does not try to seize, possess, or reduce this object, but leaves it subjective, still free" (14).

Against many critics who are skeptical of the literary merit of wonder in science fiction, largely because it classifies the genre as one geared toward provoking indeterminate emotion, David Sandner offers a similar and convincing argument for the presence of the marvelous in science fiction.[7] In his article "'Habituated to the Vast'" Sandner, a fantasy author and scholar, recalls Samuel Taylor Coleridge's endorsement of fantastic literature as a way to furnish the intellect with a comprehension of and affection for the whole. Engaged by the fictional wonders of science fiction—a genre in the fantastic mode—the imagination is trained to encounter this total, sensual world; for, wonders such as alien landscapes, the species who occupy these landscapes, or even Earth landscapes made strange through a science-fictional plot device represent a beyond-human that we must welcome, first to comprehend the fiction, then ultimately, as a result of our receptiveness, to be in an actual world comprising much more than the human species. Importantly, Sandner underscores the indissoluble relationship between the human imagination and the actual world, between suspending disbelief while encountering fictional representation and living out a real respect for the ecosystems we inhabit. Wonders in science fiction *do* provoke emotion, which, as Sandner says of imagination in general, is "a 'natural' process, embodied and so inseparable from the physical" (286).

Nevertheless, the resistance that sense of wonder has received as a definitional concept for science fiction is useful, especially if we consider it alongside environmentalist interpretations of the phenomenon. On the one hand many environmental writers share the conviction that experiencing the awe-inspiring beyond, whether real or imagined in fiction, results in a more ethical perception of and behavior toward nonhuman nature. On the other hand the science fiction scholars who remain skeptical about the validity of using the sense of wonder to define the genre do so because they are rightly unsure about what produces wonder in the first place. Depending on a number of anecdotal factors a reader of science fiction might find a work's technological marvels as breathtaking as—or more breathtaking than—its representations of the nonhuman marvelous.

For example, through the character Frank Vanderwal in Kim Stanley Robinson's second installment of the Science in the Capital trilogy, *Fifty Degrees Below* (2005), we experience the park-turned-wilderness that Frank willingly calls home: "Out in the park proper the forest now seemed wilderness, with most human sign snowed over or overgrown or flooded away. It was a whole world. Firelight in the distance the only touch of humanity. A kind of Mirkwood or primeval forest, every tree Yggdrasil, and Frank the Green Man" (356). The tableau here is sublime, recalling the woods of Norse mythology, and in these woods Frank achieves "a kind of ecstatic state, a new realm of joy" appropriately supported in the novel with a quotation from the journals of transcendentalist Ralph Waldo Emerson (404). Frank feels Abbey's "odd" and Carson's wonder. And as readers of Frank's experience we feel the beyond-oneself of the wild world. But later in the novel Frank witnesses another wonder, the "grand exercise in planetary engineering" that is the dumping of five hundred million tons of salt into the North Atlantic in an effort to restart a Gulf Stream stalled as a result of glacial melting (456–57). Rising up in a helicopter as his visit to the dumping site ends, Frank observes "the *astonishing* sight of a thousand tankers on the huge burnished plate spreading below them, an *astonishing* sight, instantly grasped as unprecedented: the first major act of planetary engineering ever attempted, and by God it looked like it" (562, emphasis added). As Moore reminds us, *astonish* comes "from the Latin *tonus,* thunder, to be struck, as by lightning; the sudden flash that startles us and, just for a moment, lights the world with uncommon clarity" (269). Here, the human creation, too, provokes Abbey's "shock of the real."

This contradictory coexistence of nonhuman and artifactual wonders in a work of science fiction—or in our actual experiences—should not deter a deeper evaluation of the implications of the phenomenon. In a book about environmental justice, Brian Baxter makes a useful historical observation:

> the objects of wonder are no longer what they once were, because the objects themselves are no longer so easily available in a world of artifacts, and wonder has been increasingly redirected to human beings and their works to the exclusion of the non-human. . . . [I]t is not a deficit of wonder from which we suffer, but a deficit of experiences of the objects which are the appropriate recipients of our sense of wonder, and of the ethical dimension to our responses. (37)

At the same time that Baxter recognizes the "appropriate" objects of our wonder, objects that from the perspective of an environmental ethic of ecological difference are necessarily the welcomed *subjects* of ecological systems or the systems themselves, he also acknowledges the power of human artifacts to evoke comparable wonder. Both nonhuman phenomena and human artifacts are often remarkable. But the ethical legitimacy of respecting as beyond-human the technologies we create to manipulate nonhuman nature is questionable, especially when examined against the environmental ethic of respecting that which is not us or ours. Are we to wonder at the Glen Canyon Dam so as to include a place in our ethics for honoring its interests or its flourishing? As Moore notes of the affective experience of human artifacts, "it's not wonder they evoke, so much as fascination perhaps, or appreciation" (269). By juxtaposing human-created and nonhuman wonders, environmental science fiction such as Robinson's asks us to consider our experiences of both, and if those experiences are indistinguishable, to consider then the ethical dimensions of a modern world in which we deem the evidence of our human presence as marvelous as the wonders that make us contemplate this presence on a deeper, more ecologically conscious level.

A complication arises with this reasoning, however. If in Robinson's *Red Mars* the human artifact that fascinates us is the space elevator, the twenty-three-thousand-mile-high traversable cable that facilities the efficient shipment of ores from Mars to Earth, then the nonhuman wonder is the planet Mars itself—"weird, lovely, fantastic," to borrow Abbey's language. The former perhaps provokes the highest appreciation owed to a feat of industrial engineering; the latter, perhaps a more meaningful reflection on humanity's cosmological place. But as Robinson's *Mars* trilogy demonstrates, we do not live in a world where such a simple opposition between human and nonhuman exists, an opposition that can easily indicate the ethical value of competing affective experiences. In the trilogy's conclusion, the character Ann walks along a Martian beach with a two-year-old child who looks up at seagulls and remarks, "Ooh! . . . Pretty! Pretty!" (760). Ann looks closely at "dark grains of basalt, mixed with minute seashell fragments, and a variety of colorful pebbles" (761). The scene is right out of Carson's magazine article, but the presence of the gulls and shells is the result of an engineering project far larger than the space elevator: the terraforming of Mars. Here, the nonhuman wonder *is* a human artifact.

This implicit narrative commentary on the artifactual aspects of nonhuman wonder does not characterize all environmental science fiction; Slonczewski's *A Door Into Ocean* and Bacigalupi's "The People of Sand and Slag" (2004), for example, make use of wonder in ways that are akin to the ways Carson, Abbey, and Moore use it. Initially reluctant to embrace his new home on the strange planet Shora, the character Spinel in Slonczewski's book begins to accept the world after witnessing its marvels:

> Now he had time to absorb the silent drama that pulsed below the waves. Hungry eels hid in wait beneath raft seedlings, which now dotted the sea like copper medals. A fanwing's egg stretched and strained until a tadpole burst out and flittered away, to swim and grow until it sprouted wings. At the coral forest, a beakfish crunched the hard stalks with enormous jaws that never tired. After some minutes of this calciferous grazing, a puff of sand would spout from its tail. Spinel wondered how long a beach a beakfish could fill, were the sand not destined to fall several kilometers below.
>
> Spinel was now more than simply curious about Shora. *Something* compelled him to come to grips with this place that was inexorably becoming a part of him. (100, emphasis added)

In Bacigalupi's short story, an ecodystopian piece set on a future Earth so polluted that humans have adapted using a technology that allows them to eat the byproducts of heavy industry, the first-person narrator admits a mysterious connection with a rare animal: a dog. Contemplating his friend's suggestion that they cook and eat the dog, the narrator says, "I don't know. That dog's different from a bio-job. It looks at us, and there's *something* there, and it's not us. I mean, take any bio-job out there, and it's basically us, poured into another shape, but not that dog. . . ." (64, emphasis added). In both cases, nonhuman wonder, expressed as an inexplicable "something," has transformative effects on the characters. Interestingly, when Sandner defines wonder he also relies on the word *something*: "wonder describes the affective moment when the individual is overwhelmed by the sense of something else, with the presence . . . of the other" (288).

But when science fiction does feature human-created nonhuman wonder—as in Robinson's work, or in Herbert's *Dune,* with its engineered biodiversity—it offers a telling insight, if indeed we comprehend environmental science fiction as cultural criticism educating us to live more ethically as ecological citizens. As Bill McKibben argued in 1989, the postnatural world is one where we face the ever-diminishing likelihood of encountering something untouched by human activity (*The End* 60). But as the *Mars* trilogy makes clear, this information need not suggest that we face an ever-diminishing likelihood of experiencing wonder and its associated ethical possibilities. If we are to experience wonder at all on Earth today, and thus exercise the environmental ethic necessary for an ecologically just present and future, we must learn how to deem as wonderful our affective experiences of places and species already touched by human activity—second-growth forests, renourished beaches, national parks, reintroduced flora and fauna, our own backyards, or even the cracks in the sidewalk. In a postnatural era such places and species make up most of the world available to us for our reflection. With Mars's beaches and Dune's rich biodiversity, Robinson's and Herbert's works, respectively, suggest that despite the human origins of natural wonders in a postnatural world, such wonders are still nonhuman, elemental things.

The speculative and affective orientations of environmental nonfiction and science fiction allow both to perform effectively the philosophical work of transformative movements that question institutionalized behavior and try to effect change in ways beyond mainstream legalistic and bureaucratic procedure. Put differently, estrangement, extrapolation, and sense of wonder constitute an ecorhetorical strategy for works of fiction and nonfiction whose interests lie in questioning deep-seated cultural paradigms. None of this is to suggest that the concerns of environmentalism are feebly grounded in fictional speculation, but instead that science fiction offers valuable representations of and critical commentary on environmental issues. If environmentalism shares rhetorical strategies with science fiction, it is because those strategies facilitate necessary critical perspective, not because the two are equally fabulated. It has become quite common for climate-science deniers, for example, to dismiss environmentalist concerns about global warming as rooted in science fiction, or, presumably, in scientific research that is made up to serve conspiratorial purposes. To read what follows as lending support to this notion would be tantamount to reading a study of feminism and science fiction—and there are many fascinating and important ones—as lending support to the view that the social inequalities about which feminism is concerned are fabulations of sociological research. Such readings would indicate fundamental, if not ideologically motivated, misunderstandings and misrepresentations of environmentalism and feminism.

Misgivings about science fiction, too, have certainly surfaced in work that would otherwise seem sympathetic to my argument in this book. In *The Ecological Rift* John Bellamy Foster, Brett Clark, and Richard York critique market-driven technological solutions to environmental degradation with these words: "The idea that technology can solve the global environmental problem, as a kind of *deus ex machina* without changes in social relations, belongs to the area of fantasy and science fiction" (116). This characterization of science fiction as technophilic is based on a popular understanding of the genre that does not seem to recognize the 1960s New Wave and its subsequent literary innovations. Prior to the 1960s the works of the genre's pulp and Golden Age eras did celebrate technological achievement. With the New Wave, which coincides historically with the rise of various social movements, including environmentalism, science fiction "generally adopted an anti-technocratic bent that put it at odds with the technophilic optimism of Campbellian hard [science fiction], openly questioning if not the core values of scientific inquiry, then the larger social processes to which they had been conjoined in the service of state and corporate power" (Latham 107). In short, science fiction has evolved, and in this evolution it has obtained a more critical view not only of modern technophilia but also of any number of sociopolitical and cultural assumptions and practices.

In "Science Fiction and Ecology" Brian Stableford mentions at least one hundred forty works of science fiction that respond to the evolving Zeitgeist of environmentalist interest over the last century, the majority of which have appeared since the 1960s. Indeed, many science fiction books and stories worthy of ecocritical analysis are not examined in this study, and there are also environmental contexts besides transformative movements within which to read these texts. Frans van der Bogert distinguishes fictions of "evolution," "disaster," "invasion," and "human nature," as well as "ecofiction" in his book chapter "Nature through Science Fiction." Perhaps the environmental science fiction that in this study represents the scope of science fiction's engagements with transformative environmentalism are closest to van der Bogert's ecofiction: fictions cognizant that "sometimes human beings themselves accidentally set into motion events that take on the character of a disaster or an invasion as they develop" (62). Environmental science fiction, however, does much more than narrate "human tampering" gone awry (van der Bogert 62). With its representative examples, *Green Speculations* demonstrates that the subgenre, like the movements it supports, reflects more deeply on ideological structures that without accident require us to forget about nonhuman nature and our uncontestable embeddedness in it. Environmental science fiction collectively chips away at the foundations of these structures to prompt an effort to rebuild them with greater attention to environmental and social ethics.

CHAPTER ONE

THE SUBVERSIVE SUBJECT OF ECOLOGY

ENVIRONMENTAL PHILOSOPHER Val Plumwood succinctly argues, "To the extent that we hyper-separate ourselves from nature and reduce it conceptually in order to justify domination, we not only lose the ability to empathise and to see the non-human sphere in ethical terms, but also get a false sense of our own character and location that includes an illusory sense of autonomy" (*Environmental* 9). Plumwood's concern about the conceptual human/nature divide is fundamental to transformative environmental movements, interested as they are in uncovering the core ideological justifications for environmentally destructive socioeconomic and cultural formations. Surely, and simply put, deep ecology's primary target of critique is anthropocentrism, ecofeminism's primary target is androcentrism, and ecosocialism's is global capitalism. But in each case the question of humanity's location in nonhuman nature is centrally motivating. Deep ecology, generally understood, "rejects the *dualistic* view of humans and nature as separate and different" (Pepper, *Modern* 17). Ecofeminism uses feminist analyses of the unequal distribution of power that is sanctioned in the dualistic gender paradigm likewise to scrutinize the Western human/nonhuman split. And drawing on Karl Marx's historical materialism, ecosocialism stresses the "'metabolic interaction' between

humans and the earth," that "'man *lives* on nature' and that in this dependent relationship 'nature is his *body*, with which he must remain in con-
tinuous interchange if he is not to die'" (Foster, Clark, and York 123). A
discussion of these movements, then, entails a look at the environmentalist
maxim that humans are part of nature, a decidedly seditious claim given
the reign of socioeconomic and cultural attitudes predicated upon notions
of humanity's exemption from nonhuman nature.

Despite popular understandings of science fiction as a technophilic
literature celebrating human achievement above all else, the genre, when
environmental, can inform this discussion quite well and, as in the case of
Frank Herbert's *Dune* (1965), make the discussion more complex. Read
collectively, Olaf Stapledon's *Last and First Men* (1931) and George R.
Stewart's *Earth Abides* (1949) make the challenging case that despite
human technological and intellectual capacities, we are still part of nature.
These books perform their (proto)environmentalist work by affirming
our embeddedness in nonhuman nature and identifying several of the key
tributaries that supply what Plumwood coined the "Illusion of Disembeddedness," including transcendental religious conviction and modern
technological and economic trends, as well as the various symbolisms and
infrastructures that grow out of and also inform this conviction and these
trends. In both works a catastrophic event leads to the near extinction of
humanity and a subsequent reflection on the reality of our embeddedness
in nature and the problems inherent in whatever enables us to act outside of this reality. Stapledon's book identifies at its outset two ideological
loci of social fantasies of disembeddedness, religious and technological. It
then traces these fantasies' paths toward environmental and social disaster, which, because we do not do well as a species afterward, illuminate
our susceptibilities to ecological change, confirming our connection to
nonhuman nature and exposing the dangers of ideological mystifications
that disclaim this connection. *Earth Abides*, however, begins with disaster. Unlike with *Last and First Men* we do not witness human recklessness
lead to tragedy, nor is the tragedy—a plague—undeniably one of folly,
though it is aided by airplane travel and presumed by many in the book
to be an accident or intentional act of biological warfare. Instead we read
about a newly primitive group of survivors who can no longer rely for
their survival on infrastructures and symbolic conventions that previously
allowed them to forget that they are fixed within nonhuman nature.

This difference between the narrative movement of *Last and First Men*
and *Earth Abides* is one of subgenre: Stapledon's book is far-future history
and Stewart's is postapocalyptic. And indeed, with the key (proto)envi-

ronmentalist features of both books being a spotlighting of some of the Illusion of Disembeddedness's constitutive forces and of the fundamental embeddedness of humanity in nonhuman nature, their subgeneric differences are nominal—at least in the reading performed here. But they are worth at least this brief rehearsal, if only because the book with which this chapter concludes, *Dune,* departs from the specific extrapolative and estranging strategies of the others to favor a more historico-political narrative that begins neither with the ideological follies of modern humanity (*Last and First Men*) nor with the moment of the end of such a humanity (*Earth Abides*) but instead with a humanity not yet fully tricked, so to speak, out of practicing its more ecocentric being. *Dune*'s Fremen live their embeddedness as best as they can given their circumstances, and as we witness their coerced shift into power politics we come to appreciate a more complex and complicated understanding of the part-of-nature thinking that *Last and First Men, Earth Abides,* and transformative environmentalism uphold. It is to this part-of-nature thinking that I now turn.

❧

The science of ecology, a subfield of biology that studies the relationships between living organisms and their environment, esteems scrupulous experimentation, quantitative reasoning, "rigorous logic in deducing conclusions, and an ever-critical attitude to both evidence and logic" (Westoby 166). As Mark Westoby argues, ecology, like all sciences, remains outside the realm of values, operating with the scientific understanding that "it is illogical to deduce 'ought' from 'is,' the normative from the substantive" (166). But in its radical mode—which since the 1960s has unfolded into a number of movements working "to break down the dualism that isolates [humans] from the rest of nature" (Worster 333)—ecology reflects on human projects and their impacts on Earth's biological and physical systems as well as overtly implicating certain values for instigating the most environmentally destructive of these projects. To better indicate its goal to define and make real more conscious and responsible material and psychological relationships with nonhuman nature, I am calling this radical ecology *transformative environmentalism.* Transformative environmentalism borrows insights from science to challenge explicitly and change those governing worldviews that to the detriment of global health fail to generate knowledge about Earth and its interconnected species.

As David W. Orr notes, "To see things in their wholeness," to possess this knowledge and the ability to ask "'What then?'" about these governing worldviews, "is politically threatening" (85, 88). "Real ecological literacy," he writes, "is radicalizing in that it forces us to reckon with the roots of our ailments, not just with their symptoms" (88). Orr's interest in his book *Ecological Literacy* is in developing pedagogies for the age of ecology and its food, water, energy, and climate crises, pedagogies that would provoke deep challenges to dominant, domineering ways of being. His project to disengage our inclinations toward disciplinary specialization, our confidence in traditional education, and most importantly for my focus in this chapter our clear acceptance of "disharmony between people and between people and the land" grows out of a culturally critical brand of ecology that became very conscious of its rebellious, radicalizing tendencies in the 1960s (88).

Recognizing the science of ecology's potential to activate normative modes of critical engagement, ecologist Paul B. Sears famously deemed the discipline subversive in his 1964 essay "Ecology—A Subversive Subject," both acknowledging the cultural need for its "continuing critique of man's operations within the ecosystem" and pointing out its threat to "the assumptions and practices accepted by modern societies" (12). Similarly, while introducing his influential 1969 co-edited essay collection *The Subversive Science* Paul Shepard declares, "The ideological status of ecology is that of a resistance movement" (9). About some of ecology's key figures he writes,

> [they] challenge the public or private right to pollute the environment, to systematically destroy predatory animals, to spread chemical pesticides indiscriminately, to meddle chemically with food and water, to appropriate without hindrance space and surface for technological and military ends; they oppose the uninhibited growth of human populations, some forms of "aid" to "underdeveloped" peoples, the needless addition of radioactivity to the landscape, the extinction of species of plants and animals, the domestication of all wild places, large-scale manipulation of the atmosphere or the sea, and most other purely engineering solutions to problems of and intrusions into the organic world. (9)

Decades have passed since Sears and Shepard articulated the latent social critique present within ecological science. However, as demonstrated in ecocritic Glen A. Love's more recent Sears- and Shepard-like assertion, the life sciences continue to serve key roles in our thinking about what is wrong with the way modern societies relate to nonhuman nature, why it is wrong, and how we might fix it. Love writes, "The social implications of biological thinking and research offer one of the great intellectual engagements of our time, sufficient to draw the attention and interest of all who are concerned with the place of humankind on the planet" (64). Here is an important caveat: the ecocritical literary scholar Dana Phillips observes that while today "Ecology sparks debates about environmental issues," ecologists themselves are accountable to objective scientific standards and are thus "less available and less pliable as spokespersons for the environmental movement" (45, 50). Ecological science produces research such as "Detection of Density-Dependent Growth at Two Spatial Scales in Marble Trout (*Salmo Marmoratus*) Populations" (Vincenzi et al.) and "Insect Diversity and Trophic Structure Differ on Native and Non-Indigenous Congeneric Rushes in Coastal Salt Marshes" (Harvey, Britton, and Minchinton). The social, political, economic, and ethical concerns about which Shepard writes in the above passage, and the "place of humankind" about which Love writes, are not the provinces of *this* ecology. While the authors of these scientific papers might express environmentalist sentiments outside their research, their research itself, as with most scientific research, does not constitute the socioeconomic or cultural criticism that environmentalist interpreters of the research might underscore.

But for Shepard, who writes at the historical moment of environmentalism's popular emergence, figures such as Aldo Leopold and Rachel Carson exemplify "the subversive science," the mode of ecological study that does engage directly with anthropogenic influences on nonhuman nature and then also draws a line from substantive scientific findings to normative cultural judgments. With her work specifically, not only did Carson destabilize widespread social and economic assumptions of her time—writing against a cultural paradigm that considered female thought, especially in the male-dominated sciences, to be inferior to male intellect, as well as calling for tough regulations on the insecticide industry and for eliminating several of that industry's staple products—she also threatened the very idea of human *being* that the modern world's most coveted attitudes resolutely protect. Implicitly invoking Charles Darwin's groundbreaking scientific thesis, which against Victorian conceptualizations thrust humanity into nonhuman nature, Carson asserts in *Silent Spring*, "Man, however much he may like to pretend the contrary, *is part of nature*" (188, emphasis added). Later, in her final speech Carson similarly declared the controversial Darwinian position that "man is affected by the same environmental influences that control the lives of all the many thousands of other species to which he is related by evolutionary ties" (Carson, "The Pollution" 245).[1]

origins
of
MAN
NATURE
dominance

theology

- expansion

As Al Gore notes, Carson worked "against the grain of an orthodoxy rooted in the earliest days of the scientific revolution: that man (and of course this meant the male of our species) was properly the center and the master of all things" (xvi–xvii). The dominant worldview against which Carson wrote—and to which ecology, as understood by Sears, Shepard, and Orr is set in contrast, thus becoming subversive—holds, among additional contentions, that "People are fundamentally different from all other creatures on earth, over which they have dominion" (Catton and Dunlap 17). Gore locates the origin of this human exemptionalism in the scientific revolution, and the historian Lynn White, Jr. notoriously censured the Judeo-Christian theology of human dominion.[2] But the preeminence of the domination mentality in modern culture suggests a more multifaceted heritage. The ideological tributaries that feed Plumwood's Illusion of Disembeddedness are indeed numerous. In addition to its origins in Baconian science and Biblical doctrine, the modern denial of human ecological embeddedness and the associated belief in humanity's right to exploit nonhuman nature is also buttressed by notions about the limitless possibilities of human enterprise in a world of perceived abundance, especially as codified in North America by the continent's European settlers, whose experience of the land's bounty contrasted sharply with their experience of Old World scarcity. The apparent differences between the intellectual capabilities of humans and animals also support human exemptionalism, as does the degree to which technology has permitted modern humanity's flight from and subjugation of nature.[3] Nourished by some combination of the abovementioned influencing factors, the dominant Western worldview asserts that humans exist apart from and superior to everything else on Earth, and that we can disavow our embeddedness even in the face of what the life sciences have taught us. To declare the inseverable integration and regulation of the human species within and by a nonhuman world of physical and biological processes and cycles is to participate in what has become a minority tradition of thinking that fights an uphill battle against rigid majority traditions pronouncing and living out an apart-from-nature mentality.

Given the fervor with which human exemptionalism has been supported in both secular and religious culture, to assert humanity's full embeddedness in and dependence on nonhuman nature is to subvert conceptions of the world that are foundational to the prevailing theological, social, cultural, political, and economic constellation. When transformative movements announce that humanity is part of nature, they do so to question ways of being that refuse to take ecological principles into consideration. Biodiversity in an ecosystem helps maintain ecosystemic health against normal environmental stressors such as fire, flood, and drought. To say that we are part of nature is a first step in positing ways of living with this nature that do not threaten biodiversity and undercut the ability of ecosystems to stay vital in the face of stress. To say that we are part of nature is to challenge especially the capitalist mode of economic production, whose extractive activities hustle along normal environmental change far more quickly than one would find such change to happen absent industrial processes, barring of course major tectonic or meteoric episodes. For a species to achieve tectonic or meteoric weight is for that species—or more accurately, for those of the species who are driving the severe change—to behave as if it is not part of nature. To say that we are part of nature, in the end, is to respond to socioeconomic and cultural forms in which nonanthropogenic ecological processes no longer structure the possibilities of human life.

Part-of-nature thinking has indeed been ill used to back objectionable ideological agendas.[4] But in the transformative environmental movements discussed throughout this study, part-of-nature thinking serves to check modes of being that, in their ignorance or denial of humanity's material grounding, threaten the processes and cycles necessary for nonhuman and human life. Even when deep ecology's part-of-nature thinking takes on a tone of spiritual kinship, it does so to root spirituality and kinship in the material world, as immanent instead of transcendent. Writing in the book *Deep Ecology and World Religions,* David Landis Barnhill and Roger S. Gottlieb note,

> When a deep ecologist makes the *metaphysical* or *psychological* claim that to be human is to be part of nature, he is opposing . . . anthropocentrism and individualism. That is, the anthropocentric view that human beings are (because of intelligence, technology, science, political life, language, the soul, etc.) categorically different from their surroundings; or the individualist view that sees people essentially as individuals, who form relationships with other beings but are not constituted by those relationships. Thus, for deep ecology our kinship with nature penetrates deeply into the essences of who we are. If as individuals and communities, we fail to realize and celebrate this fact, we will be neither truly happy nor truly sane. (7)

More strictly materialist, ecosocialism theorizes that "a large part of the answer as to why contemporary society refuses to recognize the full human dependence on nature undoubtedly has to do with the expansionist logic of a capitalist system that makes the accumulation of wealth in the form of capital the supreme end of society" (Foster, *Ecology* 9). Ecosocialism prioritizes the "full human dependence on nature" in its response to capital's restructuring of nonhuman life for the purposes of production and human consumption, which has resulted in marked ecological and social stress. Finally, while ecofeminism has one of its many roots in deep ecological conceptions of human embeddedness and one in more materialist, historical conceptions, as chapter 3 will show, the movement as a whole regards the conceptual human/nature dualism as widely problematic and of a piece with similarly problematic gender assumptions.

The two examples of (proto)environmentalist science fiction I am about to discuss—*Last and First Men* and *Earth Abides*—make humanity's embeddedness in nonhuman nature explicitly visible. I choose them for this section of chapter 1, because they reflect the interest in the nature of humankind that characterizes some of the earliest works in the subgenre. For this reason they represent the subgenre's anticipation of specifically environmentalist questions and assertions about human place that only later would prompt the birth of modern environmentalism in the 1960s. It is little wonder that many science fiction works of the late nineteenth and early to mid-twentieth century display an interest in humanity's place in nonhuman nature. Darwin's 1859 *The Origin of Species* and 1871 *The Descent of Man* forced upon nineteenth-century Victorian culture a view of humanity's relationship to nonhuman nature that radically countered conventional wisdom. In *Victorian Science Fiction in the UK* Darko Suvin analyzes Victorian science fiction as reflecting an emerging crisis of confidence in Victorian values, and Victorian scholar Herbert Sussman argues that in this analysis Suvin neglects to reveal why antihegemonic writers turned to science fiction instead of secular sermon or literary realism. Putting Suvin in conversation with Sussman, film scholar Barbara Creed writes,

> There *was* a crisis of confidence, and this arose in response to the way in which evolutionary theory—and its consequences, such as secularization and new ways of perceiving time—challenged Victorian beliefs and values. Of the science fiction texts published in the latter part of the nineteenth century, a significant number drew on Darwin's theory of evolution, particularly in the period after 1870. (43–44)

Creed upholds Suvin's position—that science fiction did grow out of anti-hegemonic attitudes—while also answering Sussman's call for a historical justification for the authorial choice of science fiction as the literary mode for the expression of these attitudes. The crisis of confidence in Victorian values grew largely out of what Darwin's science revealed about nature and the human species.

Thinking about the implications of what Darwin was teaching the Western world became a central focus for some of science fiction's early writers. These writers found in Darwin's thinking a starting point for a range of critical commentary regarding the contemporary illusion about humanity's place outside nonhuman nature, as well as the consequences of experimental efforts to make this illusion real. In *A Crystal Age* (1887), for example, naturalist William Henry Hudson imagines the end of much of humanity as the outcome of scientific attempts to control nature: "Thus did they thirst [for knowledge], and drink again, and were crazed; being inflamed with the desire to learn the secrets of nature, hesitating not to dip their hands in blood, seeking in the living tissues of animals for the hidden springs of life. For in their madness they hoped by knowledge to gain absolute dominion over nature" (79). The reference here to vivisection as a way for scientists to learn the mysteries of life and therefore to harness these mysteries in the interest of transcending nature as its managers leads us also to H. G. Wells's *The Island of Dr. Moreau* (1896). A student and admirer of the Darwinian biologist T. H. Huxley, Wells comprehended evolutionary biology and used it to think about the brand of experimental science that in this new Darwinian light could be implicated in breaking fundamental biological principles. If "As a part of nature, man was an animal—a being constituted of material structures and processes"—a finding that historian Hamilton Cravens argues is "The most important concept Darwin put forward"—then attempting to command these structures and processes might have unforeseeable costs, costs that *The Island of Dr. Moreau* vividly renders (xi).

Olaf Stapledon, as Suvin notes, is of these originators of a science fiction that has ideological and formal affinities with Darwinism (*Victorian* 407). In his *Last and First Men* a member of a civilization existing two billion years in the future narrates a history of the rise and fall of each evolutionary stage of humanity, from the First Men, through the telepathic Fifth Men and the Ninth Men of Neptune, and ultimately to the Eighteenth Men, doomed to be the Last Men when a nearby supernova threatens to destroy their planet. The civilization of the First Men, modern *Homo sapiens,* causes severe social crisis with its exhaustion of coal, which is brought about by an exuberant religious devotion to coal-intensive flying machines in the global World State. As the narrator notes while recounting the State's discovery that coal has run out, "The sane policy would have been to abolish the huge expense of power on ritual flying, which used more of the community's resources than the whole of productive industry" (70). But the First Men are unwilling to question their rituals despite worldwide raggedness and starvation created by "a world engaged, devotedly and even heroically, on squandering its resources in vast aeronautical displays" (72). When those in authority do suggest a reduction in religious flying, war breaks out and the ensuing diminished population is left to scrape a living from whatever fertile land is left.

Later in the chronicle of the First Men's fall a new Patagonian civilization moves in a direction just as unsustainable. Had they sacrificed developing an energy-intensive culture similar to that of the recently destroyed World State and instead pursued a less profligate way of life based on wind and water power, which the narrator of Stapledon's tale admits they could have done, the Patagonians "might well have achieved something like Utopia" (86). But instead this civilization opts to acquire atomic energy. Even with the possibilities of using such a "limitless source of energy" in relatively harmless ways, the Patagonians use it both as a tool for excavating from Earth materials previously made inaccessible by the World State's exhaustive mining, and as a weapon for policing the working class (89). Proletariat anger leads to the seizing of a power unit and ultimately to global atomic destruction, ending the reign of modern humanity.

Supported by religious dogma and an econocentric techno-scientific ability, respectively, the World State and the Patagonian civilization practice high-consumption ways of life, which motivate widespread ecological disaster and social unrest. *Last and First Men*'s critical commentary is clear, offering one of science fiction's earliest contributions to a culturally attentive environmentalism that was still years away from gaining traction in other modes of cultural production and public discourse. As a future history of modern humanity, the book didactically attends to the exploitive madness of the so-called rational species.

The novel's most subversive observation, though, comes in its commentary, more subtly voiced than its look at overconsumption, about the place of humans on Earth. After the Patagonians' atomic ruin, much like every other nonpolar species "the human organism had not yet succeeded in adapting itself" to the newly toxic atmosphere (92). Except for fish, some plants, and a few species of mammals and birds, every other living thing on the planet is severely affected, including humans. "[F]org[ing] ahead" despite the obstacles of this harsh, postdisaster environment, the

nonhuman life that does reemerge is represented as persistent and determined to carry on, as healthy and strong (92). But the global environmental change to which other plants and animals acclimate is one that the
First Men cannot tolerate, even though they caused it. Like the other frag-
ile species, *Homo sapiens* cannot adapt to drastic ecological change—that
is, unless the species becomes something else entirely, a "NEW SPECIES"
that after ten million years emerges in *Last and First Men* as the "Second
Men," no longer human as we know it (100). Stapledon makes the case
for the validity of human embeddedness stronger by employing Darwinian
biology in his narrative of natural selection and its implications for humanity. As the First Men, we are of the weaker animals despite our advanced
capabilities. Our susceptibility to ecological change lays bare our undeni-
able and ineradicable embeddedness in the material world. Our imagined
position outside of nonhuman nature—our "illusory sense of autonomy,"
to borrow again from Plumwood—feeds and is fed by flawed ideological commitments. The existence of these flawed commitments against
clear evidence of our embeddedness further challenges the legitimacy of
exemptionalist reasoning based in a Cartesian sense of human intellectual
superiority, a reasoning that historically broke away from pre-Cartesian
conceptions of the human subject as existing not "inside the cranium" but
instead "in a continuum with the rest of the biosphere" (Borlik 44).

Stewart's effort in *Earth Abides* to underline humanity as part of nature
is not unlike Stapledon's, and it also exposes some of the specific cultural
locations where the Illusion of Disembeddedness resides. A tale of plague
and the near extinction of humanity, the novel uses a large-scale disaster
to emphasize our embeddedness in nonhuman nature and to highlight the
ideological trends that make this embeddedness dangerously invisible. In
the book a "super-measles" plague eliminates much of the world's human
population, forcing survivors to realign themselves materially, socially,
and symbolically with natural systems previously hidden beneath modern
convenience and modern symbolism (13). The novel's main character is
Isherwood Williams (Ish), a survivor of the plague and former graduate
student whose thesis, "*The Ecology of the Black Creek Area,*" explores
"the relationships, past and present, of men and plants and animals" in a
region near San Francisco (4–5). For a student of ecology, a world without
humans as the dominant species provides an interesting opportunity for
research:

Even though the curtain had been rung down on man, here was the
opening of the greatest of all dramas for a student such as he. During

thousands of years man had impressed himself upon the world. Now man was gone, certainly for a while, perhaps forever. Even if some survivors were left, they would be a long time in again obtaining supremacy. What would happen to the world and its creatures? *That* he was left to see! (24–25)

While *Earth Abides* is also about Ish's project to navigate his existential predicament and, as critic David G. Byrd notes, "to keep the light of civilization burning," its most important characteristics as a foundational work of environmental science fiction are its affirmation that humans are indeed part of natural processes and cycles and its interrogation of a modern society that is built upon epistemological and ontological foundations that declare otherwise (par. 5). The apocalyptic and estranging end of technology and human dominance—the end of the postnatural—coupled with the concomitant estranging return of unmediated nonhuman nature instigates enormous shifts in the characters' perspectives and life ways. Ish's experiences and reflections on these new and necessarily more ecocentric ways of thinking and being force our "reckon[ing] with the roots of our ailments," as Orr puts it, by opening up a subversive critique of our own modern social and symbolic practices that the post-plague environment of *Earth Abides* renders absurd.

Although published twenty years after *Earth Abides,* wildlife biologist Paul L. Errington's entry in Shepard and McKinley's *The Subversive Science* helps set up contexts for reading Stewart's book from the perspective of a normative ecology. In "Of Man and the Lower Animals" Errington calls attention to the similarity between human populations and nonhuman animal populations, arguing against any notion that humans are "exempt from natural laws or well on the way toward becoming so" (180). He writes, "If twentieth-century society really values the things that it proclaims essential—peace, human dignity, intellectual activity, a reasonable degree of freedom and security, and a reasonable standard of living—it cannot afford to ignore the natural laws by which life continues to be bound" (180). As with many of the essays in Shepard and McKinley's book, Errington's focuses on overpopulation, specifically highlighting the trend of bobwhite quail and muskrats to develop "social evils" as their populations skyrocket (188). For Errington these animal communities are not simply metaphors for human communities. Instead, they provide a mirror image of human society, and to turn away from the reflection is to deny valuable cultural lessons.

In *Earth Abides,* speculating on the fate of humanity given the biological law *"that the number of individuals in a species never remains constant, but always rises and falls,"* Stewart's Universal Narrator concludes,

> there is little reason to think that [man] can in the long run escape the
> fate of other creatures, and if there is a biological law of flux and reflux,
> his situation is now a highly perilous one. During ten thousand years
> his numbers have been on the upgrade in spite of wars, pestilences, and
> famines. This increase in population has become more and more rapid.
> Biologically, man has for too long a time been rolling an uninterrupted
> run of sevens. (8)[5]

This passage anticipates Errington's thesis by linking *"man"* to *"other
creatures"* in a specific observation about overpopulation. But its subversive character comes above all from the linking itself, which challenges
theology and modern secular humanist philosophy alike, opening room
for urgent deliberation. The Universal Narrator likens humans to Captain
Maclear's rat of Christmas Island, the victim of *"some new disease"* that,
*"Because of their crowding and also probably because of the softened con-
dition of the individuals, . . . proved universally susceptible, and soon were
dying by thousands"* (10). Later, Ish's own reflections on ant and rat populations inform his fear for the fate of an already diminished humanity:
"'When anything gets too numerous it's likely to get hit by some plague—I
mean—' (Something had suddenly exploded in his mind at the word.) He
coughed to cover up his hesitation, and then went on, without making
a point of it. 'Yes, some plague is likely to hit them'" (114). Ish's hesitation is his, and the reader's, moment of realization: we are in the world as
much as anything else.

Earth Abides thus affirms human embeddedness. But lest we let this
affirmation press us to contemplate (natural) overpopulation and (natural)
pandemic disease as the (natural) looming fate of humanity, it is important
to read the apocalyptic scenario as the narrative's estrangement strategy,
its effort to remove from modern humans the elements that reinforce our
sense of disembeddedness and thus to draw our attention to the ubiquity
and influence of these elements in our actual world. The global catastrophe
in *Earth Abides* highlights what these things are (e.g., the grocery store,
the water faucet, Abrahamic and national holidays) and therefore enables
their interrogation. Stewart's book is not necessarily about the challenges
of reconciling growth rates in population with much smaller growth rates

in food supply. Nor is it about what disease might do to an overpopulated and underprepared human society. Surely these concerns figure into the novel, especially early on. But later, as the small group of survivors tries to establish some functional community in the absence of modernity, the novel turns our attention to what it is in this modernity that pulls us away physically and ideologically from nonhuman nature and thus feeds our imaginary sense of separation from it.

The story of Ish's emerging Californian community is largely an exploration of how modern humans lived prior to the super-measles outbreak, when complex technologies and institutions mediated individual and social relationships with nonhuman nature. The community's disconnection from this nature is confirmed when one character asks, "'Where did all this water come from anyway?'" about the San Francisco water supply, prompting the narrator to reflect, "It was curious. Here they had been for twenty-one years merely using water that continued to flow, and yet they had never given any real consideration to where the water came from. It had been a gift from the past, as free as air, like the cans of beans and bottles of catsup that could be had just by walking into a store and taking them from the shelves" (171). Modern convenience has instigated a kind of psychosocial end of nature in which the faucet and grocery store have cancelled out both the imperative to know the biosphere and to ask "What then?" about our technological implements.

The specialized knowledge required to maintain modern infrastructure dies out with the plague in *Earth Abides,* and with its death comes the slow decay of that infrastructure. Ish's community eventually adapts to life without electricity, plumbing, and the like, situating itself firmly within the ecological dictates of which its members were once unaware. With this adaptation comes also a cultural change and another set of questions: do modern language and symbols have the same power as modern technological infrastructure to lead humans toward outward and inward denials of our ecological embeddedness? If human material life is physically shaped by the same laws that shape all species populations, then what about our symbolic life—the very thing that many exemptionalists, following Descartes, say make us not part of nature? The arguments made in Stewart's book on these points anticipate recent theories linking place and discourse. As ecocompositionists Sidney I. Dobrin and Christian R. Weisser note, for example, "While discourse does indeed shape our human conceptions of the world around us, discourse itself arises from a biosphere that sustains life. That is, while discourse 'creates' the world in the human mind, the biospheric physical environment is the origin of life (and consequently, the human mind) itself" (12). So language—and by extension, all symbolic activity—both forms and is informed by nonhuman nature. The apocalyptic end of modernity in *Earth Abides* again works to underline the sources of our disconnection.

Given the reemerging primacy of wildness in *Earth Abides,* certain human symbolic constructs must disappear, especially those driven by what ultimately seem to be arbitrary aesthetic and emotional judgments. Dogs will win *"Best-of-Breed"* for physically being able to survive, not for their *"stance, and shape of head, and markings"* (27). Indigenous flora once called "weeds" and beaten back with a host of chemical technologies will outcompete *"the pampered nurslings of man"* (43). Automobiles will no longer be *"the pride and the symbol of civilization"* as entropic processes make them and their roads unusable (107). These things and more will take on different meanings as their previous meanings pass away with the disappearance of modernity.

In addition to these shifts in meaning, which are anticipated by the novel's Universal Narrator and are not specific to the story of Ish's community of survivors, the cultural adjustments of this community that do happen in the narrative also reflect a new, heightened sense of embeddedness. In her discussion of ritual, environmental philosopher Dolores LaChapelle notes, "Most native societies around the world . . . had an intimate, conscious relationship with their place," a relationship out of which their symbolisms grew (247). Ish's new native community regains this relationship as wilderness returns as the governing force. With the modern dating system deemed illogical for their current situation, Ish's community starts over with a new dating system that better reflects the conditions of their newly primitive world. As in Christian mythology, the birth of a baby marks Year One in their society; however, the parallels end there. The group understands its dependence on the land and its fundamental obedience to natural processes, thus its symbolic tendencies develop away from the human/nature dualism that Lynn White, Jr. finds in much Christian theology. Instead, one year becomes "Year of the Fires," another becomes "Year of the Bulls," another becomes "Year of the Lions," and still another becomes "Year of the Earthquake" (129, 132, 134, 143). In these cases and in several others the emerging society names its social history for events in natural history, explicitly recognizing the connection between human and nonhuman.

This recognition also appears in the community's holidays. As LaChapelle comments, "all traditional cultures, even our own long-ago Western European cultural ancestors, had seasonal festivals and rituals. The

true origin of most of our modern major holidays dates back to these seasonal festivals" (248). Ish's society abandons patriotic holidays such as
the Fourth of July but continues those holidays with roots in seasonal
cycles: "Curiously," the narrator writes, "or perhaps rather it was natural enough, the old folk-holidays survived better than those established
by law" (295). So April Fool's Day and Halloween, as celebrations of
the vernal equinox and autumnal cross-quarter day, respectively, are car-
ried on. Continued also is the celebration of winter's cross-quarter day,
Groundhog Day, modified to Ground-Squirrel Day in an area with no
groundhogs. And the "great holiday" for the group is what was "Christmas and New Years of the Old Times": the winter solstice (295). On this
day, when for those in the northern hemisphere the sun is the farthest
south, Ish's community gets together to name the passing year and begin
anew.

In a 1968 collection of anthropology papers, Richard B. Lee and Irven
DeVore conjecture that if humanity does meet an apocalyptic end, "inter-
planetary archeologists of the future will classify our planet as one in
which a very long and stable period of small-scale hunting and gathering
was followed by an apparently instantaneous efflorescence of technology
and society leading rapidly to extinction. 'Stratigraphically,' the origin of
agriculture and thermonuclear destruction will appear as essentially simul-
taneous" (3). Though not a story of nuclear catastrophe, or one of total
human extinction, *Earth Abides* does much to stage Lee and DeVore's science-fictional speculation. The extended period of cultural stability referenced by Lee and DeVore is one made possible by premodern societies
that did not possess the physical and symbolical tools that for us enable
and reinforce the Illusion of Disembeddedness. Ish's new San Francisco
represents this stability reemerging after what deep ecologist George Sessions calls human culture's "anthropocentric detour," the ten thousand
years out of two hundred thousand that humanity has strayed from its
traditionally sustainable course, inventing monocultural agriculture, anti-
ecological religions, growth-centered economies, and other constructs that
require and encourage a human/nature disconnection ("Ecocentrism"
156). Stewart's book puts humanity back on track, so to speak. In its conclusion the narrator says, "In the times of civilization men had really felt
themselves as the masters of creation. Everything had been good or bad in
relation to man. So you killed rattlesnakes. But now nature had become so
overwhelming that any attempt at its control was merely outside anyone's
circle of thought. You lived as part of it, not as its dominating power"
(281). For Ish the apocalypse necessitates a revised understanding of the

human species; for us, its representation in Stewart's book strategically
brings to light the concepts and practices that demand such revision.

❧

Last and First Men and *Earth Abides* confirm our inescapable embeddedness, and an environmentalist reading of these books leads us to identify
the truth of this embeddedness as perhaps the silver bullet with which
the pathological Illusion of Disembeddedness will be killed. *Dune,* however, steps in at the very moment of environmentalism's birth in the West
and says, "Not so fast."[6] If we actualize it in any sort of ecologically conscious individual or cultural practice, part-of-nature thinking will place us
squarely in the crosshairs of the industrial modernity about whose mechanisms of Illusion we have become critical. While all of these books direct
us toward contemplating the technological and symbolic instruments that
reinforce our sense of separation from nonhuman nature, it is only *Dune*
that encourages us to think further about how economically driven, imperialist modern ideology cannot easily be subverted by an appeal to human
embeddedness. Part-of-nature thinking loses, or at least alone it cannot
win, because (1) the Illusion of Disembeddedness is too deeply entangled
within the ideological fabric of dominant institutions, to the point of being
indistinguishable from them; (2) these institutional forms stigmatize and
discourage embedded practice using effective classist and racist fantasy
frames; and/or (3) these institutions appropriate and perpetuate a weak or
feigned ecological embeddedness to contain subversion and then continue
to forward their sociopolitical and cultural agendas. *Dune* even goes so far
as to question whether embedded practice, or living deliberately as part of
nature, is possible given both the difficulty of finding today the "nature"
of which we are a part and of negotiating the imposed burdens we face
in the shadow of a spatially and psychologically imperializing political
economy.

The overwhelming presence and necessity of the Illusion of Disembeddedness in and for dominant ideology, and the construction of reactionary
xenophobic attitudes toward more outwardly part-of-nature social and
cultural forms go hand-in-hand. In Herbert's novel this means that by their
very natures the Imperium, the CHOAM Company, the Great Houses, and
the Bene Gesserit—all of which have an interest in the spoils of *Dune*'s
central setting, in the spice melange of the planet Arrakis—cannot *not*
maintain a mystified, disconnected relationship to the material world that
they want to exploit. They must for their very existence erect a cultural

framework that keeps at a safe distance the planet's willfully and successfully ennatured indigenous people, the Fremen (*Dune* 22). The Fremen
possess a "superb knowledge of their environment" and "a kind of earth-
wisdom" that allows them to survive in the dry climate and among the
carnivorous sandworms of Arrakis (O'Reilly 42). Their "stillsuits," as
Noel Gough observes, "emphasize appropriate and environmentally sensitive technology rather than high-tech gadgetry for its own sake" ("Playing" 409). Explaining these suits, Liet-Kynes, Arrakis's planetary ecologist,
states, "'It's basically a micro-sandwich—a high-efficiency filter and heat-
exchange system. . . . The skin-contact layer's porous. Perspiration passes
through it, having cooled the body . . . near-normal evaporation process.
The next two layers . . . include heat exchange filaments and salt precipita-
tors. Salt's reclaimed'" (109). Stillsuits process urine and feces, reclaiming
most of the body's water for its Fremen wearer to drink again, all with
the energy provided by body movement. "'With a Fremen suit in good
working order,'" Kynes insists, "'you won't lose more than a thimbleful of
moisture a day'" (109).

In the same way that the new wilderness reshapes the symbolic customs of Ish's community in *Earth Abides,* Arrakis's ecology also shapes
the customs of the Fremen. In one tense scene, for example, the Fremen
leader Stilgar spits on the table of Leto Atreides, the duke whose regime
has recently moved to Arrakis from the water-rich planet Caladan and has
been appointed as the desert planet's administrative body:

> The Fremen stared at the Duke, then slowly pulled aside his veil, reveal-
> ing a thin nose and full-lipped mouth in a glistening black beard. Delib-
> erately he bent over the end of the table, spat on its polished surface.
>
> As the men around the table started to surge to their feet, Idaho's
> voice boomed across the room: "Hold!" Into the sudden charged still-
> ness, Idaho said: "We thank you, Stilgar, for the gift of your body's
> moisture. We accept it in the spirit with which it is given." And Idaho
> spat on the table in front of the Duke. (92)

Duncan Idaho, one of the Duke's men, must then remind the Duke
of the value of water, and thus of saliva, on Arrakis: "'Remember how
precious water is here, Sire. That was a token of respect'" (92). Indeed,
just as the Fremen veneration of saliva finds its origin in Arrakis's thirst-
inspiring environment, the Atreides's disgust finds its origin in Caladan's
thirst-quenching environment. Water is not in short supply on Caladan,
so bodily fluids take on a different meaning there than on Arrakis, where

one finds a whole new reverence for spit and tears.[7] This scene suggests that nonhuman nature is part of human culture always and through and through, Arrakian or Caladanian. But more than demonstrating that the Atreides regime has a distinctive cultural understanding of water that displays their embeddedness in nonhuman nature, this scene is of a piece with *Dune*'s thorough historico-political examination of power's strategic collision with whatever threatens it. The Atreides's respectful acceptance of Fremen custom is an insincere nod to an "indigenous realism," as American Indian Studies scholar Daniel R. Wildcat names it, that must ultimately be contained or eradicated if the material exploitation of Arrakis is to continue.[8]

The reality of humanity's embeddedness in nonhuman nature disrupts the ideology of those who see this nature through a distorting economic lens, or, in the case of *Dune,* through the promise of the power that the spice melange brings to those who control its harvesting and distribution. One strategy to contain or eradicate lived, practiced embeddedness and prevent its influence on modern culture is for those in power to belittle its practitioners. The Fremen are "marked down on no census of the Imperial Regate"; the Imperium does not recognize their existence (5). The Emperor describes the Fremen as "'barbarians whose dearest dream is to live outside the ordered security of the faufreluches,'" "the rigid rule of class distinction enforced by the Imperium" (78, 501). Duke Leto Atreides's son and heir, Paul, takes an early interest in Arrakis's distinctive ecology and in the Fremen as the planet's indigenous culture, but the ideological apparatuses of the power structure prevent him from forming a consciousness so divergent from the classist and racist form that consciousness must take if power over people and their places is to be maintained. Before the Atreides leave Caladan for Arrakis, one of Paul's teachers, Thufir Hawat, perpetuates contempt for the Fremen: "'There's little to tell them from the folk of the graben and sink. They all wear those great flowing robes. And they stink to heaven in any closed space. It's from those suits they wear—call them 'stillsuits'—that reclaim the body's own water'" (29). By insisting that "'A place is only a place. . . . And Arrakis is just another place,'" Hawat symbolically erases the Fremen from the land, which as "just another place" is reduced to the chance address of an exploitable resource, a location void of any meaningful human culture or intrinsic ecological value.[9]

While Hawat instills in Paul the ideological posture necessary for a future colonial leader, the Reverend Mother of the Bene Gesserit—a religious order that has its own political motives in championing the young

Duke's rise to power—makes Paul very aware of Arrakis's native culture and ecology in order to make him a good ruler who can feign embeddedness while exploiting the Fremen. It is thus with the Bene Gesserit that another one of power's defensive moves against the threat of part-of-nature thinking and being is mobilized. The Reverend Mother tells Paul, "'a good ruler has to learn his world's language, . . . the language of the rocks and growing things, the language you don't just hear with your ears'" (30). As Susan Stratton notes, Paul "solve[s] the mysteries of Arrakis ecology and learn[s] to fit into the corresponding culture of its indigenous people," though he does so not to become a careful inhabitant of the planet but instead to "accomplish his goal, which is to reclaim the planet for the Atreides" after the rival House Harkonnen wrests power from Paul's father—and to do so using an army of Fremen ("The Messiah" 307).

Before the arrival of the Atreides regime and the ensuing political power struggle that makes up *Dune*'s narrative, the Fremen are involved in a project that complicates even further the environmentalist utility of part-of-nature thinking: the terraforming of Arrakis. The issue that this project raises is not about whether humans, with our abilities to manipulate nonhuman nature almost in its entirety, really are a fundamentally ennatured species, but instead whether we can live as part of nature given modern historical circumstances that compel the management of this nature in the name of social, scientific, technological, and/or economic development. To put this issue in the form of a question, What would living as part of nature look like in today's world? Read as environmental science fiction, *Dune* asks this question. To understand the novel's answer we must grapple with its image of the Fremen as at once consciously living their embeddedness and consciously manipulating the nature within which they are embedded. This seemingly problematical image ultimately proves to be a good starting point for reflecting on contemporary part-of-nature thinking and being in productive ways. But ahead of exploring this image, we must examine what can only be our assumptions about what Fremen culture looked like before the initiation of their terraforming effort, and in the course of this examination complicate in several ways the "nature" of which the life sciences and transformative environmentalism insist that humans are a part.

We never witness the Fremen prior to Arrakis's subsumption into the Imperium. Outside of reading about their ancient technologies and customs, about the stillsuits and rituals that they continue to use and practice during the time frame of the novel, we never witness the "first" Arrakian

Fremen. However, these first Fremen seem to have once been good ecological citizens living as part of the desert planet upon which they settled as religious outcasts; their stillsuit technology and water-saving customs suggest as much, as do their methods for avoiding confrontation with Arrakis's dominant fauna, the sandworms.[10] But this presumption about the ecocentrism of the first Fremen faces an obstacle: if technology and custom mediated their relationship with nonhuman nature, making their life on the arid, storm- and sandworm-ridden planet at least bearable, then might we say that they lived some version of the Illusion of Disembeddedness, that they didn't really live as part of nature? I am not prepared to answer this question in the affirmative, because clearly the technologies and customs of the first Fremen emerged out of their lived experience in nonhuman nature and were not applied toward manipulating this nature in a way that threatened its fitness. Stillsuits and large-scale suburban water-distribution infrastructures are not equivalent technologies; revering saliva and revering the incorporeal supranatural are not equivalent customs. Stillsuits and water-saving and water-revering traditions are human artifacts, indeed, but this detail does not preclude them from constituting a part-of-nature, ecological integrity-preserving way of life. On the other hand, as *Earth Abides* demonstrates, urban plumbing and Abrahamic religious tradition can contribute to the Illusion of Disembeddedness, which does have environmental consequences.

So the first Fremen lived their embeddedness, maintaining a culture that trod lightly upon the world. But to complicate things more, the idea that the first Fremen lived as part of nature entails an examination of what this nature is in the first place. Until now the focus of this chapter has been largely on the "part of" component of part-of-nature thinking and being; as the life sciences, transformative environmentalism, *Last and First Men*, and *Earth Abides* stress, we are not apart from the other-than-human world. For the first Fremen the nature of Arrakis is desiccation, desert, sand, sandstorms, sandworms—in short, all of the interrelated ecosystemic elements from which Fremen technology and custom emerge. This arid, sandworm-populated Arrakis is the nonhuman nature to which the first Fremen migrated and within which they lived their embeddedness for millennia. But as we later find out in the *Dune* series, Arrakis is not in any sort of primordial form. It was transformed into desert by the sandworms, which are themselves not native to the planet, having been introduced in their larval phase "'from some other place,'" as Paul's heir Leto II says in *Children of Dune* (1981) (32). As such, this "second" Arrakis acts as a metaphor for an Earth that today is not in any sort of first form.

[margin annotation: what is NATURE?]

▷ When we talk about "nature," in other words, we cannot mean "some thing that is single, independent, and lasting" or "a balanced order of self-reproduction whose homeostasis is disturbed, nudged off course, by unbalanced human interventions" (Morton 20; Žižek, *In Defense* 442). With this second Arrakis, Herbert prefigures by decades the recent trend in thinking about "ecology without nature" by implicitly defining nature not as a "thing" or a "balanced order," but instead as the interdependent processes of biological and physical phenomena that constitute and comprise all life forms and make their existence possible, processes that can no longer be said to carry on fully outside a history of human influence. Read in the light of this conception of nature first as active process rather than a static entity out there, Rachel Carson's declaration that "Man, however much he may like to pretend the contrary, is part of nature" loses the romantic hues about which ecocritic Timothy Morton and philosopher Slavoj Žižek are so critical. And if we are not apart from this active, other-than-human nature, nor are we apart from the humanized nature that has emerged since humans began to abandon hunting and gathering ten thousand years ago in the Neolithic Revolution. Something we learn by thinking about the second, postnatural Arrakis of *Dune,* then, is that regardless of our individual or social ecocentric commitments we cannot live more consciously as part of a prelapsarian Earth, because such an Earth does not exist. Right now, in the modern world, we live as part of a Ciceronian "second" nature, which at once consists of pollination, decomposition, and nutrient cycling *and* agriculture and plumbing.[11]

Given that most of our food today originates in patented industrial monocultures and most of our irrigation and drinking water originates in depleted underground aquifers and dammed rivers, I would be remiss not to acknowledge again the variations of scale within the technologies that give rise to this second nature. If we cannot return to a first nature, can we—perhaps in an effort to safeguard Earth's still-functioning life-support systems—return to living as ecocentric first Fremen, so to speak, whose technologies are not of a scale that brings about drastic alterations in fit ecosystems? Environmental science fiction has ecotopian visions of such a humanity, as the next chapter will demonstrate. But before Ernest Callenbach and Marge Piercy developed compasses for more consciously part-of-nature ways of life in *Ecotopia* and *Woman on the Edge of Time,* respectively, *Dune* underscored the enormous historical challenges of realizing such a way of life in the face of scientific and political modernity. The first, ecologically literate Fremen become "second" Fremen at the moment when they are influenced by an externally imposed, modern scientific vision of terraforming Arrakis into a water-rich planet. When living, Liet-Kynes's father, Pardot—the First Imperial Planetologist of Arrakis—used the Fremen as "the tools with which he intended to remake the planet," as the means to realize *his* mental picture of ecological "*order*" (478, 477). The resulting second, managerial Fremen engage willingly in a large-scale manipulation of planetary ecology that in no way safeguards the current Arrakian ecosystem. In fact, the sandworms face certain extinction in the face of the planned planetary alterations, for their biology is such that they cannot tolerate contact with large volumes of water.

But in a sympathetic, more historically responsive reading of this project, we can say that while it is still haunted by Pardot Kynes's human-centered "Specter of Terra (Terror)Forming," the Fremen's managerial ecology is less a manifestation of an Enlightenment will-to-dominate nature and more a way of setting up an intentional, ecologically aware culture whose millennia-old respect for and knowledge of ecosystemic processes work alongside their political needs as an oppressed people (Yanarella 225). As descendants of a nomadic religious sect that has a long history of being driven from planet to planet, the Fremen have a compelling motivation for creating a more hospitable landscape on the planet they are forced to inhabit. We might also notice that the Fremen terraforming effort involves three to five centuries of collecting water and educating generations of future Fremen about the ecological system being created: "'We change [Arrakis] . . . slowly but with certainty . . . to make it fit for human life,'" Stilgar says, "'Our generation will not see it, nor our children nor our children's children nor the grandchildren of their children . . . but it will come'" (283).

Are these second Fremen living as part of nature? They have maintained the ecological literacy, technologies, and customs of their preterraforming years, and they have a profound sense of intergenerational responsibility. Or does their entrenchment also in the history of the Dune universe and their desire to do the best they can with what they (are forced to) have negate any judgment that they are living their ecological embeddedness? Again, Herbert complicates part-of-nature thinking, this time by making us aware that opportunities for living consciously as embedded ecological citizens, for asking "What then?" about our actions, are limited by the realities of the human history and the human institutions we inherit. The goal for transformative environmentalism, of course, is to change these institutions so that ecological integrity does not have to be sacrificed in the name of economy, culture, politics, justice, and so

on. With all of its complicating factors, *Dune*'s most important lesson is
that such transformation will not happen with a simple jolt of scientific
truth administered to a modern humanity that has gotten over nonhuman
nature, and more and more has gotten over science, if it does not support the hegemonic economic and cultural trajectory. It is rather the jolt of
economic and political expediency that always seems to win out in the
modern world, and *Dune* is fully aware of this, too.

What incites change?

We never get to see the planned Fremen project come to fruition in the
course of the novel and therefore to make the difficult ethical judgment
about whether the Fremen's use of managerial science in the name of their
own social justice was worth the ultimate sacrifice of the sandworms. Perhaps we are freed from making such a judgment, because in the place of a
very deliberate planetary engineering project is slammed down a promise
of quick political gains necessarily emptied of any ecologically responsive
content. Paul Atreides plays into the legend of the messiah who will lead
the Fremen to paradise, a legend that was instilled long ago in the Fremen culture by the Bene Gesserit's Missionaria Protectiva, "the arm of
the Bene Gesserit order charged with sowing infectious superstitions on
primitive worlds, thus opening those regions to exploitation by the Bene
Gesserit" (507). Paul promises the Fremen a more rapid path toward their
terraforming goals—one not tied to the geological time constraints of the
original effort—if they take up arms against the Atreides's enemies. As
Paul's mother, an Atreides and a Bene Gesserit, reflects, "Gathering water,
planting the dunes, changing their world slowly but surely—these are no
longer enough. . . . The little raids, the certain raids—these are no longer
enough now that Paul and I have trained them. They feel their power.
They want to fight" (388).

TIME

POWER

corrupt

Leonard M. Scigaj observes of *Dune Messiah* (1975), the second book
in the *Dune* series, that the Fremen Farok's "only personal motive for
enlisting in the war . . . is to realize his fantasy of immersing himself in a
real sea" (342). The reason Farok believes he will see Arrakian seas in his
lifetime, as opposed to expecting the change to come in three to five centuries, is Paul's rousing speech in *Dune:* "'What's our goal?' Paul asked.
'To unseat Rabban, the Harkonnen beast, and remake our world into a
place where we may raise our families in happiness amidst an abundance
of water'" (414). That Paul convinces the living Fremen—"we" rather
than "our future generations"—that they will raise their families in such
a paradise demonstrates the danger of modernity's drive toward expediency, and indeed, the lure of expediency is another key complicating fac-
tor when thinking about modern humans as part of nature. Paul Atreides

DREAM

EGO

PARADISE

pulls the Fremen from their deliberate ways as a culture fighting political oppression in a way compatible with their long-established, consciously part-of-nature ways of life. Paul's war does not free the Fremen from colonial subjugation and immediately lift their everyday toil. Instead, it denies them the total independence that the terraforming plan would have permitted and forces them further into the hands of the ruling class. In *Dune Messiah*, Farok admits in retrospect that Fremen participation in the war was fueled by a desire for "'experiences, adventure, wealth,'" and indeed the seas (58). And as Paul observes in that book, the Fremen had "become a civilization of . . . people who solved all problems with power . . . and more power . . . and still more power" (225). Paul's revolution acts as a social trap for the Fremen, in which "players," in this case the Fremen, "are lured into behavior that eventually undermines the health and stability of the system" (Orr 5). The second Fremen become the "third," and the second nature of Arrakis is subsumed into a political scheme that ultimately drives away the sandworms *and* undermines both the Fremen's sovereignty and their ecological intelligence.

Dune offers a complicating theorization about part-of-nature thinking and being. Rather than displaying assertions of human embeddedness as too narrow or romantic to matter in our complex contemporary moment, though, this discourse instead prompts a deeper investigation of what such embeddedness means in a world where we cannot easily put away modernity and then find a definitively natural place to settle and live more consciously as part of nature. Perhaps to acknowledge and live today our ecological embeddedness is to acknowledge and live *Dune*'s implicit, more sobering lesson: we are a part of the bee *and* the GMO crop, the water cycle *and* the faucet, the forest *and* the lumber, the ocean *and* the oil. The priority for what might be qualified as "traditional" part-of-nature thinking is to advocate for the bee over the crop and the ocean over the oil—in short, for the preservation of nonhuman nature over the proliferation of technologies that use this nature toward purely anthropo- and econocentric ends. *Dune* asserts that we cannot live this priority in the modern world without major shifts in our values and practices, at all levels of society.

As Žižek argues, "One should . . . become aware not only of the limitation of the ideology of progress, but also of the limitation of the . . . notion of the revolution as applying the emergency brake on the runaway train of progress" (*In Defense* 442). Read for their environmentalist contributions,

Last and First Men and *Earth Abides* make us aware of the limitations of a progress that requires our illusory separation from nonhuman nature. And *Dune* teaches us that the brake cannot simply be pulled. But Herbert's message is not to give in hopelessly to the driving forces of social and economic modernity; for, when the Fremen do exactly this, it undermines their ecological and political existence as Arrakian Fremen. *Dune* shows us that there is a "third" nature on the horizon—not a prehistorical "domain of balanced reproduction," not a regrowth of once wild places or an artifactual re-creation of natural processes, but finally an ecodystopian world unable to support human and nonhuman flourishing (Žižek, *In Defense* 442).[12]

CHAPTER TWO

ECOTOPIA, ECODYSTOPIA, AND THE VISIONS OF DEEP ECOLOGY

THE UTOPIAN SOCIETIES imagined in Ernest Callenbach's *Ecotopia* (1975) and Marge Piercy's *Woman on the Edge of Time* (1976) resonate with the transformative environmentalist perspective called deep ecology, which identifies anthropocentric instrumental rationality as the driver of dominant, anti-ecological socioeconomic and cultural ways of thinking and being.[1] Summarizing the philosophy of Arne Naess, the environmental philosopher who coined the term *deep ecology* in the early 1970s, David E. Cooper writes, "Among the policies advocated by Naess are radical reduction of the world's population, abandonment of the goal of economic growth in the developed world, conservation of biotic diversity, living in small, simple, and self-reliant communities, and—less specifically—a commitment 'to touch the Earth lightly'" (213). Callenbach's and Piercy's utopias display almost programmatic commitments to such ideals, advocating in the mid-1970s a way of conceiving and being in the world that is still widely influential among environmentalist scholars and activists. These novels think deep ecology with their mutually supportive ideas on population reduction, alternative modes of economic production, biodiversity (as a material and spiritual-psychological imperative), communal life ways, and reducing human impact on Earth.

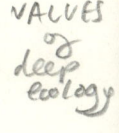

VALUES
of
deep
ecology

It would be anachronistic to claim that *Ecotopia* and *Woman on the Edge of Time* grew out of their respective authors' direct engagements with the deep ecology movement, because in 1975 and 1976 deep ecology was not yet a codified philosophical perspective. But finding a direction in the relationship between deep ecology and the utopian fictions discussed here is of lesser value, in my view, than recognizing the set of interests and concerns that gave rise both to deep ecology and these books at proximate moments in Western history. As deep ecologist Bill Devall notes, the 1960s and 1970s saw the development of environmentalism in response to "the effects of the explosive growth of human population; the effects of toxic wastes and pollution on air, water, and soil as well as on human health and well-being; and deforestation and human-caused extinction of other species" ("Deep Ecology" 51). But by the mid-1970s this environmentalism became an institution, with many of its already existing and new membership organizations (e.g., the Sierra Club, the Natural Resources Defense Council) bureaucratically advocating for policy changes but not leading a charge for fundamental transformations in "our society's basic culture" (Devall, "Deep Ecology" 52).[2] The *deep* in deep ecology thus countered what many grassroots environmentalists deemed to be an ultimately *shallow* reformist environmental movement. Growing ecological degradation coupled with an ineffectual effort to address this degradation's core ideological inputs motivated deep ecology to take a different route to meaningful environmental activism. Callenbach's and Piercy's books are literary utopian embraces of this deep environmentalist commitment. They question and repudiate socioeconomic institutions and cultural attitudes that continue to dominate modern life today, disagreeing with the ideologies that inform modern being and positing substitute social and cultural arrangements.

By virtue of the precision with which *Ecotopia*'s and *Woman on the Edge of Time*'s utopian communities align with deep ecology's ideals, the books can serve a pedagogical function for the movement as well as a critical function for uncovering the movement's limitations. Reflecting the neo-Malthusian worries that constituted 1960s and 1970s environmentalism, *Ecotopia* and *Woman on the Edge of Time*, like deep ecology, posit a declining human population as essential for ecological and social vitality. While the books, again like deep ecology, are also critical of economic growth as a major influence on ecological and social degradation, they do little to presage the virtual disappearance of reactionary, apocalyptic overpopulation myths against recent criticisms of capitalist production and other origins of this degradation.[3] Both books also raise the specter of violence as a necessary liberatory strategy, something not endemic to deep ecology but indeed a lurking possibility given especially the combination of deep ecology's antithetical orientation and the Western political establishment's efforts to reject the kinds of alternative socioeconomic and cultural possibilities that deep ecology sponsors.

This chapter thus ends with a look at John Brunner's dystopian novels *Stand on Zanzibar* (1968) and *The Sheep Look Up* (1972), which can be interpreted to theorize prefiguratively a reconstruction of deep ecology by thinking more explicitly than the ecotopias do about demographic challenges and problems of radical environmentalist praxis. In addition to motivating deep ecology with their harrowing, dystopian images of ecological and social breakdown, Brunner's books make it clear that (1) within our contemporary moment human overpopulation demands less of our attention than does the dominating mode of globalized economic production and (2) violent engagement in the interest of ecological or social liberation might appear as activists embrace a deep ecological ideological orientation, and thus the fundamentally nonviolent movement must contend with such a possibility. Again, it would be anachronistic to suppose that Brunner's dystopias, which predate deep ecology and the utopias discussed here, responded directly either to deep ecology's shortcomings or to Callenbach and Piercy. But reading *Ecotopia, Woman on the Edge of Time, Stand on Zanzibar,* and *The Sheep Look Up* as manifesting and/or challenging the visions of deep ecology is more an exercise in highlighting the value of mingling these works in a dialogical interplay ultimately to synthesize an ecological, activist perspective that each book alone—and deep ecology alone—cannot provide.

As Devall and Sessions note in their deep ecology manifesto, *Deep Ecology,* the movement finds its philosophical influences in many places: the Pythagorean, Platonic, Spinozan, and Huxlian "metaphysics of interrelatedness," which places "humans in the wider scheme of things" (80); the literature of the British and American Romantic periods, as well as more recent literature that reflects comparable suspicions about modern, industrial life; ecological science and newer models of physics that reject the notion of scientific objectivity; Franciscan Christianity and Eastern spiritual traditions; feminism; and the knowledges and experiences of indigenous peoples (83–108). Deep ecology "recognizes the fundamental interdependence of all phenomena and the fact that, as individuals and societies, we are all embedded in (and ultimately dependent on) the cyclical processes of nature" (Capra 6). To its understanding of human *being* deep ecology adds a spirituality not confined to top-down, institutional religiosity, but expanded to practice "the mode of consciousness in which the individual feels a sense of belonging, of connectedness, to the cosmos as a whole" (Capra 7). As a transformative environmental movement, deep ecology encourages significant ethical, epistemological, and ontological reorientations in a modern world where scientific quantification and manipulation, economic expansion, and human domination persist as central creeds.

Telling influences on deep ecology exist not only in canonical Romantic or spiritual writing, Huxlian philosophy, or indigenous epistemology, but also in utopian science fiction literature that attends to the illusory divide between humans and other-than-human nature. The societies imagined in these ecotopias avow both the intrinsic value of nonhuman nature—its value apart from its utility for humans—and the importance for humans to act within, not outside of, natural dictates. The value of ecotopian vision has not gone unnoticed by Devall and Sessions; they discuss the importance of ecotopian narrative in their book: "Creating ecotopian futures has practical value. It helps us articulate our goals and presents an ideal which may never be completely realized but which keeps us focused on the ideal. We can also compare our personal actions and collective public decisions on specific issues with this goal" (162). Though not scholars of utopia, Devall and Sessions echo academics who assert the importance of the utopian imagination in modern culture. They do for ecotopian fiction what utopian literary scholars do for utopian fiction—that is, declare the significance of what one such scholar, Lyman Tower Sargent, calls "social dreaming" for the realization of an alternative, more just or ethical, society (1). As Tom Moylan writes, by producing images "that radically break with prevailing social systems . . . utopian discourse articulates the possibility of other ways of living in the world" (*Demand* 26). And extending Moylan's analysis, Phillip E. Wegner demonstrates the ways in which the imaginary communities of Thomas More's *Utopia* (1516), Edward Bellamy's *Looking Backward* (1888), Ursula K. Le Guin's *The Dispossessed* (1974), and other texts have transcended imaginary possibility and have figured into modern nation-building:

> in the narrative utopia, the presentation of an "ideal world" operates as a kind of lure, a play on deep desires, both immediately historical and otherwise, to draw its readers in and thereby enable the form's educa-

tional machinery to go to work—a machinery that enables its readers to perceive the world they occupy in a new way, providing them with some of the skills and dispositions necessary to inhabit an emerging social, political, and cultural environment. (2)

Utopian fiction is fiction of possibility; it envisions optional cultural paths, "catalyzes desire" for these paths, and instructs cultural and political progress with its "visionary glimpses of how our real world could be changed" (Mohr 278).

Deep ecology's endorsement of ecotopian fiction stems from the ideal worlds that ecotopias imagine. A movement grounded in a critique of what it sees as the outmoded, unsustainable Western worldview and in a combination of scientific and spiritual notions of embeddedness, deep ecology finds in ecotopian texts the narration of its appraisals and desires. Unlike the space of the modern developed world, ecotopian space intrudes little on other species and their habitats. Its human inhabitants participate in communal governments and promote economic systems that are not growth-centered and resource-intensive. Ecotopian fiction portrays worlds far different from the originary world that it contests, articulating ecologically conscientious life ways hitherto contained or eradicated by modern social, political, economic, educational, and religious life. Ecotopian fiction is an instructive "educational machinery," a cognitively estranging lens through which readers can compare their world with that proposed in fiction and as a result better perceive the inadequacies of current worldviews and practices. Devall and Sessions's confidence in ecotopian fiction stems from their understanding of the genre's possibilities for narrowing "the distance between what ought to be and what is now reality in our technocratic-industrial society" (162).

While ecotopian fiction occupies an important place in deep ecology, ecodystopian fiction holds similar and potentially greater value as an instructional literature of deep ecology. According to Sargent, dystopian narrative describes in detail nonexistent societies "that the author intended a contemporaneous reader to view as considerably worse than the society in which the reader lived" (9). Despite its dreadful extrapolations, dystopian narrative maintains the utopian impulse: as Moylan notes, "a dystopian text can be seen as *utopian* in tendency if in its portrayal of the 'bad place' it suggests (even if indirectly) or at least stimulates the potential for an effective challenge and possibly change by virtue of human efforts" (*Scraps* 156). And as Dunja M. Mohr observes,

Where utopia uplifts the reader, dystopia holds up a hellish mirror and describes the worst of all possible futures. Although both utopian and dystopian imaginings of the future refer readers to the present and seek to implant a desire for societal transformation, they evoke different effects: the utopian defamiliarization takes the avenue of arousing readers' desire for utopia, whilst the defamiliarized dystopian society appalls readers.

Where utopia compares social vision and reality by creating difference, dystopia presupposes and thrives on the correlation and similarity of the present social order and the near-future scenario. Using opposed strategies, both utopia and dystopia, however, share the same objective: sociopolitical change by means of the aesthetic representation of a paradigm shift. (27–28)

Dystopia fuels opposition to unethical systems of domination and oppression by portraying worlds where readers might live if steps are not taken to change these systems, and, I will add, by imaginatively rendering current global situations that demand immediate attention.

Ecodystopia, as a version of dystopia functioning under the same definitional rubric, offers something ecotopia cannot, because of the latter's generic constraints: extended reflections on the issues that give rise to deep ecological sentiments, including overpopulation, species extinction, and air and water pollution. Ecodystopian science fiction stages dystopian presents and futures, frightening worlds not disengaged from the now but instead very much extrapolated out of some current and real, anti-ecological trend—whether that trend is social, scientific, economic, religious, or a combination of these and others rehearsed daily in the contemporary order of things. Significant, too, is that ecodystopia's generic imperative to represent consequences also initiates important reflections on the viability and ethics of solutions that deep ecological philosophy can be interpreted to support, such as population controls or acts of violent ecotage against inflexible social and cultural institutions. This characteristic aligns ecodystopia with what Sargent, Moylan, and others have deemed the "critical" trend in dystopian narrative, though not in the same sense of being like more recent dystopias that are "self-reflexively 'critical'" of traditional dystopian tendencies (Moylan, *Scraps* 188). The works by John Brunner examined below indeed move ecodystopian science fiction in such a direction, but critical ecodystopia reflects more so on ecotopian (im)possibility given the sociopolitical realities of the spaces upon which ecotopian thinkers want to layer their dreams. Thus, much like *Dune*, this type of fiction is a powerful tool for stimulating new, more ecologically and socially conscious ways of thinking and being in the world.

❖

Ecotopia chronicles the visit of the *New York Times-Post* reporter William Weston to Ecotopia, geographically the area once comprising Washington, Oregon, and northern California. Ecotopia seceded from the United States twenty years prior to William's visit, and William's purpose there is to write a series of articles documenting the unusual practices of the nation's people. These practices include, among other things, maintaining an antigrowth economy and fulfilling a national goal to reduce population. Early in the book, William's newspaper articles—which along with an italicized private notebook make up the book—are openly critical of Ecotopian ways: their lack of traffic and billboards is drab and isolating; their recycling requires too much personal effort; and their elimination of processed foods and putting certain foods on "'Bad Practice lists'" is "a loophole that might house a large and rather totalitarian rat" (19). Despite the reporter's early judgments, later he admits a change in attitude toward the nation: "*the more closely I look at the fabric of Ecotopian life, the more I am forced to admit its strength and its beauty*" (95). Though William's visit to Ecotopia is supposed to last just six weeks, in the end he stays there. In a farewell letter to his editor he writes, "*I've decided not to come back, Max. You'll understand why from the notebook. But thank you for sending me on this assignment, when neither you nor I knew where it might lead. It led me home*" (167).

A similar reevaluation of ecotopian life occurs in Piercy's *Woman on the Edge of Time* as the book's main character, Connie Ramos, admits she wishes her young daughter could grow up in Mattapoisett, the novel's near-future ecotopia to which she travels:

> She will be strange, but she will be glad and strong and she will not be afraid. She will have enough. She will have pride. She will love her own brown skin and be loved for her strength and her good work. She will walk in strength like a man and never sell her body and she will nurse her babies like a woman and live in love like a garden, like that children's house of many colors. People of the rainbow with its end fixed in earth, I give her to you! (133)

Connie has reasons to want such a future for her daughter, because Connie has grown up in fast-paced New York City, has lived on the streets, has been abused physically and mentally by men, has had the one man she ever loved taken away from her by the prison system and killed in a medical experiment, and during the course of the novel is forced into a medical experiment while living in a mental health facility. Despite the aversion Connie should have toward existing institutions, similar to William in Callenbach's book, she is reluctant to accept the promises of ecotopia. Her friend from Mattapoisett in the year 2137, Luciente, informs her of the fundamental social changes that have occurred in the alternative future; living under modernity's ideological supremacy, Connie can only doubt the viability of these changes. She questions the city's lack of social hierarchy, of patriarchy, and of centralized government. But the revolutionary thinkers living in the ecotopian future ultimately assist Connie on a journey to free herself from the forces that have dominated her life for so long. In the end, while she does not get to live in the future ecotopia, she thinks of Mattapoisett as she revolts against her oppressors at the hospital.

One of the concerns shared by these ecotopias and deep ecology is human demographics. Following a host of writers who in the 1960s and 1970s attended to the potential consequences of human overpopulation, both Naess and the deep ecologist, poet, and essayist Gary Snyder agree that taking steps to reduce world population is necessary for the realization not only of deep ecology's ecocentric ideals but also of general ecosystemic health.[4] In his 1973 essay "The Shallow and the Deep, Long-Range Ecology Movements," Naess sketches his deep ecological concept of biospherical egalitarianism, which to him is fundamental to environmental movements wanting to do more than institute shallow legislative efforts to cut pollution and resource depletion, efforts really aimed at preserving natural resources for the people of affluent nations. Biospherical egalitarianism requires "a deep-seated respect, or even veneration, for ways and forms of life" (151–52). It eschews anthropocentric hierarchies of being, instead observing the equal right to flourish for all species. Importantly, biospherical egalitarianism "implies the reinterpretation of the future-research variable, 'level of crowding,' so that *general* mammalian crowding and loss of life-equality is taken seriously" (152). Life-equality necessitates the protection of appropriate life-space requirements (physical space and resource availability) for all organisms. And since life space for any one species is reduced as another species overcrowds and infiltrates, human overpopulation violates such egalitarian principles.

Because human crowding threatens the abilities of other species to flourish, Snyder, in his essay "Four Changes," suggests cutting world population—about 3.6 billion at the time of the essay's publication in 1969— in half. His reasoning is similar to Naess's:

> Position: Man is but a part of the fabric of life—dependent on the whole fabric for his very existence. As the most highly developed tool-using animal, he must recognize that the unknown evolutionary destinies of other life forms are to be respected, and act as gentle stewards of the earth's community of being.

> Situation: There are now too many human beings, and the problem is growing rapidly worse. It is potentially disastrous not only for the human race but for most other life forms. (141–42)

The population problem can be addressed on the social and political levels worldwide, Snyder believes, by convincing governments that human overpopulation is a serious problem, by legalizing abortion and promoting sterilization, by questioning and correcting cultural ways of thinking that press women to have children, and by refusing to see a nation's growing population as a sign of a good economy. Advocating changes in community structure, Snyder endorses alternative marriage arrangements, sharing "the pleasures of raising children widely, so that all need not directly reproduce to enter into this basic human experience," limiting family size, adopting children, and as Naess also encourages, developing kinship with nonhuman species (142).

In Callenbach's book, after seceding from the United States, Ecotopia engages in a national effort to reduce its population. Ecotopians want to decrease population to minimize pressure on resources and on other species, and to improve the quality of life for their nation's people. They begin their efforts by legalizing and lowering the cost of abortion, as well as universalizing female contraceptives. Both prove effective, as deaths begin to outnumber births. The Ecotopian population declines during one measured period by seventeen thousand, while in that same period American society gains three million. The national goal to reduce population is coupled with a move away from centralized, metropolitan social organization and toward more deliberate living in dispersed small communities. As a result, and to give only one example from the book, "instead of massive hospitals in the city centers, besieged by huge lines of waiting patients, there were small hospitals and clinics everywhere" (62). Finally, Ecotopians rethink the concept of family, disintegrating the nuclear ideal that obligates as a moral, if even economic, responsibility the replacement of oneself with single, or more often multiple, consuming progeny. Instead, Ecotopians value family as "a group of between five and 20 people, some of them actually related and some not, who live together" (64).

The efforts to reduce population in *Woman on the Edge of Time,* and to value family structures not dependent on one's own reproduction, also mirror the ideas of deep ecology. Though Mattapoisett's use of "brooders," tanks in which human fetuses are grown, is more formulaically science fictional than Ecotopia's political and social mechanisms, it nevertheless stages deep ecology's position on population reduction and control. The brooder becomes not a real option, but instead an estranging *novum* that provokes environmentalist, and feminist, reflection on the possibilities of reproductive technology. For feminism, the brooders free women and men from biological enchainment, indicating Piercy's "faith in the liberatory potential of reproductive technologies" (Sandilands 9)—women, liberated from "the power to give birth," and men, from never being "humanized to be loving and tender" (Piercy 98). For deep ecology, such technology also liberates nonhuman nature from human overpopulation, a liberation that is central to the movement's platform.[5] Further, similar to the communal groups of Ecotopia, and to the community childrearing Snyder proposes, Mattapoisett's children are assigned three "mothers," or nurturers, who can be male or female.[6] This restructuring of family life to extend and value nurturance beyond genetic relations, coupled with the deliberate move to shrink population, grows out of a conscious social effort to minimize the effects of material culture on Mattapoisett's material base, its ecology.

For deep ecology, maniacal economic growth and consumerist trends have likewise distressed the world's ecosystems, this time by encouraging an excessive mining of natural material. As Sessions notes in his preface to *Deep Ecology for the 21st Century,*

> Government leaders and economic elites in Industrial Growth Societies continue to push for endless economic growth and development. . . . Third World countries are now entering global markets and trying to become First World countries by destroying their ecosystems and wild species as they emulate the industrial and consumer patterns of the ecologically destructive unsustainable First World. (xx)

Earth Policy Institute president Lester R. Brown speaks also to this point: "Over the last half-century, the sevenfold expansion of the global economy has pushed the demand on local ecosystems beyond the sustainable yield in country after country" (79). Brown's specific concern is with the growth economy's more recent injurious effects on oceanic fisheries, forests, and rangelands. But even the deep ecologists of the 1970s recognized economic growth as responsible for overtaxing vital ecosystemic processes and damaging the systems necessary for human and nonhuman life. They advocated, then as now, for fundamental changes in the ways developing and industrial societies view such growth. Rather than valuing economic expansion and consumerism, deep ecologists and the ecotopian writers discussed here look toward more ecologically and socially conscientious economic paradigms.

Naess, for example, outlines several requisite lifestyle changes for transforming modernity's growth-centered economy into an ecologically viable system: "Anticonsumerism and minimization of personal property"; "Endeavor to maintain and increase sensitivity and appreciation of goods of which there is enough for all to enjoy"; "Absence or low degree of 'novophilia'—the love of what is new merely because it is new. Cherishing old and well-worn things"; "the attempt to avoid a material standard of living too much different from and higher than the needy"; and "Appreciation of lifestyles which are universalizable, which are not blatantly impossible to sustain without injustice toward fellow humans or other species" ("Deep Ecology" 260). Also writing against the grain of production-driven consumerist ideology, Snyder offers a Thoreauvian maxim: "True affluence is not needing anything" (146). With an assertion about the cancerous nature of economic growth, Snyder suggests that rather than promoting such growth without considering its deleterious effects on ecosystems, the economy should handle production, distribution, and consumption "with the same elegance and spareness one sees in nature" (146). For Snyder, hoarding personal possessions must be surrendered to communal sharing, and the modern fascination with new technologies must be surrendered to a high esteem for old ways: "handicrafts, gardening, home skills, midwifery, herbs—all the things that can make us independent, beautiful and whole" (146).

In his first newspaper article on the subject of Ecotopian society William displays his growth-centered culture's fear of the utopian nation's antigrowth economy: "Ecotopia still poses a nagging challenge to the underlying national philosophy of America: ever-continuing progress, the fruits of industrialization for all, a rising Gross National Product" (4). William perceives Ecotopia's stable-state system in this way because "*it means giving up any notions of progress. You just want to get to that stable point and stay there, like a lump*" (31). With his censuring of economic systems that see industrialization and a rising GNP as unnecessary and unhealthy, William exhibits his U.S. culture's marriage to the growth model. What William cannot see in Ecotopia's economy—rather, what his upbringing prevents him from seeing—is its agents' primary motivation to preserve ecological integrity and to fulfill an ecological ethic of species equality. He can at least communicate the Ecotopian point of view, a fact that fore-shadows his ultimate acceptance of it: "humans were meant to take their modest place in a seamless, stable-state web of living organisms, disturb-ing that web as little as possible" and "People were to be happy not to the extent they dominated their fellow creatures on the earth, but to the extent they lived in balance with them" (43–44). But William's defense of "the underlying national philosophy of America" reflects more the attitudes of the system from which he comes. He analyzes Ecotopia's stable-state economy using capitalist language, inevitably condemning any contrary economic possibilities. If William's American readers believe that Ecoto-pia cannot maintain a decent *standard of living* with its twenty-hour work week, that Ecotopia's system cannot *attract capital,* and that the nation will suffer *financial collapse,* then they are too deeply fixed in the language and rationalizations of capital to see or admit the triumph of Ecotopia's divergent economy, which does not subscribe to capital's exact notions of standard of living, investment, and financial success (48). Interpreted with the language of capital, the stable-state system will always fail; but inter-preted with its own ecocentric logic, the Ecotopian economy realizes Sny-der's "true affluence."

In Piercy's book, Connie's expectations when she first arrives in Mat-tapoisett demonstrate her faith in a booming economic future: "Rocket ships, skyscrapers into the stratosphere, an underground mole world miles deep, glass domes over everything" (62). But opening her eyes she sees instead the village of a bucolic past, prompting her to ask Luciente, "'You sure we went in the right direction? Into the future?'" (62). Luciente assents and Connie replies questioningly, "'Forward, into the past? Okay, it's better to live in a green meadow than on 111th Street. But all this striv-ing and struggling to end up in the same old bind'" (64). This sentiment repeats William's initial attitude about Ecotopia's seemingly backward sys-tem. Both protagonists reflect the capitalist tendency to view as economi-cally and socially regressive any alternative mode of economic production that does not depend on, and thus relentlessly provide, a constant flow of commodities through markets and a constant reinvestment of capital into new, marketable stuff and exploitable places and cultures.

In addition to its concerns about overpopulation and growth-centered economics, deep ecology advocates a *"relational, total-field image,"* a perception of "Organisms as knots in the biospherical net or field of intrin-sic relations" that at once reflects the materialist, part-of-nature thinking reviewed in chapter 1 and a related ecospirituality that is central to deep ecology and, as chapter 3 will demonstrate, cultural ecofeminism (Naess, "The Shallow" 151). Snyder, who derives his ecophilosophy from Bud-dhist concepts of organic unity and Animist ideas about the spiritual matrix that connects all life and material (Taylor, "Snyder"), writes, "Man is but a part of the fabric of life—dependent on the whole fabric for his very existence" (141). While this is true scientifically, for deep ecology the properly ecocentric attitude is also one that makes spiritual the ecologi-cal connections among nature's varied, and often instrumentally valueless, elemental parts. As Bron Taylor and Michael Zimmerman write,

> Naess and most deep ecologists . . . trace their perspective to personal experiences of connection to and wholeness in wild nature, experi-ences which are the ground of their intuitive, affective perception of the sacredness and interconnection of all life. Those who have experienced such a transformation of consciousness (experiencing what is sometimes called one's "ecological self" in these movements) view the self not as separate from and superior to all else, but rather as a small part of the entire cosmos. (456)

Deep ecologists apprehend the human self by identifying the ecological and cosmological totality within which this self exists.

In Callenbach's book, Ecotopians educate their children in a manner consistent with deep ecology's scientific *total-field image,* and they worship in a way consistent with the movement's ecospirituality. About Ecotopian schoolchildren, William writes, their experiences

> are closely tied in with studies of plants, animals and landscape. I have been impressed with the knowledge that even young children have of such matters—a six-year-old can tell you all about the "ecological niches" of the creatures and plants he encounters in his daily life. He will also know what roots and berries are edible, how to use soap plant, how to carve a pot holder from a branch. (35–36)

An Ecotopian ten-year-old knows "how hundreds of species of plants and animals live, both around their schools and in the areas they explore on backpacking expeditions" (120). Such knowledge, even in young children, would be taken for granted in an ecologically literate soci-ety. But traditional education instead practices conservative pedagogical

models, which according to environmental educator C. A. Bowers emphasize not ecological literacy but rather human achievements of the past,
social engagement, and job training (37–38). Just as ignorant of ecology
are liberal models of education, which focus on social development, individualism, and rational, linear thinking (Bowers 74–76). Whatever their
merits, these pedagogical trends become harmful in their neglect of ecology and of understanding human achievement, social engagement, the
individual, and so forth within the context of ecological relationships. Perhaps William writes "'ecological niches'" within quotation marks because
of his *Times-Post* readers' unfamiliarity with the term. Their education
presumably has not accounted for ecology in the same way the Ecotopians' has. Ecotopian adults can be heard saying, "'*Knowing yourself as an
animal creature on the earth, as we do. It can feel more comfortable than
[William's] kind of life*'" (80–81) and "'*We don't think in terms of 'things,'
there's no such thing as a thing—there are only systems*'" (81).

Rooted also in a cosmology that, as critic Jim Dwyer notes, "inspires
people to consider themselves intrinsic parts of nature and act accordingly," Ecotopian spiritual life reflects the ecocentric tenets of its educational system (565). This correspondence makes sense from the perspective
of deep ecology, which connects pedagogy with spiritual growth: "Education should have as its goal encouraging the spiritual development and
personhood development of the members of a community" (Devall, "The
Deep" 134). Never in *Ecotopia* does William submit to his *Times-Post* editor an extended reflection on Ecotopian religion; he mentions spirituality
peripherally in his discussions of economy, population, and health care.
And when he does touch on the issue, either in an article or in his personal
journal, he does so with an Abrahamic discomfort with nature-based spirituality. Ecotopians hold pagan charms, eschew the clear-cutting of forests
for their apparent worship of trees, build shrines to various spirits, and
embrace death as a part of the cycle of life. Similarly, in Piercy's book,
the people of Mattapoisett live their cosmology "as partners with water,
air, birds, fish, trees," professing nothing of an institutional religion but
instead deeply integrating themselves in ceremonies "to heal the world we
live in with so many others" (118, 269). Aligned in *Ecotopia* and *Woman
on the Edge of Time* with an overall superior quality of social and ecological life, such ecospirituality—and indeed its educational complement—is
contrasted with those religious and pedagogical systems of modern life
that deny human embeddedness in other-than-human nature.[7]

Deep ecologists hope to engender a new notion of community. For
them, community goes beyond human social interaction. A community

is instead a total ecological field, a life system, and even a form of life. And because "The vulnerability of a form of life is roughly proportional to the weight of influences from afar, from outside the local region in which that form has obtained an ecological equilibrium," our current tendency to import commodities and consumer ways of life into established human–nonhuman ecological fields disturbs the evolutionary self-sufficiency of these fields (Naess, "The Shallow" 153).[8] The result is a social degradation that is both a symptom and a source of ecological degradation. To solve this problem Naess advocates strengthening local self-government and community self-sufficiency. Snyder supports similar moves: "Division by natural and cultural boundaries rather than arbitrary political boundaries" and "land-use being sensitive to the properties of each region" (147).[9] Such bioregional thought pervades contemporary environmentalist discussions, which often advocate using locally available resources, rebuilding local economies, and establishing participatory democratic communities.

Callenbach reflects on the strengths of community and bioregional autonomy in three ways in his book. First, all Ecotopian food, energy, and building materials are locally harvested, and the nature of this practice is such that local systems remain healthy and distant systems remain untouched—at least by Ecotopians. Second, attesting to the importance of self-in-community, William eventually becomes aware of his and his culture's unfulfilling disconnectedness from what could be called Stegnerian place.[10] He writes, "*I'm beginning to see that to an Ecotopian, who always has a strong collective base to return to, a place and the people of that place, my existence must seem pathetically insecure*" (127). When William admits "*I have never cried about it. But maybe I should,*" Callenbach issues a compelling request for readers to evaluate their own disconnectedness and to envision life in community, with a strong sense of belonging (127). Finally, Ecotopia decentralizes the operations of local regions, getting rid of national spending and putting control of "basic life systems" into the hands of local communities (62). As a result of these changes, communities arrange their lives more deliberately, population density drops, medical services improve, and previously threatened ecosystems flourish.

Mattapoisett is also community- and bioregionally-oriented. As Jackrabbit, one of the town's dwellers, says, "'A sense of land, of village and base and family. We're strongly rooted'" (116); and the village is "'Own-fed,'" "'Self-sufficient as possible in proteins'" (64). In their recognition of themselves as part of community, as part of (deep ecological) nature, Mattapoisett's people fulfill a central goal of deep ecology: self-realization in other-than-human nature. As Sessions notes, "human individuals attain personal self-realization and psychological-emotional maturity when they progress from an identification with narrow ego, through identification with other humans, to a more all-encompassing identification of their 'self' with nonhuman individuals, species, ecosystems, and with the ecosphere itself" ("Deep Ecology" 211). Connie's desire for her daughter to grow up in Mattapoisett and William's choice to stay in Ecotopia are largely functions of the psychological completeness each experiences in their respective new communities. This completeness results from the conscious social, political, economic, educational, and spiritual policies and practices of ecotopia, all of which lead to the most general but materially significant consequence of ecotopian deep ecology: the small human footprint.

With its appraisals of overpopulation and growth and consumer tendencies, as well as its ecological-ecospiritual practices and redefinition of community, deep ecology hopes ultimately to lessen human influence on the nature within which a particular kind of (utopian or whole) human, and even nonhuman, identity emerges. With ecological integrity comes social and individual integrity; any utopian hope for the latter necessarily entails the former as the result of a practiced ecocentric ethic, which, following Aldo Leopold's land ethic, argues for the protection of "the long-term flourishing of all ecosystems and each of their constituent parts" (Taylor and Zimmerman 456). What matters most to Ecotopians, according to William, "*is the aspiration to live in balance with nature, 'walk lightly on the land,' treat the earth as a mother*" (29). And summing up the critical stance of ecotopian deep ecology in general, Bolivar, a key spokesperson for social opinion in Mattapoisett, states, "'I guess I see the original division of labor, that first dichotomy, as enabling later divvies into haves and have-nots, powerful and powerless, enjoyers and workers, rapists and victims. The patriarchal mind/body split turned the body to machine and the rest of the universe into booty on which the will could run rampant, using, discarding, destroying'" (203).[11] The collective story written by *Ecotopia* and *Woman on the Edge of Time* narrates deep ecology's stance on these dominant conceptual dualisms. It is a story that always reveals the disparity between a "balanced" ecotopian society and a disembedded, displaced modern society. With William contrasting his lived experiences in Ecotopia against his lived experiences in the United States, and Connie living two experiences as she bounces back and forth between polarized worlds, these ecotopias transport us back and forth between our known world and the world of possibility. Indeed and as such, ecotopia offers another dualism, but it is one that strategically privileges subordinated sociopolitical and ecologically conscious options. Callenbach's and Piercy's books demonstrate the value of ecotopian fiction for communicating and exploring the changes advocated by a transformative environmental philosophy that will have nothing less than comprehensive change to dominant socioeconomic and cultural practices.

Following the previous discussion of ecotopian fiction, this section of chapter 2 highlights what is precisely deep ecological in ecodystopian fiction, the question being, "How does such fiction also motivate deep ecological dreaming?" Dystopia always contains an implicit utopian drive, as Moylan and Mohr argue, but while this feature of John Brunner's *Stand on Zanzibar* and *The Sheep Look Up* leads them to go together with ecotopia and deep ecology, the books cannot be read in complete alignment with deep ecology's espoused principles. Even if we read utopia as a compass rather than a blueprint, as political scientist Marius de Geus argues we must, we still need to be critical about the direction in which the compass points us.[12] Brunner's ecodystopias enable this corrective. Extrapolating atrocious global futures from some very present and real situations, they not only concentrate our attention on the most critical matters but also question the viability of the ways we choose to act going forward.

As demonstrated earlier, population reduction is a key interest in *Ecotopia, Woman on the Edge of Time*, and deep ecology, emerging as they do out of a cultural moment that also produced Paul Ehrlich's *The Population Bomb* (1968) and other demographic studies, fictional and nonfictional. Ecotopians make it a national goal to decrease population; Mattapoisett controls population scientifically, growing its future generations in brooders; and deep ecology holds as one of its eight basic principles that "The flourishing of human life and cultures is compatible with a substantially smaller human population. The flourishing of non-human life *requires* a smaller human population" (Naess, "The Deep" 68). *Stand on Zanzibar*'s insights into overpopulation soften deep ecology's and ecotopia's strong, if not dogmatic, attention to population controls by highlighting the growth economy and modern consumption habits as much more detrimental than overpopulation to ecological health and by drawing attention to the ethical problems inherent in controlling population. The book challenges the emphasis on population reduction that characterized many early works of environmental fiction and nonfiction, encouraging critical readers not to deemphasize the global harm of overpopulation—to be sure, the book's title is a direct reference to overpopulation—but to recognize modern economic doctrine as demanding greater attention.[13] Human overcrowding jeopardizes appropriate life space requirements for other species, but it is certainly feasible and in fact historically accurate to find that more damaging consequences arise from the encroachment of economic systems that liquidate human and nonhuman life space in the name of economic policy, even using demographic trends to justify increased production.

In the novel, the multinational corporation General Technics (GT) wants to transform a small, peaceful, and economically disadvantaged African nation named Beninia into a processing center for an offshore mining project. GT and its enterprise represent the economic trend that deep ecology does indeed target: elite nations pushing third world countries to participate in their market interests and fantasies of a global consumer society while erasing any chance of developing alternative economic forms that are more ecologically sustainable and socially just. As critic Neal Bukeavich notes, "the Beninian enterprise enacts a kind of economic imperialism that renders it unlikely to initiate any revolutionary shift in global environmental politics" (59). With the initiation of GT's scheme, Beninia will be swept into an economic system that not only gobbles up existing social relations—and in Beninia's case, peaceful social relations—but also exhausts material nature. Nowhere in GT's plan is there a discussion about developing an economy that will lift Beninia out of poverty without sacrificing its already limited resource base. But it is *predominantly* such an exhausting economic system and the culture it creates and then feeds that wreaks the ecological havoc, and this insight is the specific contribution of *Stand on Zanzibar* to deep ecology's population concerns.

Throughout *Stand on Zanzibar* Brunner gives readers fragments of the consumer culture that economic projects such as General Technics's Beninia plan support. It is a culture deep ecology would find harrowing in contrast to its ecotopian images of strong communities and ecologically sustainable ways of living. Certainly it is the kind of culture against which Ecotopia and Mattapoisett define themselves, but as a dystopia Brunner's work fully explores this culture, rendering many of its terrifyingly feasible possibilities. Communities as dynamic collections of participating individuals with senses of ecologically inspired self do not exist in the mass culture of *Stand on Zanzibar*. Instead, the dominant culture is an actualized capitalist fantasy of a world unified in its consumption habits. Images of Mr. and Mrs. Everywhere, "construct identities, the new century's equivalent of the Joneses," fill television screens sold by the media giant Engrelay Satelserv, allowing viewers to see themselves in a variety of more desirable places

(*Stand* 9). And a "Colliderscope" "turns your drab daily environment into a marvelous mystery" (172). These simulation technologies demonstrate a point made in the novel by Chad Mulligan, one of the characters who is critical of the society: "'the whole of modern so-called civilized existence is an attempt to deny reality insofar as it exists'" (251). The apparatuses of this "so-called civilized existence" allow two obfuscations: material reality, as in humanity's necessary embeddedness in nature, is forgotten; and social reality, as in the lived consequences of this amnesia, is masked.

The latter obfuscation occurs with a technology that ubiquitously promotes cultural and individual homogeneity. Song lyrics in Brunner's novel show this:

Like the good Lord God in the Valley of Bones
Engrelay Satelserv made some people called Jones.
They were not alive and they were not dead—
They were ee-magi-nary but always ahead.
What was remarkably and uniquely new—
A gadget on the set made them look like you!
Watching their sets in a kind of a trance
Were people in Mexico, people in France.
They don't chase Jones but the dreams are the same—
Mr. and Mrs. Everywhere, that's the right name!
Herr und Frau Uberall or *les Partout*,
A gadget on the set makes them look like you. (309)

Mr. and Mrs. Everywhere provide the society of *Stand on Zanzibar* with capitalist utopian experiences, Disneyesque escapes to the Moon, Mount Everest, or Martinique, all conveniently liberated from despoiled material reality. For Tom Moylan, in the mid-twentieth-century, utopian visions—which originally opposed "the affirmative culture maintained by dominant ideology"—dissolved into the corporate-driven utopias of shopping malls and the Disney empire (*Demand* 1). Co-opted by capital, utopia was diluted with images of "pleasurable weekends, Christmas dreams, and goods purchased weekly in the pleasure-dome shopping malls of suburbia," all visions compatible with growth-centered, capitalist ideology and, incidentally, as Brunner shows, redirecting social attention away from the degradation required for this ideology's upkeep (8).

As simulated culture in Brunner's dystopia has replaced genuine social relations and effectively canceled political critique among the now tuned-out masses, simulated nature (third nature?) has replaced nonhuman nature. Synthetic grass carpets General Technics' headquarters, and a clinic in London has a floor "covered by tiles with a design of dead leaves embedded under a clear plastic surface" (158). Interestingly, this "only touch in the place which suggested nature" is trampled, "a failure," the leaves disappearing "behind a mist of scratches and scrapes, the legacy of uncountable feet that had crossed the room" (159). Given that this clinic is one that pregnant women must visit to be eugenically tested, the results dictating whether they must terminate their pregnancies, it and its trampled floor of faux fallen leaves symbolize all at once human population pressure (there are a lot of scratches and scrapes), the ecological harm such pressure induces (nature is now only a tiled image), and most importantly the ethical quandary of population control (a central authority is deciding who can and cannot have children).

Stand on Zanzibar considers the growth economy and modern consumer culture to be the most detrimental pressures on global ecological and social health, and it makes this claim stronger by emphasizing population control as a directive far more unethical to institute than deep ecology and ecotopia appear to recognize. Deep ecology seems to treat overpopulation and excessive production and consumption as equally worthy of sustained critical attention, but Brunner's work argues otherwise. Alongside the consumerist ideology broadcasted globally in Brunner's ecodystopia is a praise of eugenic legislation. A "Greater New York Times editorial slot" hails Puerto Rico for cracking down on population growth and "for joining the majority of us who have seen the danger [of overpopulation] coming and resolved to put up with the minor inconveniences it entails when we decide to control the human elements of the big scene we inhabit" (15–16). Such "minor inconveniences" include a cultural stigma on fertility, mandatory abortion, and other top-down methods of enforcing obedience to government-mandated controls. Perhaps, then, *Stand on Zanzibar* issues a needed reality check for readers impressed with deep ecological utopia.

Stand on Zanzibar does not discount the importance of a declining population for social and ecological health, but it does imagine the danger of treating overpopulation and modern economic doctrine as equally accountable for environmental despoliation. The book stages the dystopian upshot of such an evenly distributed critique: governments end up working to cut population growth while allowing economic growth to continue unimpeded. Given the hegemony of an economic system that fundamentally cannot be shifted away from the imperative to exploit people and material nature, popular attention to drastic and global social and

ecological degradation—an attention driven by this economy's media complex—will turn toward overpopulation as the primary threat, thus absolv-
ing the capitalist economy from its hazardous global expansion. Brunner's
implicit take on the implications of what has since become deep ecology's
neo-Malthusianism anticipates that of deep ecology's staunchest critic,
Murray Bookchin, who asks,

> would the grow-or-die economy called capitalism really cease to plun-
> der the planet even if the world's population were reduced to a tenth
> of its present numbers? Would lumber companies, mining concerns, oil
> cartels, and agribusiness render redwood and Douglas fir forests safer
> for grizzly bears if—given capitalism's need to accumulate and produce
> for their own sake—California's population were reduced to one million
> people? ("The Population" par. 38)[14]

His answer: no. Whales are extinct in *Stand on Zanzibar*, and Manhattan is
under a dome. One character reflects on "when he last saw the stars" and
"got wet in the rain," and with this we are left to contemplate the death
of human experiences of nonhuman wonder, and thus of the ethical possibilities of such wonder, as a consequence of industrial pollutants (262). A
cosmetics manufacturer brags, "'we have taken control of our entire environment, and what we choose by way of fashion and cosmetics matches
that achievement'" (60). The world of the novel represents Bill McKibben's
"end of nature," in which the modern way of life "now blows its smoke
over every inch of the globe" (*The End* 60). McKibben, like Brunner, sees
modern economic doctrine as the biggest threat to global social and ecological integrity. "There is no place on the planet now," he writes, "that
does not fall under the enchantment of our images of the good life" (*The
End* xxii). The "good life" is a life of production-driven consumption, and
ultimately the life that makes overpopulation the serious threat that it is.

If *Stand on Zanzibar* is Brunner's indictment of the growth economy
and production-driven consumer culture as sources of extreme social and
ecological despoliation, then *The Sheep Look Up* is his most thorough
exploration of the extent and effects of this despoliation. As in *Stand on
Zanzibar*, *The Sheep Look Up* imagines a world in which modern ideological commitments to economic growth, its requisite mass consumption,
and human/nature disconnect play out fully, despite (or, because of) devastating environmental and social injustices. But while *Stand on Zanzibar*
can be read as an effort to upset the myth that human overpopulation is
more responsible for ecological and social breakdown than modern eco-

nomic doctrine, *The Sheep Look Up* is less focused on overpopulation and instead surveys what is harmful in contemporary socioeconomic and cultural paradigms. It expresses anxieties about loss of community, the effects of unchecked economic growth, and the lack of ecological knowledge in modern society, as it also explores contrasting strategies for environmentalist action. While these concerns demonstrate the novel's alignment with deep ecology's concerns, and thus ecodystopia's pedagogical function for the movement, it is the latter exploration of environmentalist action that allows Brunner's book to operate also as a corrective or warning for deep ecology.

The Sheep Look Up details the effects of a U.S. military hallucinogen leakage. Countries whose citizens consume a synthetic food produced in the area of the leak have mass rioting. The military's cover up of the chemical spill is one of several attempts by the U.S. government and the corporations it supports to deny their roles in bringing on ecological and social disasters. Insecticide-resistant worms devastate crops worldwide, and nearly all Americans suffer from ailments caused by environmental contaminants. Fighting to expose the misdeeds of corporations and the complicit government is the environmentalist and cult figure Austin Train, who also condemns emerging environmentalist violence. For the former activities Austin is labeled a subversive by the right-wing U.S. president, Prexy. Falsely accused of kidnapping the son of Roland Bamberley—a businessman whose company manufactures water filters and whose brother, Jacob, manufactured the contaminated food—Austin is put on trial publicly and uses the opportunity to address his television audience with a plea: "'at all costs, to me, to anyone, *at all costs* if the human race is to survive, the forcible exportation of the way of life invented by these stupid men must . . . be . . . *stopped*'" (353). Shortly after this declaration Prexy orders the broadcast to be cut off and the courthouse crumbles from a bomb built by one of the real kidnappers. The novel's ending begins in a fury of American civil disorder, chaos one character claims fulfills his computer-generated forecast of "the best thing we can do to ensure a long, happy, healthy future for mankind" (363). "We can just about restore the balance of the ecology, the biosphere, and so on—in other words, we can live within our means instead of on an unrepayable overdraft, as we've been doing for the past half century," says Dr. Thomas Grey in the novel, "if we exterminate the two hundred million most extravagant and wasteful of our species" (363).

Implicitly through its dystopian strategy and explicitly through Austin Train, *The Sheep Look Up* offers sympathetic deep ecological critiques of a range of modern ideologies and practices. One of its key critiques is of the type of thinking that, against the ecological imperative to maintain biodiversity, declares the expendability of certain nonhuman animal species. The novel opens with a poem that announces,

> The day shall dawn when never child but may
> Go forth upon the sward secure to play.
> No cruel wolves shall trespass in their nooks,
> Their lore of lions shall come from picture-books. (2)

The domestication of wilderness celebrated here is an ideal central to Western modernization. As Jessica Wilkinson, Sara Vickerman, and Jeff Lerner write,

> Taming wilderness to suit human needs was part of the value system European settlers brought to [North America]. The new nation's vast natural resources were valued, but early settlers were concerned primarily with exercising control over the landscape, its indigenous human inhabitants, and its natural resources. . . . Wild animals and plants were more often seen as threats or competitors than as objects worthy of protection. (285)

This taming has been called one of the "hallmarks of modernization," and we can see it confronted in Callenbach's and Piercy's ecotopias, which like deep ecology imagine economic, demographic, and spiritual models that encourage knowledge of and respect for biodiversity regardless of the instrumental value of species (Baker 2). In *The Sheep Look Up*, Austin calls himself a "commensalist," building his environmentalist philosophy on the idea that "you and your dog, and the flea on the dog's back, and the cow and the horse and the jackrabbit and the gopher and the nematode and the paramecium and the spirohete all sit down to the same table in the end" (18–19).

After the celebratory poem that begins Brunner's novel is a scene critical of the antiwilderness vision to which the poem rejoices. In a dislocating incident that would initially reinforce the fear of carnivorous nature in any reader of the novel's opening poem, a man finds himself hunted by wild animals "In broad daylight on the Santa Monica freeway" (3). Petrified and with "monstrous menacing beasts edging closer," the man hides from cougars, jaguars, cobras, falcons, and barracudas—the beasts that the writer of the opening poem wants to relegate to children's fairy tales

(3). Trying to run, the man is killed by a stingray. Is this a scene of some science-fictional, fantastical California now taken over by the savage crea- tures that the poem demonizes? No. The beasts are cars: Mercury's Cou- gar, the Jaguar, AC's Cobra, and so forth. The predation often associated with wild nature is given a different look, an ecocritical reevaluation dem- onstrating that automotive, industrial society, not wilderness, is the threat to life.

The Sheep Look Up links global ecological degradation to modern habits that have grown out of an ideology of man as conqueror, to bor- row Aldo Leopold's concept, instead of man as biotic citizen. This lack of ecological intelligence enables economic progress in Brunner's imagined future, but as Brunner shows, it also leads to a disabling of ecological sys- tems and creates an atmosphere conducive only to perpetual corporate profiteering. Lead, chemical byproducts of various industries, and DDT have brought about the poisoned world imagined by Rachel Carson in *Silent Spring*. As a result clean air, water, and filtermasks are commodities in *The Sheep Look Up*, purchased from vending machines. And a food producer, Puritan Foods, uses the public's growing fear of pollution to market falsely its brand of "uncontaminated" food. These examples reveal a central capitalist phenomenon: the omnipresent (il)logic of capitalism permits big industry to profit from its own poor environmental record, but in no way are the resulting cleanup industries altering their profit motive or developing an ecologically and socially conscious economy, despite the obvious necessity to do so. As one character states, "'they shit in the water until it's dangerous to drink, then make a fucking fortune out of selling us gadgets to purify it again'" (187).

Similar to *Stand on Zanzibar*, corporate offices in *The Sheep Look Up* boast of modernity's containment of nonhuman nature: "cosmoramic pro- jections," simulated views of the outside world "Superior to the natural article," "prevent the intrusion of untasteful exterior reality" (133). Again, this exterior reality is McKibben's postnatural world at its dystopian extreme, in its third nature. Deep ecology finds intimate, spiritual con- nections between all forms of life, connections that allow for human self- realization. Callenbach's Ecotopia and Piercy's Mattapoisett nurture these connections. Fields and natural gardens serve as places for reflection and identity-building. In Brunner's world, however, exterior space is poisoned, lifeless but for "rodent" species whose extreme populations are due to the loss of biodiversity. A child in Brunner's novel cuts her foot while playing in an old garbage dump; a woman dies from exposure to pollutants at the beach. In such an atmosphere, fostering a recognized human–nature connection and an ecocentric consciousness of nonhuman wonder becomes improbable, if not impossible.

Influenced by Austin, the "Trainites" of *The Sheep Look Up* mount a genuine ecotopian response to the custodians of the disastrous economic and political policies. A loosely organized group manifesting itself shortly after the Vietnam War, Trainites live out a number of environmentally sustainable practices in small collectives called wats. As if taking a cue from Naess and Snyder, Decimus—the man killed in the opening scene—was a Trainite who promoted, as Naess would say, a "global solidarity of lifestyle" ("Deep Ecology" 260): "His principle, at the Colorado wat, was third-world oriented; his community grew its own food, or tried to—crops had a nasty habit of failing because of wind-borne defoliants or industrial contaminants in the rain—and likewise wove its own cloth, while its chief source of income lay in handicrafts" (*Sheep* 34). The presence of Trainite wats gives Brunner's novel a utopian quality. Wats are Brunner's Ecotopias or Mattapoisetts, spaces apparently insulated from what is "Out There," from "death and destruction" and "poison in the rain," as one character thinks (171). But what makes *The Sheep Look Up* different from *Ecotopia* and *Woman on the Edge of Time*—what makes the wats spaces of ecodystopian worry rather than of ecotopian hope—is that at the moment of optimism, the Out There breaks through the insulation and intrudes upon utopian space. Despite the Trainites' ecological consciousness and foresight, the wats cannot keep acid rain at bay, nor can they prevent the intrusion of a crop-threatening worm imported into the United States by a careless company.

Brunner uses the wats to insist on the potential for ecotopian enclaves and ecotopian ideas to stimulate cultural work in the world. His exploration into this potential is not simplistic and unidirectional, though. Instead, *The Sheep Look Up* speculates about contrasting forms that environmentalist opposition, influenced by ecotopian social dreaming, might take. The first of these narrative explorations shows the journalist Peg Mankiewicz becoming discouraged with the polluted and corrupt state of modern life. Her extended investigation of Decimus's death draws the ire of her editor, Mel Torrence, who is hostile to the Trainites. Mel views public resistance, the most violent of which he carelessly and wrongly associates with Austin's supporters, as a nuisance. As he declares, "'They block traffic, they foul up business, they commit sabotage, they've even gone as far as murder'" (92). Seeing the merit in the Trainites' actual methods of nonviolent dissent, the falsity of Mel's allegations of murder, and the fact that the real killers "'are the people who are ruining the world to line their pockets,'"

[margin annotations: ECOTOPIAN VISIONARY POSSIBILITIES]

[margin annotations: #4 Research + public education]

Peg quits the newspaper and heads to the Colorado wat (93). Encouraged by the undemanding and ecocentric way of life at the wat, but ultimately dissatisfied with its people's lack of civic engagement with the world Out There, Peg leaves to carry on the fight started by Austin and Decimus. The Colorado wat is indeed an ecotopian space, but for Peg such a space is not enough for a world in need of sweeping change. In the end she channels her energies into critical journalism, researching and revealing the effects of rich nations on poor nations. With the public educative possibilities of such exposures she hopes to address the ecodystopian nightmare.

Peg's story is one in which an individual draws inspiration from an ecotopian ideal and moves into the world to instigate change through journalistic endeavor. Like Peg, Hugh Pettingill becomes disgruntled with the conditions of society. Speaking out against his adoptive father, the food producer Jacob Bamberley, Hugh voices the anger of many in the novel: "'Because of you and people like you we sit here in the richest country in the world surrounded by sick kids—. . . . You and your ancestors treated the world like a fucking great toilet bowl. You shat in it and boasted about the mess you'd made. And now it's full and overflowing, and you're fat and happy and black kids are going crazy to keep you rich. *Goodbye!*'" (112). Hugh also flees to the Colorado wat, but instead of seeing the aggressive activism he falsely associates with the Trainites, he witnesses a community "rehearsing for tomorrow, devising a viable lifestyle by trial and error" (148). But Hugh wants direct action now; he wants an oppositional movement whose actions, we can say in retrospect, go beyond the sabotage that Edward Abbey later dramatized in *The Monkey Wrench Gang* (1975) and that has since been associated with groups such as the deep-ecology-inspired Earth First! and Earth Liberation Front.[15] He leaves the wat and joins a small group of activists who employ the violent resistance he desires, including kidnapping Roland Bamberley's son Hector and demanding for ransom that Roland freely distribute twenty thousand water filters to citizens.

Peg and Hugh act upon an understanding that broader social transformation entails crossing utopia's spatial or intellectual boundaries and working in the world Out There to effect change. Tellingly, the ecodystopian elements of acid rain and an imported invasive insect have already crossed into the utopian wat, essentially dissolving ecotopian space and making such direct engagement with the Out There the only viable option for such transformation. But this direct engagement takes on two appearances in *The Sheep Look Up*. Peg's tactic is journalistic disclosure, hoping for change by educating people. Hugh's tactic is direct action in the extreme, physically confronting those responsible for environmental and social degradation. With its staging of both activist possibilities, *The Sheep Look Up* inserts an important question into environmentalist discourse: what liberatory strategies might activists engage in the interests of eco-systemic and social liberation? Interestingly, all of the fictions discussed in this chapter raise this question in some way, but only *The Sheep Look Up* highlights its centrality. Ecotopia could not maintain its independence from the United States if not for the fear among citizens and leaders of the latter country that Ecotopians have mined major U.S. cities with atomic weapons. Callenbach's book closes, though, with William vowing to shift his writing toward educating readers about Ecotopia, about *"things [in] Ecotopia that the rest of the world needs badly to know"* (166). The threat of violence maintains Ecotopian liberty, but William wants to educate the non-Ecotopian public about Ecotopian ways and, presumably, in so doing nonviolently enable the country's existence and perhaps even its influence on the world. In *Woman on the Edge of Time* Connie engages a sort of personal revenge liberation by poisoning her doctors with an insecticide that she stole from her brother, thinking of Luciente and Mattapoisett as she does so. Billie Maciunas rightly sees Connie's violent strategy as a poor course for implementing change, but the implicit reflection in the conclu-sion of Piercy's book is on the difficulty of realizing utopia-inspired change against hegemonic dominance and oppression (256). Brunner's ecodysto-pias also display this systemic, obdurate dominance and oppression, with *The Sheep Look*, of all the books, most clearly positing divergent activist directions to which the utopian compass might point.

Perhaps the full question raised in these narratives is about more than what environmentalist activism might look like when its motivating atti-tude reflects deep ecology's disdain for the dominant Western worldview. Deep ecology provides an ideological orientation for activism against the agents of ecological destruction and a likewise socially destructive instru-mental rationality. Whatever its specific critiques (e.g, demographics, eco-nomics, disembeddedness), its core aim, as Naess writes, is *"a substantial reorientation of our whole civilization"* (*Ecology* 45). *The Sheep Look Up* makes it clear that such an orientation might take on physically aggressive shapes when confronted with the intractable pervasiveness of ecological and social domination and oppression in modern political and economic forms. Brunner's ecodystopian strategy brings him to imagine dissent in its worst state of uncontrolled violence acted out by those who "wanted to wreck and burn and kill" (*Sheep* 123). As such, Brunner offers critical dys-topian reflection on the possibility of violent rebellion arising from those who, much like Connie in Piercy's novel, ultimately discover the obstinacy of those in power toward utopian possibility or any sociopolitical alternatives. The novel does not condemn all forms of active opposition. Austin supports demonstrators, whereas he denounces violence. But the manifestations of extremist pandemonium in Brunner's work illustrate social disorder that is a symptom of both the failure of those in power to open a dialogue with activist groups whose concerns are about legitimate ecological and social issues and of an activist perspective that, given this failure, has the potential to instigate misanthropic aggression.

As Wegner suggests, imaginary communities "are real . . . in that they have material, pedagogical, and ultimately political effects, shaping the ways people understand and, as a consequence, act in their worlds" (xvi). Ecotopian fiction is a place where deep ecology can find a motivational imaginary space for similarly shaping its theory and practice. In ecotopia human society does its best to exist unobtrusively as one part of a complex and necessary ecology. Doing this requires new patterns of being that reduce the human footprint and allow for the flourishing of all species. New rituals and new pedagogical models emerge in ecotopia. More sustainable economic practices prevail over the modern push for economic growth and consumption. Political decisions are localized and all people are encouraged to participate in democratic process. But as David Pepper writes, "To be truly transgressive, rather than lapsing into reactionary fantasy, ecotopias . . . must be rooted in existing social and economic relations rather than being merely a form of abstraction unrelated to the processes and situations operating in today's 'real' world" ("Utopianism" 18). This is where ecodystopia can help.

While indeed "Deep ecological and bioregional literature . . . can seem regressively removed from today's world" (Pepper, "Utopianism" 18), if read in dialogue with ecodystopia's constructive insights, deep ecological utopia can become refined enough to transcend its remove—and even its suspected "eco-brutalism"—and then to play a role in prompting change Out There (Bookchin, "Social Ecology" par. 15). In "Social Ecology versus Deep Ecology," Bookchin writes,

Deep ecologists see . . . humanity essentially as an ugly "anthropocentric" thing—presumably a malignant product of natural evolution—that is "overpopulating" the planet, "devouring" its resources, and destroying its wildlife and the biosphere—as though some vague domain of "nature" stands opposed to a constellation of nonnatural human beings, with their technology, minds, society, etc. (par. 14)

Such charges against deep ecology stem especially from the tendencies in the movement to posit an all-encompassing "humanity" and to overlook global challenges in favor of local, bioregional reform. The former tendency blurs the complexities of human cultural difference and the various political structures and social hierarchies that sustain relations of socio-economic power; some humans are more responsible for severe social and ecological degradation than others. The latter tendency can lead to a bioregional isolationism and a disregard for the plight of distant cultures. Brunner's novels shape our understanding of the dynamics of worlds opposite those of Callenbach's and Piercy's, and they even teach us that such worlds are out there and need to be attended to. But an extreme faith in the growth economy, an enforced cultural homogenization, and an authoritative government and corporate leadership inhibit the possibility of new patterns of being. Without ecotopian dreaming—or, in the case of *The Sheep Look Up*, with ecotopian dreaming present but dismissed and criminalized—damaging systems are allowed to flourish at the expense of sustainable ecological and social possibilities. Balanced against each other, ecotopia and ecodystopia provide deep ecology with a more complete sense of its visions and of the challenges it faces and must thoroughly consider while pursuing these visions.

CHAPTER THREE

ECOFEMINIST THEORIES OF LIBERATION

I N THIS CHAPTER I move from deep ecology to ecofeminism, a transformative environmentalist philosophy that likewise emerged within
the post-Carson atmosphere of the 1970s, matured in the 1980s, and
continues to thrive today. As philosopher Karen J. Warren argues, male-
centered thinking follows a "logic of domination" that promotes the
oppositional pair male/female, places a higher value on males in this pair,
and as a result justifies inequalities between men and women (47). The
superiority granted to males under this logic excuses the use of social,
political, and economic power to subordinate women, and it sanctions a
privileged socioeconomic and political stance for men. For Warren and
other ecofeminists, the projects of feminism and environmentalism must
notice the similarities between this androcentric logic and the cultural logic
that constructs a culture/nature opposition, places a higher value on culture, and as a result authorizes human domination over nonhuman nature.
Because both feminism and environmentalism are fundamentally critical
of domination, each one can find in the other one resources for expanding its attentions and energizing its methods, ultimately to join hands in
a coproductive ecofeminism that denounces oppressions of women and
nonhuman nature as well as addresses these oppressions with theory and
practice. In the words of Greta Gaard, "no attempt to liberate women (or

any other oppressed group) will be successful without an equal attempt to liberate nature" ("Living" 1).

Ecofeminism is a diverse body of critical thought, though, in some modes aligning with deep ecology's ecospirituality and critique of anthropocentrism and in other modes proposing an emancipatory politics that rejects deep ecology's normative principles. Ecofeminist theorists propose and contest contrary positions. As such, ecofeminism cannot be said to have linked feminism to environmentalism in any consistent or universal way. But this characteristic of ecofeminism does not harm its productiveness as a critical method. In feminist literary scholarship, efforts to negotiate particularly the tension between "affinity" and "constructionist" ecofeminisms have produced some rich results. For example, Karla Armbruster argues that whether our ecological politics is informed by a perception of an affinity—a deep ecological kinship or continuity—between women and nature, or by a broader attention to the way differences in race, economic class, ethnicity, gender, and species construct our ideas about human–nonhuman relationships, we will still end up validating the conceptual dualisms and hierarchies that we are critiquing. In the former case the continuity perspective creates "yet another dualism: an uncomplicated opposition between women's perceived unity with nature and male-associated culture's alienation from it" (98). In the latter case the constructionist "emphasis on differences in gender, race, species, or other aspects of identity can deny the complexity of human and natural identities and lead to the hierarchical ranking of oppressions on the basis of importance or causality" (98).

I want to follow Armbruster's lead in discovering and fleshing out possibilities for thinking about this longstanding ecofeminist discussion. Methodologically, however, I want to travel down a different path, not because Armbruster's is not clear and fruitful enough. To be sure, her call for ecofeminism to embrace poststructuralist theory in order to resist "recontainment" by dominant dualisms and hierarchies is an invaluable theoretical boundary crossing (99).[1] And her reading of Ursula K. Le Guin's "Buffalo Gals, Won't You Come Out Tonight" (1987) is equally an invaluable and successful application of her poststructuralist ecofeminism to a work of literature. My effort in this chapter is to show how certain works of science fiction read alone or in combination have engaged with central ecofeminist issues at the same time as, and even before, such issues provoked theoretical deliberations in more academic settings.

As ecofeminist works, Sally Miller Gearhart's *The Wanderground* (1979), Le Guin's *Always Coming Home* (1985), and Joan Slonczewski's *A Door Into Ocean* (1986) envision healthy ecological spaces as the outgrowths of the cultural valuing of the "feminine" and the containment and/or absence of the "masculine"—a move characteristic of affinity ecofeminism. These books narrate affinity, or as I will continue to call it, *cultural* ecofeminist possibility, all portraying women—and societies—who define themselves in ways encouraged by that branch of ecofeminism: against the dominant logic of patriarchy and through their own personal and local experiences, through collective histories, and/or through Earth-based spiritual traditions. But these texts do not represent exclusive, uncontested cultural ecofeminist positions. They balance and at times struggle with their cultural ecofeminist ideas and other ecofeminist positions. For this reason, Gearhart's, Le Guin's, and Slonczewski's works perform within and among their narratives the critical dialogue important for ecofeminist theory then, in the formative years of ecofeminism, and even now, when such discussions remain pedagogically and politically important. They stage within their fictions the very debate that ecofeminism grapples with as a transformative environmentalist movement searching for ways to challenge the oppressions of women and nonhuman nature effectively, and to perform this challenge while maintaining the best theoretical and practical work of ecofeminism's many iterations.

Sherry B. Ortner's 1974 essay, "Is Female to Male as Nature Is to Culture?," helps set up contexts for discussing the differences between cultural ecofeminism and more constructionist, rationalist ecofeminisms. An anthropologist, Ortner finds men's subordination of women to be universal and asks what it is in every culture that leads to this subordination. She reasons that the pancultural oppression of women follows from the likewise pancultural tendency to identify women with nonhuman nature. Ortner borrows from Simone de Beauvoir to show that breasts, the uterus, menstruation, and pregnancy highlight humanity's fundamental animality, our inescapable belonging to the class Mammalia. Since *culture,* by definition, values human engagement "in the process of generating and sustaining systems of meaningful forms (symbols, artifacts, etc.) by means of which humanity transcends the givens of natural existence," patriarchy emerges as culture's defense against whatever would remind civilization of humanity's inability to fully realize this transcendence, including the menstruating and lactating female (40). Women are thus forced to remain in the home, where they can exercise their "natural" roles as mothers to animal-like infants that are "utterly unsocialized," "unable to walk upright," and unfamiliar with social language (45–46). "[W]oman's body," Ortner concludes, "seems to doom her to mere reproduction of life" (43). On the other hand, "the male . . . lacking natural creative functions, must (or has the opportunity to) assert his creativity externally, 'artificially,' through the medium of technology and symbols. In so doing, he creates relatively lasting, eternal, transcendent objects, while the woman creates only perishables—human beings" (43). Under the logic of patriarchy, men are the agents of privileged, nonanimal culture; women are of a lower order.

Anthropologist Melissa Leach is among those who have since critiqued Ortner's argument, mainly because of its claims about the universality of patriarchally constructed woman–nature connections. And without a doubt Leach's analysis of the Mende-speaking people of Western Africa, whose relationships with nonhuman nature disturb any simplified conception of culture as dependent upon oppressing women and nature, does much to dismantle such claims. But as a context for discussing the cultural and rationalist threads of ecofeminist thought, Ortner's research is still useful; for, by highlighting a perceived connection between women and nature, Ortner raises important questions about whether that connection should be welcomed as valuable for social and ecological transformation or challenged as falsely construed and in the end hazardous for feminist and environmentalist projects. Ortner favors the latter, characterizing what Stacy Alaimo deems "feminist theory's flight from nature" (4).

Drawing from many of the same sources as deep ecology, cultural ecofeminism posits an innate woman–nonhuman nature link and argues that this link should be embraced as a way of dealing with the social and environmental problems inherent and evident in patriarchal culture.[2] Developing in the late 1970s and early 1980s out of radical feminism's repudiation of oppressive social systems and accentuation of ways of knowing and being that contest harsh masculinity, cultural ecofeminism dismantles patriarchy by prioritizing "feminine" values. Cultural ecofeminists "elevate what they consider to be women's virtues—caring, nurturing, interdependence—and reject the individualist, rationalist, and destructive values typically associated with men" (Gruen 77). Lori Gruen, a critic of cultural ecofeminism, argues that the belief that women and nonhuman nature are connected works to devalue men as unconnected from nature and thus does nothing to restructure the hierarchal relation of privilege that feminism and other social movements have challenged for years. As Val Plumwood notes, ecofeminists of this "Cavern of Reversal" define their identities "by reversing the valuations of the dominant culture" (Feminism 3). For cultural ecofeminists, though, the hierarchal relation of privilege is not what is troubling. The direction of the privilege is. Judith Plant writes as a cultural ecofeminist: "Women's values, centered around life-giving, must be revalued, elevated from their once subordinate role. What women know from experience needs recognition and respect. We have had generations of experience in conciliation, dealing with interpersonal conflicts in daily domestic life. We know how to feel for others because we have practiced it" ("Searching" 160).

Plant does not challenge the validity of the presumption that strong interpersonal communication and empathy are innate in women, which other types of feminism and ecofeminism do challenge by labeling such characteristics as imposed upon women in patriarchal social systems. Her essay in Irene Diamond and Gloria Feman Orenstein's *Reweaving the World* is about what women, specifically, can bring to the bioregionalist project, a project advocating a more life-centered, interpersonal, and connected view of local place. The thought that women are inherently closer to nature and are thus invaluable for the realization of bioregional ways of life is not a problem for cultural ecofeminists. What is a problem is when culture devalues its feminine categories and thus devalues the virtues necessary for a more viable human relationship with nature. While still manifesting hierarchical thinking, cultural ecofeminism argues that privileging care and empathy for all human and nonhuman life, instead of privileging self-interest and the production of marketable goods, are reversals necessary for an ecocentric, life-affirming culture to emerge.

Asserting so-called feminine values is central to Andrée Collard's ecofeminism, too. Much like Plant, Collard centers her theorizing on the importance for environmentalism of accenting an essential woman–nature connection. She writes, "Ecology is woman-based almost by definition. *Eco* means house, *logos* means word, speech, thought. Thus ecology is the language of the house. Defined more formally, ecology is the study of the interconnectedness between all organisms and their surroundings—the house. As such, it requires a thorough knowledge and an intimate experience of the house" (137). As speakers of the language of the house, Collard argues, women endure the domestic burdens relegated to them under patriarchal convention. Women can therefore empathize with the similarly abused nonhuman nature, making them better positioned to address and correct this latter abuse. Relatedly, cultural ecofeminism stresses the need for a collective history of women's oppressions in patriarchy. One project of feminism as a whole is to draw attention to women's history, but the goals of this attention vary. Cultural ecofeminism breaks from the liberal feminist endeavor to achieve equal rights and representation for women using the methods of already existing sociopolitical institutions and instead seeks change by contrasting the modern history of women's oppression with an ancient history allegedly permeated with prepatriarchal ideals such as kinship, egalitarianism, and nurturance. The goal of this juxtaposition is epistemological; lacking knowledge of "what [women] were and therefore what [women] can be . . . encourages women to want incorporation into man's world on an 'equality' basis, meaning that woman absorbs his ideologies, myths, history, etc. and loses all grounding in her own traditions" (Collard 8).

Much of the work done in cultural ecofeminism involves revaluing matriarchal principles historically documented in archeological studies. In its spiritual forms cultural ecofeminism promotes the reemergence of ancient matriarchal belief systems that coincided in Minoan Crete and Old Europe, for example, with peace and respect for all life. Along with Marija Gimbutas, Riane Eisler, Starhawk (the author of the deep ecological and cultural ecofeminist science fiction book *The Fifth Sacred Thing* [1993]), Charlene Spretnak, Joanna Macy, and Carol P. Christ, Collard is a thinker in this tradition. She and others call on modern culture to embrace or at least adopt some values of Earth-based spiritualities historically seen in goddess-worshipping cultures. "In cultures where the cycle of life is the underlying metaphor," Starhawk writes, "religious objects reflect its imagery, showing us women—Goddesses—ripe in pregnancy or giving birth. The vulva and its abstracted form, the triangle, along with breasts, circles, eyes, and spirals, are signs of the sacred" (175). According to Spretnak, many feminists came to ecofeminism after their exposure, through historical and archeological research, to such an ancient religion "that honored the female and seemed to have as its 'good book' nature itself" (5). What was intriguing for early ecofeminists "was the sacred link between the Goddess in her many guises and totemic animals and plants, sacred groves, and womblike caves, in the moon-rhythm blood of menses, the ecstatic dance—the experience of knowing Gaia, her voluptuous contours and fertile plains, her flowing waters that give life, her animal teachers" (Spretnak 5).

That cultural ecofeminism is caught up in idealism is one of the main criticisms leveled against it. Critics of cultural ecofeminism believe that valuing a woman–nature connection is an ineffective liberatory strategy that fails to consider and dismantle rationally the logics of the social, political, and economic systems responsible for dominations of all types. Susan Prentice identifies cultural ecofeminism's idealism as its worst characteristic. Advocating an understanding of systems of power and domination more sophisticated than what cultural ecofeminism offers, she writes, "By locating the origin of the domination of women and nature in male consciousness, eco-feminism makes political and economic systems simply derivative of male thinking" (9). For Prentice the assumption that men "'think wrong'" and that "'biology is destiny'" "trivializes several centuries of history, economics and politics by simply glancing over the formidable obstacles of social structures" (9). Janet Biehl also voices this critique. She chides cultural ecofeminism for narrowly and crudely focusing on patriarchy as *the* cause of oppression, and for assuming that prioritizing women's supposed biologically determined predispositions is a way to eradicate oppression. What about the state, Biehl asks, which historically as an institution has oppressed women, nature, and men alike? Racism is rooted in ethnic chauvinisms and economic motivations unrelated to gender conflict. And capitalism's profit motive and growth imperative have instigated an entire range of oppressions directed at whoever and whatever gets in the way of their realization. Drawing on Prentice's analysis Biehl concludes, "Systems of domination like capitalism, statism, and ethnic oppressions—and sexism itself—have a 'history, logic, and struggle' of their own"; in no way does elevating women's values above men's values engage the procedures necessary to foster real change (50).

A strong advocate of rationalist feminism, Biehl also questions the validity of cultural ecofeminism's historical references. Goddess worship does not guarantee a benign culture, she argues, yet cultural ecofeminists seem to honor such worship as "the magic carpet by which we can reclaim the 'women's values' of the Neolithic" (33). Nor does the presence of "full-figured female figurines" in ancient archeological sites confirm that the relative peacefulness of early Neolithic cultures resulted from an embrace and worship of "a generative female principle" (34). The societies of the early Neolithic were complex, and to suggest that their sociopolitical dynamics grew simply out of goddess worship is to ignore the range of social, political, and cultural intricacies that constructed the Neolithic temper. Biehl also references archeological evidence of human sacrifice in Minoan Crete, which suggests a cruelness in that society overlooked in cultural ecofeminism's idealizations.

Biehl concludes, "With an ecological ethics grounded in the potentiality of human beings to consciously and rationally create a free ecological society, we can begin to develop an ecological political movement that challenges the existing order on the grounds that it denies both humans and nonhumans their full actualization" (130). Biehl's loyalty to reasoned democratic process is crucial, as she values the modes of critical engagement necessary for transformation while at the same time denying legitimacy to gender valuations that would lock women's identities onto eternal, nonnegotiable, and politically feeble concepts of femininity. But as Elizabeth Carlassare points out, such loyalty comes at the expense of discounting "the work of cultural ecofeminists with their emphasis on transforming consciousness, reclaiming women's history, and fostering a woman-based culture and spirituality" (229). Perhaps there is something valuable not in locating a simple continuity between women and nonhuman nature, but at least in esteeming as a vital part of the ecofeminist dialogue those ideas that have come about as a result of thinkers whose intellectual tendencies move them toward more personal and spiritual transformative modes.[3] As Carlassare notes,

> Criticism of ecofeminism's essentializing tendencies is important to insure critical self-reflexivity and for examining the ways in which essentializing may sometimes work against the goals of women's liberation by homogenizing the diversity of women's experiences. Dismissing cultural ecofeminism on this basis, however, precludes the possibility of learning from this position and obscures the legitimacy of the variety of positions and discursive forms under ecofeminism's umbrella. (231)[4]

Published five years after Ortner's anthropological study of patriarchy, and a decade before ecofeminism rose to prominence as a critical perspective in the late 1980s and early 1990s, Gearhart's *The Wanderground* is the story of the Hill Women, an all-female society living nomadically in a wilderness far away from the "City" and its oppressions. Driving the plot is the encroachment of men from the City into the wilderness where, years before, various expressions of male potency—aggressive sexuality, militarism, and destructive technologies—were made impotent by what the Hill Women call both the "Revolt of the Earth" and the "Revolt of the Mother," a juxtaposition of "Earth" and "Mother" characteristic of cultural ecofeminism (158). Explaining the Revolt one of the Hill Women says, "'Once upon a time . . . there was one rape too many. . . . The earth finally said 'no.' There was no storm, no earthquake, no tidal wave, no specific moment to mark its happening. It only became apparent that it had happened, and that it had happened everywhere'" (158). Guns no longer worked in the wilderness, machines broke down, animals refused to serve men, and the male libido waned. As imagined by Gearhart, this

Revolt represents disdain for mythologies of Earth and its processes as tools of a violently retributive god, demonstrating instead Earth as a Gaian female subject peaceably protecting herself against men, who have brought violence upon women, animals, and land. The effects of the Revolt are disappearing, however. Rumors of male virility's return outside the City are leading men to test their sexual strength through acts of rape and group "Cunt Hunts" in the country, generating a fear in the Hill Women that "woman energy might again be drained as it had been for millennia before the Revolt of the Earth" (130).

The Wanderground supports an inverted masculine/feminine value hierarchy. The novel is self-reflexively aware of its good women/bad men dichotomy, presenting one character, Jacqua, who says to herself early in the book, "'It is too simple . . . to condemn them all or to praise all of us'" (2). But right away Jacqua declares, "'for the sake of earth and all she holds, that simplicity must be our creed'" (2). This condemnation of men and praise of women is a necessary defensive and offensive mantra for the Hill Women, for their historical experiences do not reveal anything decent in the male sex. In addition, this mantra is key for the novel as a cultural ecofeminist thought experiment and radical feminist speculative text motivated by its historical moment to narrate female subjectivity against patriarchal society's male gaze, as well as to narrate female possibility when released from this gaze's physical and psychological oppressions.

As a result of the Revolt and the subsequent escape of the Hill Women's predecessors to the wilderness, women have been left free to evolve independently of the patriarchal logic of domination. This narrative move facilitates Gearhart's speculation on the qualities inherent in women as free subjects living on what Alaimo discusses as "undomesticated ground," nature as "a space of feminist possibility" (23). Although to be expected in a science fiction novel bordering on fantasy, these qualities, these estranging *nova*, stand out as being more ecological, more embedded and interrelational, than the qualities that the text argues men possess as members of a fundamentally disconnected sex. The Hill Women fly, or "windride." They have a built-in instinctual mechanism called a "lonth" that acts as a flight response allowing involuntary kinesthetic control, demonstrating their return to an animal nature that modernity has sedated. The Hill Women can also communicate telepathically with other Hill Women and with flora and fauna, a phenomenon called "mindstretch" that requires traits associated in cultural ecofeminist thought with the feminine: "'Meaningful communication,'" a Hill Women lesson goes, "'is the meeting of two vessels, equally vulnerable, equally receptive, and equally desirous of hearing'" (115). Finally, the Hill Women engage in a ritual called "earthtouch" that uses mindstretching to send energy drawn from Earth by one Hill Woman to another in need of this energy. Combined, mindstretch and earthtouch represent a dynamic, deep ecological spiritual and communicative web of interdependencies between one woman and other women, and women and nonhuman nature. This web is an ecological phenomenon permitted to develop as a result of the absence of anti-ecological and enforced patriarchal power.

Just as cultural ecofeminism does more theoretically to elevate what it conceives as women's values than simply to connect women and nature in an essential bond, so too does *The Wanderground* go beyond just conceptualizing women as windriders with more ecologically sound instinctual and communicative awarenesses. The novel also offers up programs for reviewing and challenging modern cultural tendencies that oppress women and nonhuman nature. The apparent essentialism of Gearhart's book thus borders on being "a positive tool of liberation," as Noël Sturgeon notes of selected essentialist rhetorics (9). This political possibility ultimately wanes, as I will show below, but the first of these programs motivates ecofeminist practice by uniting the oppressed through their individual histories. Against a destructive patriarchal memory that recalls the potency men used to have outside the City, and thus reinstates the violent misogyny of the past after the effects of the Revolt have worn off, the women of *The Wanderground* stress the importance of a collective and constructive memory that allows members of their liberated society to understand their social history and what motivates their emancipatory project. Thus, while the men of the City continually seek to impose and perpetuate a master narrative of patriarchal history—requiring every woman to be married, allowing men to have several wives, and instituting curfews on women— the women of the country seek local stories that will illustrate what they are escaping from and to, as well as inform their future. Nowhere in this collective history do the women subscribe to a master narrative of their culture's experience. Instead,

> From countless seemingly disconnected episodes the women had pieced together a larger picture so that now they had some sense of what had happened during those last days in the City. Over the years as women had joined them the memory vessels had been added to: more and more stories, more and more horrors, and sometimes a narrative that brought with it some hope or humor. As a woman shared, she became part of all their history. (23)

As a cultural ecofeminist text, then, *The Wanderground* posits competing historical paradigms—one masculine, one feminine—that use historical references either to recreate the social conditions of a predetermined, univocal social system or to create freeing conditions based on an ecology of private experiences.

Second, as the earthtouch ritual shows, the Hill Women are rooted in a deep ecological, Earth-based spirituality that is vital to their selfhood, their kinship, and their sense of place. Indeed, advocating such a spirituality is imperative for cultural ecofeminism. Earthtouch emphasizes what Riane Eisler, a cultural historian, calls a "partnership model of society" (33). Developing out of the Gaia tradition, which regards Earth as "a living system designed to maintain and to nurture life," the partnership model opposes the "dominator society," favoring instead a worldview founded upon ancient spiritualities in which "the world was viewed as the great Mother, a living entity who in both her temporal and spiritual manifestations creates and nurtures all forms of life" (Eisler 30). Partnership requires empathetic nurturance, and thus from a cultural ecofeminist perspective can only emerge given a revaluing of the feminine. In *The Wanderground,* partnership in earthtouch is exclusive to those whose feminine capacities have been permitted to develop in the absence of masculine power. As a political statement Gearhart's is radically essentialist. To posit a separatist, feminist space where a spiritual ecological conscience can thrive is a key theoretical move for ecofeminist science fiction. As unsophisticated as this move may be, it initiates speculation on what it is in modern culture that undermines the human potential for realizing such an ecological conscience: masculine aggression, perhaps, but ideologies of dominance more accurately. So while Gearhart's story "reinforces the exclusivity of the categories of male and female"—something that science fiction scholar Jenny Wolmark sees as problematical for its adherence to the same-old gender assumptions and the resulting failure to question these assumptions—such reinforcement is a viable starting point for an ecofeminist project that endorses a worldview contrary to prevailing dogma (85).

Rounding out Gearhart's programs for instituting change is *The Wanderground*'s look at the dominant ideology against which the Hill Women elevate their collection of personal histories and their feminine partnership, an ideology embodied by men and their collective space, the technological City. The dystopian City is the institutional space for both men, the oppressors, and technology, the tool of their oppressions. Answering why the Hill Women, with their extraordinary powers, refuse to seek violent revenge on the City with technological weaponry, one of the Hill Women insists, "That's the mistake the men made, sisterlove, and made over and *progres or growth imperative* over again. Just because it was possible they thought it had to be done. They came near to destroying the earth—and may yet—with that notion" (145). Thus, the essential quality of men in the novel is being "'Driven in their own madness to destroy themselves and us and any living thing'" with whatever technology is available (3). Even using the tool of language, men in the novel impose oppressive aesthetic standards upon women ("streamlined," "limited," "dependent," "constantly available") (63).

The Wanderground succeeds as a radical statement of cultural eco-feminism. It establishes and contrasts what it means to be a woman both in the oppressive context of patriarchy and in a liberated context. As women unchained, the Hill Women restore and develop further their innate feminine potentials. Vulnerable, receptive, pacifist, interconnected, wild—these terms describe both the natural world that Gearhart imagines and the women she envisions evolving free from masculine oppressions, women empowered by a Revolt of the Earth-Mother to create themselves as subjects who value the qualities of the feminine traditionally disparaged in patriarchy. To make this empowerment clearer, Gearhart sketches a woman living in the dystopian City as an unmistakably powerless object of the male gaze: "a thickly painted face, lacquerstiffened hair, her body encased in a low-cut tight-fitting dress that terminated at mid-thigh" (63). This image of stiffness, encasement, and termination reveals the misogyny against which the Hill Women are fighting, a misogyny that permits men to exercise reckless power over women and sustain a civilization of dominance over women and other-than-human nature.

Prefiguring the anti-essentialist insights of Prentice and Biehl, feminist literary critic June Howard notes of Gearhart's book,

> The evaluation of "feminine" and "masculine" qualities asserted by radical feminism and by *The Wanderground* . . . lends support to the idea that differences between men and women are "natural," and thus endangers the basis of our critique of existing social relations and our belief that they can be changed. The disagreement is between those who accept and build upon the common-sense observation that the sexes differ, and those . . . who argue that gender identity is constructed by complex, socially and historically specific structures. (72)

From Howard's point of view *The Wanderground* promises nothing transformative and is actually dangerous in its maintenance of ahistorical gender divisions. To achieve successfully a more fully developed ecofeminism,

Gearhart could have further contemplated the simplicity of her novel's universal condemnation of men—the simplicity that her character Jacqua admits. But she passes up this opportunity in favor of cultural ecofeminist polemic. In the novel there exists briefly a potential dissipation of essentialist definitions of men: the book's Gentles are "Men who knew that the [Hill Women] were the only hope for the earth's survival" (2). However, this potential is quickly weakened by a subsequent description of the Gentles as "Men who, knowing that maleness touched women only with the accumulated hatred of centuries, touched no women at all" (2). The Gentles understand their instinctive male aggressiveness and thus choose to abstain from physical contact with women altogether. They know themselves as innately hostile male bodies that require self-policing to ensure the protection of women and nonhuman nature.

Of course, this understanding of the Gentles is Jacqua's, revealed in the passage in which she reflects on and endorses the simplicity of the Hill Women's denunciation of all men. Gearhart's ecofeminist project still shows promise of theoretical complexity, though, when it introduces other Hill Women who question inscribing a predetermined, inborn aggressiveness on the Gentles. Reacting to the developed communicative powers of one of the Gentles, the Hill Woman Betha admits that "her absolutes began to get fuzzy around the edges when she tried to make them apply to a man like Aaron" (115). But again Gearhart does not explore gender difference as more complex than cultural ecofeminism declares. Only women can share power peacefully, her novel insists: "men—even Gentles—found it difficult or impossible really to share power" (115). What Betha sees in this Gentle does not instigate a revision of the Hill Women's established beliefs. Rather, his "understanding of the essential fundamental knowledge [that] women and men cannot yet, may not ever, love one another without violence" instead impresses on her a slightly different perception of the Gentles than her perception of men in general (115). The Gentles are different from the men of the City merely because they realize and contain their natural brutality as well as share the Hill Women's view of human sexual relations.

Gearhart's final opportunity to render a more complex ecofeminism comes when the Hill Women engage with the Gentles in political process. The Gentles have noticed that the increased violence against women outside the City correlates with the number of Hill Women on rotation in the City, and they want to meet with the Hill Women to discuss this trend. As fewer women from the Wanderground make their way in disguise into the City to keep an eye on the conditions there, more abuses against the Hill

Women happen in the country. Before the meeting in which the Gentles share this crucial observation, the Hill Women debate whether they should grant the Gentles this meeting at all. Though the meeting does happen, it does not take place without opposition: "to some of the women it did not matter that the gentles were men sworn to isolate themselves from women; if they were men then there was no reason for concourse with them" (126). But the eventual decision to let several women meet with the men—while greeted unenthusiastically and permitted only under the assurance that the individual women speak only for themselves and not for the group as a whole—signals a step toward a more socially conscious ecofeminism.

In the end, however, the women maintain their essentialism. Their fear of universal masculine aggression prevents them from opening up productive conversation with the Gentles about how both groups can work together to dodge the intruders from the City. Moments after their pledge to communicate the Gentles' observations to other Hill Women, the women return to their separatism after learning that the Gentles have discovered in themselves telepathic powers similar to the Hill Women's. Responding to the Gentles' claim that these powers are nonviolent, Evona says, "'Nonviolent? Never. You know what will happen. You'll use your new power all right. You'll use it, perfect it, manufacture it, package it, sell it, and tell the world that it's clean and new because it comes from a different breed of men. But it's just another fancy prick to invade the world with'" (179). Evona's response is laden with the types of ideological barriers that other modes of feminism and ecofeminism avoid in their drives to add more complexity to ecofeminist conversations. The Hill Women's attitude toward the Gentles does not encourage the breakdown of their essentialism into a mode of thought more open to recognizing the potential for anyone, man or woman, to exercise social and ecological consciousness, and thus for progressive social and ecological change to grow out of democratic conversation.

The *Wanderground*'s brand of ecofeminism defines men as inherently oppressive and liberated women as ecologically conscious. *Always Coming Home*'s ecofeminism is more critical than that, even though Le Guin does reflect several facets of cultural ecofeminist thinking. The Kesh society of her future history interweaves human culture and nonhuman nature in a way that breaks down the culture/nature dualism to favor instead a spirituality of individual, social, and cultural embeddedness in nonhuman nature. This deep ecological, cultural ecofeminist ecospirituality informs the Kesh's social organization and treatment of Earth, as it also combats a patriarchal quest for dominance over nature that would undermine the lived union with nonhuman nature that the Kesh have achieved. Further, the Kesh's gender identifications are analogous to those of cultural ecofeminism: the Kesh connect "woman and animal . . . throughout [their] sexual and intellectual teaching," a connection that the narrator of this passage declares is *not* used to devalue woman (420).

A complex symbol, the "heyiya-if," illustrates Kesh spirituality and gender identifications. Signifying ecological connection with its dual spirals growing inward, as well as openness to change with its center empty and refusing to finalize that connection, the heyiya-if permeates and defines the Kesh's cultural activities, their dance choreography, stage productions, town planning, art, musical instruments, and meditative practices. The heyiya-if informs the practices of the Kesh. They make "no provision for a relation of ownership between living beings," arranging their society around not just a respect for life—a cultural ecofeminist care ethic—but also a deep ecological sense of their place within the ecosystem (43). The "Earth People" of the Kesh's "Five Houses of Earth" include "the earth itself, rocks and dirt and geological formations, the moon, all springs, streams and lakes of fresh water, all human beings currently alive, game animals, domestic animals, individual animals, domestic and ground-dwelling birds, and all plants that are gathered, planted, or used by human beings" (43–44). The "Sky People" of their "Four Houses of the Sky" include "the sun and stars, the oceans, wild animals not hunted as game, all animals, plants, and persons considered as the species rather than as an individual, human beings considered as a tribe, people, or species, all people and beings in dreams, visions, and stories, most kinds of birds, the dead, and the unborn" (44). Here, Patrick D. Murphy's thoughts on matrilineal societies are useful: "In matrilineal societies among the first nations, . . . kinship is observed in terms of extended families, lodges, clans, and entire tribes, not nuclear family structures. As a result, it is more accurate to say that there are not others in such cultures, only anothers, that is, beings who are neither self nor other in any absolute dichotomy but are familiar, related, and connected with us" (*Farther* 88).

▷ A specter haunts the ennatured Kesh in the form of a masculinity once prevalent in the aptly named "City of Man"—our own Industrial Age, our now—and now reemerging in the future world of the Kesh in a patriarchally organized warrior group called the Condor, or the Dayao.

Representing a time "'when [people] lived outside the world,'" "a sort of peninsula sticking out from the mainland, very thickly built upon, very heavily populated, very obscure, and very far away," the City of Man still exists in the world of *Always Coming Home* in the form of the dangerous industrial toxins modernity left behind (Le Guin, *Always* 153). With the Condor this City of Man takes its present form in militaristic aspiration. They want to resurrect the "Great Weapons" of the past, a project identified in Le Guin's book with the essence of masculinity. One weapon, a tanklike vehicle named the "Destroyer," "push[es] through a wall of bricks, thundering and shaking through the ruins it made, huge and blind, with a thick penis-snout" (349–50). A figurative rape this is, one also extended to the other-than-human world: "the Destroyer push[es] against the oak trees . . . , push[es] them over" (350). In the masculine culture of the Condor, a "man-dominant" culture, the "identification [of woman and animal] *is* used to devalue" (420, emphasis added).

Le Guin's book traces one Kesh woman's navigation through this masculine "outside the world" as well as her experiences of living life under the cultural paradigms dominant during the City of Man and now resurfacing as a force against which the Kesh's ecologically conscious Valley culture must struggle. North Owl is the daughter of a woman of a Valley House, Willow, and a man of the oppressive Condor people, Terter Abhao. As one of the Kesh she is among the world as a child enough to recognize "the dirt [as] the mother of [her] mothers" and to make her coming-of-age ritual one of absolute in(ter)dependence in the wilderness (19). However, because North Owl's father left the Valley so early in her life to command an army, she has grown up with the title "half-person" (19). At eight years old she feels incomplete. Terter's return to the Valley with his army prompts North Owl to reflect, "He was home, he was here, our family was whole; now everything was as it should be, balanced, complete; and so it would not change" (30). But she soon finds out that her fantasies of familial completion, informed by a patriarchal concept of the family, contradict the greater ecological union valued in Kesh culture.

When North Owl leaves the Valley to join her father and experience Condor culture we get a deeper view of this culture's supporting structures, the linguistic, religious, and social configurations that underlie Condor tyranny. In this way, Le Guin's ecofeminism moves away from strict cultural ecofeminist reasoning and into a more critical mode of ecofeminist understanding, one motivated to explore the [historically contingent, rather than fixed, features of patriarchy.] First, unlike the Kesh's language, the Condor's recognizes hierarchy; Terter renames North Owl "'Ayatyu,'" "'woman born above others,'" while he also refers to the people of other towns as "people of no account" (186, 189). Condor is a hierarchal designation symbolizing people who "go in silence, above all the others" (189). Second, this linguistic encoding of hierarchy goes hand in hand with the patriarchal religion of the Condor people, a monotheism with only one person—a man, "The Condor"—able to interpret the word of "One" (193). Of religious practice North Owl observes, "Women were not allowed into the sacred parts of their heyimas, which they called *daharda;* we could come no nearer than the vestibule in front of the daharda to listen to the singing inside on certain great festivals. Women have no part in the intellectual life of the Dayao; they are kept in, but left out" (200). Furthermore, "True Condor warriors were to be one thing only, reflections of One, setting themselves apart from all the rest of existence, washing it from their minds and souls, killing the world, so that they could remain perfectly pure" (201). And finally, with such language and religion comes an attendant social and familial structure. North Owl narrates,

> Certain men belonging to certain families are called True Condors, and others like them are called . . . One-Warriors. No other people are called Condors. Men who are not of those families are all called *tyon,* farmers, and must serve the True Condors. Women of those families are called Condor Women, and must serve Condor men, but may give orders to tyon and hontik. The hontik are all other women, foreigners, and animals. (193)

In contrast to the "anotherness" of which Murphy speaks, the Condor's social reasoning embraces an otherness steeped in a strict division between male warriors—and their approved servants—and "women, foreigners, and animals."

Tied to such linguistic, religious, and social structures, the Condor's masculine oppressiveness loses the ahistoricity and immovability of the masculinity that is represented in *The Wanderground.* The Condor's living "outside the world" is indeed a product of a certain masculinity, but grounded in historically contingent structures, this masculinity is not rigid. That the Condor "believed that animals and women were contemptible and unimportant" and that "Condors' wives were expected to have babies continuously, since that is what One made women for" demonstrates that beliefs and expectations motivate such patriarchal notions (345). If patriarchy is a sociopolitical construct driven by belief and expectation, then it proves to be far more malleable than if it were biologically defined and, as

Gearhart's book largely suggests, inevitable. In the same way, the apparent feminine qualities of Kesh culture are more the product of the pervasive heyiya-if—a linguistic, religious, and social device—than they are of an inevitable feminine principle.

In addition to its content, the form of Le Guin's book draws attention to the artifactual nature of gendered categories. *Always Coming Home* contains excerpts of literature, artwork, maps, and other objects of Kesh and Condor existence. The effect of this cutting and pasting is an emphasis on the constructedness of the Kesh's ecological conscience and the Condor's tyranny, both of which are products of a set of historical relics and not fundamental to sex. The heyiya-if produces and is produced by the ecological mind-set of the Kesh just as the Condor's crimes feed and are fed by their hierarchical religious language. Social change, it seems, is possible given transformations in the frameworks that make up any cultural system. While North Owl's journey from living with the Kesh and inside the nonhuman community to living with the Condor and outside this community, ultimately to return to the Kesh, represents a journey between opposite ends of a gendered spectrum, *Always Coming Home* does not frame this spectrum as natural and something to be dealt with using separatist strategies. As a result, Le Guin's book contributes much to ecofeminist theorizing, embracing much in cultural ecofeminist thought but positing additional, more complex theoretical questions.

If we evaluate *The Wanderground, Always Coming Home,* and Slonczewski's *A Door Into Ocean* using a strict cultural ecofeminist rubric, then their authors' creations of separate spaces for the ideological positions they critique and celebrate display quite adequately the gender associations upon which cultural ecofeminism bases its thinking. *The Wanderground*'s potently masculine, aggressively sexual, and technological City invades an ecofeminist wilderness of liberated and highly evolved women. *Always Coming Home*'s reestablished City of Man, which like its ancestral Industrial Age lives "outside the world," intrudes upon a revived ecocentric culture and this culture's Earth-based spirituality. *A Door Into Ocean*'s colonialist and patriarchal culture of planet Valedon threatens the sovereign, all-female, all-water world Shora, whose inhabitants have a remarkable knowledge of ecology and a strong sense of place. Slonczewski's clear gendering of colonialist politics and ecological wisdom as male and female, respectively, operates in much the same way as Gearhart's and

Le Guin's gendering of similar ideological stances—as cultural ecofeminist polemic. But like *Always Coming Home*'s ecofeminism, *A Door Into Ocean*'s goes beyond this polemic to fashion more complex understandings of gender and thus more effective liberatory strategies for women and nonhuman nature.

A shift toward a more critical position characterizes Slonczewski's ecofeminism, but as with *Always Coming Home* this shift does not involve a wholesale dismissal of cultural ecofeminist ideas. Read together, Le Guin's and Slonczewski's books provide a full sense of what I believe is the ecofeminist position they both ultimately participate in and argue for, a position that is aligned with the ecofeminist Ynestra King's resistance to an academic fragmentation of the movement into dichotomous theoretical brands. I will explicate *A Door Into Ocean* within this context shortly, after taking a moment to note that King's *dialectical* ecofeminism—a label I am adopting from Catriona Sandilands—at once rejects essentialist gender associations and revalues nurturance, interdependence, and other subordinate yet more ecologically conscious precepts.[5] What sets this ecofeminism apart from the cultural ecofeminism of Plant, Collard, and Gearhart is its anti-essentialist stance; what sets it apart from the rationalist feminism of Prentice and Biehl is its open-mindedness to alternative forms of critical engagement, such as spirituality, intuition, passivity, and emotion.

King argues that ecofeminism must be revised to embrace the more complex social conscience of rationalist positions while still preserving the ecological conscience of cultural ecofeminism. She admits that in choosing nature over culture and feminine values over masculine values, cultural ecofeminism does not adequately question these illusory dualisms. Demonstrating a more constructionist standpoint she writes, "women's ecological sensitivity and life orientation is a socialized perspective that could be socialized right out of [them] depending on [their] day-to-day lives" (23). Continuing, she notes, "There is no reason to believe that women placed in positions of patriarchal power will act any differently from men" (23). Women's ecological sensitivity is context-specific, not universal. Just as women can be healers, nurturers, or defenders of nonhuman nature, given different cultural contexts they might also oppose these traits. Likewise, whereas men can be culturally programmed to be militaristic, other contexts might determine them to be caring.

Such critical positions on gender and gendered value categories help free ecofeminism from some potentially devastating theoretical and practical limitations, the same limitations that hinder *The Wanderground* from today providing a more effective and applicable critique. In King's eco-feminism the transformative impulse is not tied to the idea that change can happen only within a supposedly universal feminine social or spiri-tual framework, and in the absence of an equally universal masculinity. Instead, ecofeminist reform begins in comprehending gender assumptions as constructed social phenomena. King's final image of a more effective ecofeminism is one that welcomes a multiplicity of views not strictly con-structionist or rationalist:

> Ecofeminism suggests . . . a recognition that although the nature-culture dualism is a product of culture, we can nonetheless *consciously choose* not to sever the woman-nature connection by joining male culture. Rather, we can use it as a vantage point for creating a different kind of culture and politics that would integrate intuitive, spiritual, and rational forms of knowledge, embracing both science and magic insofar as they enable us to transform the nature-culture distinction and to envision and create a free, ecological society. (23)

King blends cultural ecofeminism and rationalist feminism in a way that creates a new category for the movement, a category deeply concerned with removing the extremes of these two positions while embracing what is most valuable in each. Such an ecofeminism understands woman–nature connections, man/nature disconnections, and nature/culture dualisms as malleable cultural products that must be evaluated using a range of criti-cal voices and tools, from the engaged democratic processes of rational-ist feminism to the deeply personal, ecospiritual reflections of cultural ecofeminism.

As with Gearhart's and Le Guin's speculative fictions, Slonczewski's novel shares with cultural ecofeminism the dual goals of censuring patri-archy's social and ecological oppressions as well as highlighting the eco-logical conscience associated with women. And like Le Guin's book, Slonczewski's develops its ecofeminist position further by adding a level of complexity characteristic of the dialectical ecofeminism just reviewed. Shora's inhabitants, Sharers, are much like the women of *The Wander-ground* and the Village dwellers of *Always Coming Home* in that they have traits demonstrating their deep connection to place. Physically, the "breathmicrobes" of the Shoran atmosphere turn Sharers' skin deep pur-ple, a preventable phenomenon they accept as part of dwelling on Shora. Their lungs have evolved to allow long stints of breathlessness under water. Conceptually, the notion of sharing that gives Shora's inhabitants their name erases the hierarchies inherent in dualistic, patriarchal think-ing; their expressions "learnsharing, worksharing, [and] lovesharing" nul-lify any paradigm denying that "'Each force has an equal and opposite force'" (36). And intellectually Sharers understand their lives as dependent on an intact ecological web. When asked why she does not spray the liv-ing rafts, upon which Sharers make their homes, with an insecticide when parasites threaten them, Merwen—a native of Shora—responds, "'Then seasilk would choke the raft. And fingershells would go hungry, and tube-worms die of the poison; then fish and octopus would have nothing, and what would Sharers eat?'" (60). Their physical, conceptual, and intellec-tual embeddedness in ecological place sets the Sharers apart from their patriarchal oppressors, whose intrusion into Shora constitutes much of the plot of Slonczewski's novel.

Valedon's people, Valans, know the Sharers as "women-like creatures who lived in the endless sea, women whose men were never seen, who subsisted on seaworms and could dive deep beyond light's reach with-out going mad" (9). This perspective shrouds the Sharers in a mystery of otherness that for the Valans justifies attempts at their exploitation by a patriarchy cemented to hierarchical value structures. Historically Valedon had a native population, known derogatorily as "Trolls," that "passed away when the godlike Primes"—who were modern humans, but are now extinct due to nuclear catastrophe—"came to remodel the planet . . . to human standards" (36). As "creatures," Sharers, too, are threatened by a new manifestation of power; the rulers of the universal political system of which Valedon is a part—the Patriarchy—want to open up Shora for min-eral exploration and textile markets. Sharer compliance is necessary for this to happen, but since increased economic exploitation threatens the life forms of Shora, such compliance will not happen. Valan trade there has already brought on much ocean noise, drowning out the communications of animals essential to Shoran ecological integrity. The traders' applica-tions of poisons to the Shoran sea has also threatened life. Thus the Shar-ers defend their planet against these, and many more, intrusions.

The Patriarchy was formed to regulate independent governments away from the dangerous uses of military power that ended the reign of the Primes. But the events of *A Door Into Ocean* suggest little distinction between the violent use of nuclear weaponry by the Primes and the violent use of economic weaponry by those now in the Patriarchy. The Patriarchy claims to follow "the lesson of the dead gods: too many people smashed too many atoms—and planets, in the end," but its support of Valedon's social, political, and economic exploitation of Shora demonstrates that it fails to see this exploitation as another way of smashing planets (21). In the same way that Le Guin extrapolates the Condor from the poisoned society of the Industrial Age, Slonczewski relates the Patriarchy to the extinct Primes to urge a radical move away from the logic of domination and its consequential social, political, and ecological abuses. This concern about patriarchy is not specific to cultural ecofeminism. As a feminist mode, ecofeminism is always critical of patriarchy's logic of domination. But explicit in *A Door Into Ocean* is the cultural ecofeminist view of "feminine" ways of knowing and being as promising an alternative needed to move toward a more ecologically conscious society and politics. In this way the cultural ecofeminist moments of Slonczewski's book share much with their equivalent moments in Gearhart's book.

The stark contrast between Valedon's social and political norms and the life ways of the Sharers leads to gendered ideological collisions as Valans attempt to take possession of Shora. While the outcomes of these collisions seemingly favor masculine power, in the end the Sharers overthrow their colonial oppressors by using what Slonczewski's book overtly considers a feminine will. Most tellingly indicating the radical cultural ecofeminism of this novel, the Sharers live in a female separatist ecotopia where the absence of men permits certain values to thrive: respecting social and ecological interconnectedness, affirming and nurturing life, and building communicative networks. Sharer science is a science of life, their intellectual supremacy in biology used not to destroy but to nurture ecological systems. Their politics is one of open communication between all of Shora's raft communities during events called Gatherings. And Sharers are pacifists. In an instance that reveals the intertwining of their scientific knowledge and valuing of life, their political methodologies, and their pacifism, at one Gathering a Sharer named Yinerva proposes to use biological warfare to rid Shora of "'the Valan pestilence'" that threatens "'Not only Sharer children and survival . . . , but all the other creatures of Shora, the lesser sisters, seaswallowers, fanwings, rafts—from snail to swallower'" (309). The group, however, ultimately chooses to preserve their nonviolent ways and instead to conquer the Valans with what the defeated Valan general calls "bloodless 'invasions'" (395). The Sharers' nonviolent techniques for resisting Valan aggression include whitetrance—a form of "Gandhian discipline" in which a Sharer grows pale, still, and unresponsive to outside threats—as well as boycotting Valan goods (Slonczewski, "Study Guide" par. 31).

Read as a cultural ecofeminist text *A Door Into Ocean* demonstrates the potential for "feminine" values to triumph over "masculine" impositions. But because the reason for Shora's ultimate defeat of Valedon and the Patriarchy is only partially tied to gendered values, it would be an incomplete judgment to deem Slonczewski's novel a work of hard cultural ecofeminism without considering the range of its critical thinking. For one, Valedon's racism also instigates its military's retreat. While Valan patriarchy indeed cannot beat down Shoran ways of life, Valan racism cannot permit Valedon's army to succeed in its colonialist task. One of the most effective ways the Sharers defeat the Valans is not by conscious tactic but by possessing a racial characteristic that signifies for the Valans various substandard associations: purple skin. From the perspective of the Valan mind-set, Sharers are low creatures. They are natives who "'don't think like civilized people,'" who are "'just naked women,'" and who do not "'acknowledge the authority of Valedon'" (275, 253, 249). When the skin of the Valan occupiers begins to take on the marker of Sharer nativeness, they fear the "Purple Plague" (299). Troop morale plummets, contributing to the ultimate withdrawal of the army.

While this particular criticism of racism is perhaps and at first odd in its suggestion, against history, that colonialist fears of the predefined Other can protect colonized cultures—rather than justify and prompt militaristic and/or economic endeavor against them—it is nonetheless crucial in its recognition that colonial power is a conglomeration of several oppressive forces, including racism and patriarchy. Thus, A Door Into Ocean shares the theoretical positions of Prentice, Biehl, and King, who also do not limit their critiques of oppression to patriarchy alone. Prentice's and Biehl's rationalist feminisms, and King's dialectical ecofeminism, complement Murray Bookchin's social ecology, which targets hierarchy as the foundation upon which sexism, racism, and other modes of domination are built (hence his attacks on deep ecology, a movement that wants to reorder the anthropocentric/ecocentric hierarchy). According to social ecology, interrogating any one of these forms of oppression alone does not achieve the complete critical assessment and revision that interrogating their underlying motivating force can. As Mellor observes, "Patriarchy only exists as one form of hierarchy, it is neither the original, nor the primary oppression" (158). Gaard also makes this point when defining social ecofeminism: "Features unique to social ecofeminism include . . . its analysis of the hierarchical structure of oppression as even more descriptive than the specific forms of oppression" (Ecological 43). A Door Into Ocean moves into such a critical territory, beyond the limited range of cultural ecofeminism's exclusive focus on patriarchy—and often its support of alternative valuations that are hierarchical nonetheless—and into a

focus on questioning together patriarchy, racial essentialism, and anthropocentrism. Such a complete critical evaluation is necessary for the total
dissolution of hierarchy, in general, that would liberate nonhuman nature
from human tyranny as it also liberates oppressed humans from oppressive ones.

Though *A Door Into Ocean*'s focus on race, or hierarchy more generally, is secondary to its primary focus on gender and patriarchy, the novel
still moves strongly away from strict cultural ecofeminism. Operating on
patriarchy not simply to reverse its assumptions, but more so to include
it in a broader critical analysis of gender assumptions in general, Slonczewski's book tests cultural ecofeminism and patriarchal essentialism alike
with two of its characters, the male Spinel and the female Jade. As Susan
Stratton notes, "Gender duality [in *A Door Into Ocean*] is challenged both
by the successful adaptation of a Valedonian male teenager to Sharer ways
and by the fact that the most vicious of Valedonian soldiers is female"
("Intersubjectivity" par. 22). These characterizations complicate essentialist notions and open the door for ecofeminism to look more at the social
than the so-called innate origins of male and female behavior and relationships with nonhuman nature.   "coming of age" or "evolution"

Slonczewski's novel is in part a bildungsroman about Spinel, an adolescent boy from Valedon who goes to Shora, experiences life there, and
ultimately chooses to stay. Spinel's acceptance of Sharer ways, however,
comes after his interior battle with himself over the patriarchal ideology
that defines him. Going through hard times financially, Spinel's parents
arrange for him to seek opportunity on Shora. The Sharers promote the
move, for Spinel presents them with the opportunity to study masculinity and to prove that a man can become a Sharer. But Spinel is not so
excited. It is outrageous to him that there are not any men on Shora, and
he believes that "'A world without fathers could have no place for him'"
(22). Coming from a hierarchical society Spinel sees the equality among
Sharers as the product of "bizarre logic"; to him the planet is "ridiculous"
(61). And as Spinel's exposure to the Shoran atmosphere turns him purple,
he demands a medicine that will curtail the phenomenon.

With his compulsory defense of the heterosexual family unit, his
hierarchical logic, and his unwillingness to experience difference, Spinel
embodies essentialist notions of masculinity. But Spinel is not the subject
of essentialist contention. Central to Slonczewski's argument is that masculinity is a socialized characteristic, and this is made obvious as Spinel
embeds himself more and more into Shoran life, shedding his socialized
masculinity and adopting a social and ecological conscience. Interestingly,

this embedding begins after he witnesses the wonders of Shoran ecology.[6] Afterwards, "Spinel was now more than simply curious about Shora. Something compelled him to come to grips with this place that was inexorably becoming a part of him" (100). That "Something" is likely the very nonhuman nature within which he overtly experiences his embeddedness as his skin deepens to purple and his ocean dives increase in depth and duration. Spinel's newfound sense of place ultimately leads him to join the Sharers in defending their planet against Valan exploitation, his sea change expressed in the final words of the novel as he swims away from the spacecraft that would have taken him back to Valedon: "a friendly fanwing dipped and soared overhead like a hand beckoning, Come, lovesharer, come home" (403).

That a male can become a "lovesharer" is one part of the constructionist ecofeminist claim of *A Door Into Ocean*. The other is that given the cultural atmosphere a woman can embody the worst of masculine aggressiveness. As Chief of Staff of the Valan army, Jade is a woman whose militarism challenges essentialist notions of femininity and the idea that violence and hostility are sex-specific. About militaristic conditioning, ecofeminist scholar Janis Birkeland writes, "men are taught to despise and distance themselves from their 'feminine' side, or their emotions and feeling" (35). Slonczewski's narrative shows that such conditioning is inscribable on both men and women. Jade derogatorily nicknames the Sharers "catfish," placing them at the bottom of an ontological hierarchy that denies species equality and justifies Valan oppressions against Shoran natives. "'Catfish aren't human,'" Jade says, "'they're Vermin, and that's how to treat them'" (323). Jade admits that it is her duty to kill, as she also administers a range of tortures in an attempt to crack the Sharer's nonviolent protests. In Slonczewski's world masculinity is a socialized trait; militarism and violent aggression do not emerge simply from being male but are characteristics etched on any sex by genderless oppressive institutions.

Stephanie Lahar asks,

Is there a way to know whether there were ever times and places when human beings lived in easy cooperation with each other and the nonhuman environment, without the sexist, oppressive, and exploitive complex of power relations we call patriarchy? Is seeking such times and

places useful in empowering women today, by portraying model societies in which women either shared or held primary power? (97)

As works of science fiction, Gearhart's, Le Guin's, and Slonczewski's novels all imagine such times and places. But their positions, like ecofeminism
itself, are diverse. Espousing the multiplicity of perspectives within ecofeminism, Lee Quinby notices that ecofeminism "has combated ecological
destruction and patriarchal domination without succumbing to the totalizing impulses of masculinist politics," embracing as political strategy a plu-
rality of theoretical positions rather than a single, hegemonic stance (123).
The ecofeminist texts reviewed in this chapter confirm Quinby's point, at
least regarding science fiction's ecofeminist theorizations.

Often challenged as essentialist in its judgments, *The Wanderground*
embraces as political strategy the spatial separation of men and women as
well as the safeguarding and uninhibited self-realization of both women
and nonhuman nature associated with this separation. Ecotopian? Perhaps. But as discussed in chapter 2, ecotopian visions have transformative potential, if not to lay a literal groundwork then certainly to posit
an intellectual compass for moving toward a new ground. And in Gearhart's novel, that compass is one necessitated by the experiences of women
and nonhuman nature during the time of the book's composition—the
1970s—when both feminists and environmentalists were pushing the
boundaries of dominant ideology and reaching for new and effective critical methodologies.

Always Coming Home and *A Door Into Ocean* also embrace cultural
ecofeminism, positing as a critical strategy the consideration of gender difference. But these books intrinsically question their own considerations.
Le Guin's work does not locate gender difference in inflexible biological
determinations, instead highlighting the malleability of the structures and
symbolisms determining female and male relationships with nonhuman
nature, and with each other. Slonczewski's book expands the ecofeminist
critique of patriarchy to a broader social critique of hierarchy as it also
underscores gendered behavior as specific to the atmospheres constructing
such behavior, regardless of sex. By doing so, *Always Coming Home* and
A Door Into Ocean develop on cultural ecofeminism without watering
down what is most important in its message: the liberation of women and
nonhuman nature from oppression. These liberations demand theoretical
and practical diversity. *The Wanderground, Always Coming Home,* and *A
Door Into Ocean* together offer us literary explorations of this diversity.

CHAPTER FOUR

ECOSOCIALIST CRITIQUE

A S THE PREVIOUS chapters have shown, environmental science fiction recurrently criticizes capitalist economic productivism and/or the ideological positions that enable this productivism. Olaf Stapledon's *Last and First Men* comments on the economic exploitation of nonhuman nature. George R. Stewart's *Earth Abides* contains a critique of the myth of human supremacy, which morally justifies capitalist exploitation. *Dune* raises questions about whether we can even locate something called "nonhuman nature" in our contemporary economic situation, when imperial dominance threatens an already second nature with a dystopian third one. Both Ernest Callenbach's and Marge Piercy's ecotopias abandon capitalist economies, favoring instead a qualitative affluence; and John Brunner's books express clear anxieties about capitalist production and consumption patterns. Fredric Jameson observes the identification of patriarchy with capitalist imperialism in Ursula K. Le Guin's *Always Coming Home* (67), and Sally Miller Gearhart's and Joan Slonczewski's ecofeminist novels likewise connect patriarchy to economically motivated imperial aggression toward nonhuman nature.

Much environmental science fiction attends to the "tensions between the economic forces of production and local ecological conditions" highlighted by sociologist James O'Connor and environmental historian Carolyn Merchant (*Radical* 9). Historically considered, the subgenre is an environmental literary movement that has emerged in response to the degradation of nature that characterizes the capitalist productivism of the last one hundred years. Each story, as with each transformative movement reviewed in this study, responds differently to this degradation. Nevertheless, this degradation seems most often to be perceived in environmental science fiction as born if not always in productivism, then certainly in the deep-seated values that make the destruction of nonhuman nature for economic gain morally tolerable.

Spanning the second half of the twentieth century, a period of time that saw the largest increases of economic production and consumption in human history, the novels analyzed in this chapter look critically upon the historical economic circumstances within which each was written, and which collectively enabled such massive economic growth. Frederik Pohl and C. M. Kornbluth's *The Space Merchants* (1952) offers a satirical look at "the new emphasis on consumption in the post-war American economy" (Luckhurst 110), particularly calling out the advertising industry whose self-admitted goal was—and still is—to "maintain the multiplicity and intensity of wants that are the spur to the standard of living in the United States" (Lebow 9). Twenty years later in *The Word for World Is Forest* (1972), Le Guin reads "the ethic which approved the defoliation of forests and grainlands and the murder of noncombatants in the name of 'peace'" during the Vietnam War as "a corollary of the ethic which permits the despoliation of natural resources for private profit or the GNP" (Le Guin, "Introduction to" 151). And Kim Stanley Robinson's *Mars* trilogy (1993, 1994, 1996) appears about another twenty years later in the post-Reagan era of global capitalist expansion to think about the ecological consequences of economic hyperactivity and to imagine political solutions to rampant, unfettered capitalist development. As a result of their critical engagements with the capitalist mode of production, these books can be read within the context of the final transformative environmental philosophy that I will discuss in this study: ecosocialism.

Ecosocialism stands for the supersession of capital by a system of democratized socioeconomic organization that assures social justice and maintains ecological integrity. Joel Kovel, author of the ecosocialist manifesto *The Enemy of Nature*, defines an ecosocialist society as "a society that is recognizably socialist, in that the producers have been reunited with the means of production in a robust efflorescence of democracy; and also recognizably ecological, in that the 'limits to growth' are finally respected, and nature is recognized as having intrinsic value and not simply cared for, and thereby allowed to resume its inherently formative path" (10). Ecosocialism is necessarily a class movement, finding in capital's state-supported class structure the social foundation for an inherently repressive mode of economic production—that is, an elite-driven system that denies workers (and with colonization, indigenous peoples) their control of the tools, raw materials, and sites of material production and with wage labor exploits their labor power in an effort to realize a profit in a globalized network of commodity exchange.

As an ecological movement ecosocialism highlights the effects of such tendencies on ecosystemic integrity. First, severing workers from a collectively owned and democratically managed means of production enables the production of commodities with value only as things to be exchanged globally for the profit of the owner class (exchange values) rather than as goods necessary to satisfy human needs (use values) and, importantly, obedient to local ecological limits. In capitalism, exchange is the privileged value. As O'Connor writes,

> This means that (1) in the workplace, land use practices, divisions of labor, and so on, are governed first and foremost by the need *to produce exchange value,* or profit. The needs to preserve ecological diversity, avoid ecological debts to other workplaces and future generations, promote the intellectual development of the worker, and the like are subordinated to production for profit; and (2) in the sphere of consumption . . . clean air and water, uncongested transport, and other social and ecological "goods" are sacrificed to the need *to realize exchange value* in the market. (327)

Second, in capitalist wage labor, workers—who because of the ubiquity of capitalism are under economic compulsion to seek employment in producing surplus value for the owners of private enterprise—are alienated from nonhuman nature, and nonhuman nature is alienated from the creative, ecologically sensible human. Wage labor relegates workers to the status of interchangeable factory, monocultural plantation, or cubicle occupants who are thus psychologically and physically removed from their place within the ecological field of relations that for ecosocialism, and deep ecology, defines a whole human self. While ecosocialists indeed find much wanting in deep ecology, both movements encourage the de-alienation of humans as a prerequisite for realizing our selves within the mesh of ecosystemic relationships.[1] As Kovel argues, the "human trade-mark"—which is different from the trademarks of other species only in terms of varying capacities and ways of fitting into the ecological whole—is characterized by inwardness and acting upon imagination in materially transforming ways (109). The realization of our full humanity is a func-tion of the degree to which we participate freely in the production of use values, in the production of the necessities of our own lives, and the com-munity's life, as integral components of ecosystems. Under capitalism the private owners of the means of production, following the profit motive and a market whim instigated largely by capital's sophisticated advertising and marketing complex, disunite workers from nonhuman nature and use value, defeating their beings as "organismic totalities . . . who act in the ecosystemic world and are acted upon by the world" (Kovel 99). And if capitalism is dehumanizing because it prevents workers from being in eco-systemic relationship, then it is anti-ecological in part because by contriv-ing and mandating the privately owned wage laborer it denies ecosystems the ecological creative capacity of human beings, replacing this capacity with "consumption habits artificially produced by advertising" (Löwy 7).

Finally, the profit motive of capital's owner class commands a growth imperative that sees social and ecosystemic boundaries as opportunities for new investment and commodification. Capital thus proceeds with an atti-tude of limitlessness, wreaking social and ecological havoc in the process. Noncapitalist cultures are penetrated and contained within the ruling capi-talist totality as "Other—barbarians, savages, human animals, and eventu-ally (with the growth of science), ethnicities and races," thereby justifying their place at the bottom of a class hierarchy where uncreative wage labor prevails and social life remains perpetually deteriorated despite the prom-ises of trickle-down theory (Kovel 122–23). Capital "alters [life worlds] in ways that foster its accumulation, chiefly by introducing a sense of dissat-isfaction or lack—so that it can truly be said that happiness is forbidden under capitalism, being replaced by sensation and craving" (52). Kovel continues,

> The culture of advanced capital aims to turn society into addicts of com-modity consumption, a state 'good for business,' and, *pari passu*, bad for ecologies. The evil is doubled, with reckless consumption leading to pollution and waste, and the addiction to commodities creating a soci-ety unable to comprehend, much less resist, the ecological crisis. (66)

Capital's movement to commodify new pools of labor and to appeal in so many ways to untapped markets parallels its intrusions into nonhuman nature, which along with human labor constitutes what Karl Marx called "conditions of production." Such intrusions, as ecosocialism argues, are responsible for ecological degradation.

O'Conner's "second contradiction of capitalism" and Merchant's "first contradiction" of contemporary society are parallel observations on the tendency for productivist economic activity to be in tension with ecological integrity. Capitalist activity has increased atmospheric warming, decreased soil fertility, exterminated species, polluted oceans, poisoned groundwater, and more.[2] The agents of capital thus damage the external physical conditions of capitalist production. This damage, combined with further injury to social and personal conditions (e.g., intensified urban congestion, increasing healthcare costs, divorce, crime) raises the economic system's costs. Operators of the system therefore create a crisis that "has more to do with *external* or natural barriers than with the *internal* or class antagonisms of the system" (Foster, "Capitalism" par. 9). Important here is O'Connor's and Merchant's theoretical split from traditional Marxism, in which internal economic crisis and class antagonisms are perceived to instigate historical transformation. Instead, the economic mode's inherently anti-ecological and antisocial activities instigate, as Merchant notes, "new ecological social movements: environmental health and safety, farm-workers' antipesticide coalitions, ecofeminist protests over groundwater toxins, leftwing green parties, and so on" (*Radical* 149).

"The root of ecological crisis is economic," Derek Wall asserts (7). A transformative solution to such crisis is thus to expose capitalism by highlighting its methods and effects, and then to challenge the economic system with a newly imagined democratic mode of production. This new mode would oppose a prevailing global capitalism that, as the dominant force behind anthropogenic pressures on planetary boundaries today, is socially and ecologically unsustainable. As responses to capitalism's second contradiction, the following science fiction works do much to navigate capitalism's problems, and in the case of the *Mars* trilogy, point the way forward toward a different economic system.

Suji

#1
The Space
Merchants

Deemed by M. Keith Booker and Anne-Marie Thomas as "a founding text of environmentalist science fiction," *The Space Merchants* presents an ecologically dire future Earth where freshwater is in severe decline, coal is still a big industry, and polluted air necessitates nasal antisoot plugs (207). Overpopulation has people yearning for the more roomy past, and wood is so rare that oak and pine jewelry signify the status that precious metals and jewels signify today. And to meet global food-supply needs in the absence of land fit enough to grow food organically, one company, Chlorella Proteins, develops and maintains Chicken Little, once a small piece of heart tissue and now a gigantic blob of protein-rich meat sliced, weighed, shaped, frozen, cooked, flavored, packaged, and shipped all over the world. The atrocious ecological conditions of this future Earth have not instigated any sort of broadly accepted revolutionary or ecotopian economic program, however. Despite the strain of the growth-centered economy on Earth's limited life-support systems, and thus on most of the planet's human and nonhuman population, the wheels of this economy keep turning in what David Mogen, the author of a book about mythologies of the American West in science fiction, identifies as a frontiersmanship imported from the past to drive the modern economy.

Where *The Space Merchants* is most acute in its criticism is not in condemning the ramping up of capitalist production and the associated consumerist ethos in post–World War II America but in illustrating the pernicious nature of capital's principal instigator of this ethos. This instigator is an advertising institution motivated both to pave the way for global economic expansion into regions of disparate cultural attitudes and practices, and to obfuscate empirical evidence that would otherwise implicate the economic system it serves in a range of misdeeds. Read as a work of environmental science fiction's economic critique, *The Space Merchants* is most effective when it shows how much the capitalist economy depends on an advertising industry whose foremost obligation is to facilitate social amnesia about the regrettable origins of whatever this economy produces or never to admit that such origins exist in the first place.

In *The Space Merchants* advertising perpetuates at least two of the mythologies necessary for capital's expansion: (1) there is a pancultural desire and need for the capitalist mode of production, and (2) capitalist production processes and their resulting commodities are harmless. In the book the large advertising agency Fowler Shocken Associates makes its fortune pioneering for economic globalization. One of Fowler Shocken's favorite accounts is Indiastries, for which the agency prepared "'a whole subcontinent'" to merge "'into a single manufacturing complex'" (3). Fowler Shocken himself outlines the "history of advertising—from the simple handmaiden task of selling already manufactured goods to its present role of creating industries and redesigning a world's folkways to meet the needs of commerce" (6). While Fowler celebrates marketeering efforts to expunge social and cultural difference around the world to facilitate capitalist growth, such efforts are a key target of critique for contemporary critics of the global economy. Jerry Mander and Edward Goldsmith, editors of *The Case Against the Global Economy and for a Turn Toward the Local,* write, "For corporations, the overwhelming drive is constantly to expand their resource bases and their markets to create globally homogenized consumerist life-styles" (295). Developing this point in the same collection, social justice advocate Tony Clarke observes the effect of the growth economy's homogenizing objectives: "a global monoculture is emerging, which not only disregards local tastes and cultural differences but threatens to serve as a form of social control over the attitudes, expectations, and behavior of people all over the world" (300).

Fowler's brief history of advertising demonstrates what critics of globalization notice today: in the interest of profit and the perpetuation of capitalism, the agents of capital are annihilating cultural tradition. Of the many problems with this subordination of difference to economic purpose, one is indeed ecological, especially if that difference is one of a culture's desire to maintain its aboriginal place and maintain its indigenous economy. Referencing environmental thinker and activist Vandana Shiva, Brian Tokar writes in *Earth for Sale,* "development . . . systematically degrades the knowledge, skills and cultural practices that have made it possible for people to thrive completely outside of a commercial context for thousands of years" (170). Indeed, capital's systematic degradation of knowledge and skills is what leads Daniel R. Wildcat to call for an "indigenous realism," mentioned earlier in this study as lived embeddedness. Epitomizing Shiva's point and making Wildcat's efforts more urgent, apologists for global capitalism believe, as global money manager Peter Marber demonstrates in his book *Money Changes Everything,* that because citizens of economically disadvantaged nations sport American brand-name clothes they must desire to throw away their culture and enter the global marketplace (158). In replacing the noncommercial with an omnipresent commercial, or subsuming noncommercial cultural practices into commercial exchange as identity commodities, the development policy that extends from Marber's attitude—indeed, the very attitude that Fowler Shocken fosters in Pohl and Kornbluth's novel—erodes not only cultural integrity but also ecological integrity, since the latter is often a core concern of the groups that capitalism's extractive industries target.

The exhausted ecology represented in *The Space Merchants* is the result of the reckless consumption encouraged by advertising's ubiqui-

[handwritten annotation: narratives can be fictional & concealing. can they also be revealing — in their simplicity — or hard to see truth?]

tous fictional and concealing narratives. After defining early the motivation that drives the advertising industry, Pohl and Kornbluth show this industry in action. Having "'actually and literally conquered the world" with Indiastries and other accounts, and "'Like Alexander, [weeping] for new worlds to conquer'" (6), Fowler initiates his next project: the "development and exploitation of the planet Venus" (7). With "Sales" as their god, Fowler's agency begins its marketing. To start, Mitchell Courtenay, the agency's language man and the novel's narrator, consults with Jack O'Shea, the only person to have travelled to Venus, to locate in O'Shea's experiences images that will appeal to prospective immigrants to, and consumers of, the planet. O'Shea's honesty about Venus, though, is not what Mitch wants to hear. Asked to "'Suppose [he] wanted a lot of people to go to Venus. What would [he] tell them about it?'" Jack replies, "'I'd tell them a lot of damn big lies'" (17). How else to sell an atmosphere of "'embalming fluid,'" heat that "'averages above the boiling point of water—if there were any water on Venus, which there isn't,'" and winds "'clocked five hundred miles an hour'" (17)? Mitch, however, trusts that "'there are answers for all those things'" and instead wants Jack to give him "'the feel of the place'" (17).

The contrast between the actual Venus of Jack's experience and the imaginary Venus that Mitch wants to sell speaks to a fundamental strategy of global capital to conceal physical and or social reality using appealing, marketable symbolic values. But Mitch soon gets to experience the deceptiveness of advertising language when he is thrust into the authentic environment of another one of his accounts, Chlorella Proteins. Kidnapped and given a new identity as a laborer at the oppressive Costa Rican factory that houses Chicken Little, Mitch cannot help but recall the words he wrote to sell Chlorella's products: "'From the sun-drenched plantations of Costa Rica, tended by the deft hands of independent farmers with pride in their work, comes the juicyripe goodness of Chlorella Proteins'" (68). In contrast to the advertising language, Chlorella Proteins greets laborers—not family farmers—with "a gush of disinfectant aerosol," a team of condescending guards, and number plaques to wear around their necks (67). The factory is eighty stories high and its photosynthesis mirrors create working conditions too bright to be safe.

Opposing Fowler Shocken Associates and the consumer culture that the firm promotes, the World Conservationist Association (W.C.A.) works to curtail the "reckless exploitation of natural resources" that it believes "has created needless poverty and needless human misery" (80). However, in the world of *The Space Merchants,* a world in which the ideology of capital permeates social consciousness, the W.C.A. offers a criticism too contrary to be adopted comfortably.[3] As with the Trainites in *The Sheep Look Up,* the W.C.A. is demonized by those in power who control public discourse, thus neutralizing their message. A W.C.A. pamphlet attempts to debunk myths about the organization:

> You have probably heard that "the Consies" are murderers, psychotics, and incompetent people who kill and destroy for irrational ends or out of envy. None of this is true. W.C.A. members are humane, balanced persons, many of them successful in the eyes of the world. Stories to the contrary are zealously encouraged by people who profit from the exploitation which we hope to correct. (80)

As a key player in capital's mind control Mitchell knows the W.C.A. only as malcontents. His resentment of the "Consies," as well as his position as an enabler of hyperactive consumer behavior, comes out when he reflects on the fellow factory worker and secret W.C.A. member who handed him the abovementioned leaflet:

> I hated the twisted minds who had done such a thing to a fine consumer like Gus. It was something like murder. He could have played his part in the world, buying and using and making work and profits for his brothers all around the globe, ever increasing his wants and needs, ever increasing everybody's work and profits in the circle of consumption, raising children to be consumers in turn. (82)

Mitch must feign sympathy with the W.C.A. cause to escape the Costa Rican factory, and though he seems too firmly embedded in capitalist ideology to adopt any conservationist sentiment while intermingling with members of the organization, in the end he does just that.

Once he is outside his corporate physical and ideological space, Mitch sees a reality that his entrenchment within the capitalist fantasy prevented him from seeing. Interestingly, Mitch's experiences in and realizations about this reality attest to a worldview so different from the worldview of global capital that Fowler Shocken writes them off as imagined. Contrary to the mythologies perpetuated by capital, "The interests of producers and consumers are not identical," "Most of the world is unhappy," "Workmen don't automatically find the job they do best," "Entrepreneurs don't play a hard, fair game by the rules," and "The Consies are sane, intelligent, and well organized" (135). But Sales is to Fowler a Truth that "could do no wrong" (136). As Mogen argues, Fowler's "convictions are part of a system of culturally-reinforced delusions that provide rationalizations for the system from which he profits" (65). Embodying the global capitalist hegemony, Fowler dismisses Mitch's disclosures the same way capital has dismissed economic alternatives throughout the novel, discounting Mitch's new conscience as the product of a "wicked, untamed id" (136).[4] The novel ends after Fowler dies and leaves Mitch with majority shares in Fowler Shocken Associates. With his new ecological and social conscience, Mitch exercises his advertising aptitudes and financial resources to convince the public to stay away from Venus. Using the government-sponsored Venus rocket, he relocates to the planet with a group of W.C.A. members—an ending that prompts Mogen to reflect, "Though *The Space Merchants* spends much of its time lampooning the absurdity of importing myths from our frontier past into the context of the Space Age, it finds its resolution in the tried and true American solution to social and personal problems: escape to the frontier" (66).

In the second edition of her book *Screening Space,* Vivian Sobchack draws from Ernest Mandel and Fredric Jameson to define the "postindustrial" age and to characterize the cultural dynamics of what is often called "late capitalism." She notes, "With the 1940s . . . and coincident with the technological development of nuclear and electronic power marked progressively by the atom bomb, the television set, and the computer, comes a new moment of capitalist expansion" (243). Marking this late capitalism is "The totalizing incorporation of Nature by industrialized culture . . . into a visible and marketable 'desire' produced as media spectacle" (244). When in *The Space Merchants* Mitch stares through the window of a tourist rocket at the Amazon valley and Tierra Del Fuego only to be interrupted with advertisements that opaque his view, he is experiencing late capitalism. These places are already capitalist spaces in the book—the Amazon basin home to the world's biggest power dam and Tierra Del Fuego a whale fishery—and are thus doubly commodified when Mitch's gaze is subjected to advertisements. Indeed, with their imaginative descriptions of scarcity, sterility, and pollution amid the hypercapitalist symbolic strategies that overwrite this ecological reality in every way possible, Pohl and Kornbluth underline the problems of a late capitalism too caught up in an ideology of perpetual economic growth to notice, or even care about, the physical limits of its activities.

Mogen highlights the irony of *The Space Merchants*'s social and personal escapism in the face of its biting critique of what is ultimately that same escapism used to enable capitalist expansion. But given Mitch's seemingly intractable grounding and participation in an economic mode that commodifies nonhuman nature and human culture in ways that go beyond overwriting them with marketing language, his adoption of a conscience critical of capitalist production at least signals a hopeful shift in social consciousness. The frontier is not literally the new world of Venus, but instead the new world of thinking beyond capitalism. Mitch's physical relocation from a completely commercialized and dominated Earth to a Venus he vows not to compromise to corporate interests symbolizes the possibility of a movement in culture from a productivist ideology unwilling to confront its inherent hazards—and a resulting consumer conscience unaware of the effects of economic growth on ecosystems and cultures—to an ecological conscience awake to the effects of capital's global supremacy and willing to meet this supremacy with new ideas.

"One of the major [science fiction] denunciations of the American genocide in Vietnam" and thus of the cultural attitudes that helped sustain that war, Le Guin's *The Word for World Is Forest* could be discussed within the context of part-of-nature, ecological thinking, deep ecology, and ecofeminism (Jameson 274). Its description of the forest on the planet Athshe, the novel's setting, expresses a biological reality that challenges modernity's taming of wild nature in the interest of economic development. In the forest,

> No way was clear, no light unbroken. . . . Into wind, water, sunlight, starlight, there always entered leaf and branch, bole and root, the shadowy, the complex. Little paths ran under the branches, around the boles, over the roots; they did not go straight, but yielded to every obstacle, devious as nerves. The ground was not dry and solid but damp and rather springy, product of the collaboration of living things with the long, elaborate death of leaves and trees; and from that rich graveyard grew ninety-foot trees, and tiny mushrooms that sprouted in circles half an inch across. (25)

Here, complexity and decay mark the actuality of the nature from which life is born, the wild nature of which humans are a part and that must be preserved if life is to continue to be born. The book also reflects on deep ecological concerns. When one character, Kees, worries that Don

Davidson's Terran logging crew is breaking ecological protocol when it poaches deer on Athshe, Davidson argues his point with anthropocentric reasoning (5): "'it's the men that count. Not the animals'" (4). Continuing his dispute with the ecologically conscious Kees, Davidson declares, "'You worry about deer and trees and fibreweed, fine, that's your thing. But I like to see things in perspective, from the top down, and the top, so far, is humans. We're here, now; and so this world's going to go our way'" (5). This reasoning is coupled in Davidson with an androcentrism that imposes hierarchical sexual relations in the same way it imposes top-down human–nonhuman nature relations. In fact, the novel begins with Davidson anticipating his visit to the "new shipload of women . . . breeding females . . . 212 head of prime human stock" (1).

While Le Guin's novel invites readings from the perspectives of normative ecology, deep ecology, and ecofeminism, its central conflict demands a reading critical of capitalist expansion and production—an ecosocialist reading. The book's success as a work of environmental science fiction comes mostly from its insistence that it is foremost the ideology of capital, with its constituent ways of thinking about human and nonhuman nature, that enables the erosion of biological systems and the oppression of human and nonhuman Others. If *The Space Merchants* is chiefly about the symbolic strategies used to disguise capitalism's malignancies while expanding its reach, then Le Guin's *The Word for World Is Forest* is a closer exploration of these malignancies. It argues that the capitalist mode of production necessitates ecophobia, speciesism, racism, and misogyny. To build firm inter- and intraspecies hierarchies authorizes the dominant species and the dominant class and race to behave only in its own interests; to objectify women makes them available for consumption. Put differently, capitalism needs understandings of human and nonhuman Others that allow these Others to be commodified in the first place. Capital's knowledge of people and place—indeed, Davidson's knowledge in the novel—is strictly economic, fed by a fetish for markets and the emptying of cultural and ecological meaning that turns people and places into objects of exchange.

Demonstrating this emptying of meaning, Davidson reflects on the motivations of those exploiting Athshe: "men were here now to end the darkness, and turn the tree-jumble into clean sawn planks, more prized on Earth than gold. Literally, because gold could be got from seawater and from under the Antarctic ice, but wood could not; wood came only from trees. And it was a really necessary luxury on Earth. So the alien forests became wood" (7). Davidson's explanation of capital's intentions on Athshe characterizes capitalism's perception of nonhuman nature and of itself. Terms such as "darkness" and "tree-jumble," disassociated from their signification of the life-giving qualities of nonhuman nature highlighted in the blocked passage above, are imposed on the Athshean woods, writing off their place within a complex ecological totality to serve instead a mythology in which production saves the day by taming the forest and transforming it from a locale of "primeval murk and savagery and ignorance" to "a paradise, a real Eden" (3). Seeing themselves as honorable in disinfecting the forest and its people, the agents of capital in Le Guin's novel provide the necessities of human life—wood—and are thus all the more pious. To say wood is a "necessary luxury," though, is oxymoronic, for as the consumer culture theorist James Twitchell contends, luxuries are "totally unnecessary" (1). The logging of the forest is necessary only in that it serves the very economic system that imposes a rhetoric of need upon its products.

With the capitalist vocabulary lifted from Davidson's project, no longer is it a noble endeavor to sanitize Athshe and fulfill human necessity. Instead, it is a deforestation project supported by "the Development people" whose real interest in Athshe is the one hundred twenty million dollars' worth of lumber that the planet provides the Terran market annually (76). Certainly, this project has a number of ecological and cultural ramifications. His thoughts focused on "212 buxom beddable breasty little figures," Davidson is inconvenienced by news of the ecological consequences of his venture: "Dump Island"—the first Terran colony on Athshe—cannot sustain crops or a healthy ecology with its forest logged (1). Missing the ecological network of root systems and fibreweed that stabilizes the topsoil, Dump Island dies as quickly as the rain can wash its soil into the sea. Concerned about the ecology of Athshe and critical of the Terran development plan for the planet, one character, Raj Lyubov, admits, "As for the total land ecology . . . I say we've irrecoverably wrecked the native life-systems on one large island, have done great damage on this subcontinent Sornol, and if we go on logging at the present rate, may reduce the major habitable lands to desert within ten years" (71).

Lyubov is an anthropologist for the Terran colonies and his ultimately inaccurate assessment of the Athsheans as a passive and consequently exploitable species leads those in power to disregard his ecologically literate observation as another erroneous judgment. But Lyubov's speculation exhibits one of environmental science fiction's key environmentalist features, and it returns us—as any extrapolative assessment could—to the issue of extrapolation I discussed in the introduction to this book. As Frank M. Robinson avows, science fiction writers are "our early warning system for the future" (255), and Carol P. Hovanec maintains, "This is certainly one of Le Guin's purposes"—to offer a theoretical case study "of what might happen in the future if humanity continues to exploit the environment" (84). Science fiction does ask imperative questions about the future, but as Le Guin asserts, "Science fiction is not predictive; it is descriptive" (Introduction par. 7). By depicting spaces ravaged by economic production, environmental science fiction authors raise questions about how we should behave now to avoid such consequences in the future. But, importantly, they also engage in such depictions to make us aware that much of what they portray or forecast is happening now.[5] Lyubov's prediction operates on both levels. It serves as a warning to the Terrans (and us) about the consequences of current extractive activities, and it reminds them that these consequences have already been experienced somewhere else. Disputing the argument that the Terran development plan for Athshe can progress with minimal ecological impact, Lyubov asserts, "'That's what the Bureau of Land Management said about Alaska . . . The survival percentage of Native Alaskan species in habitat, after 15 years of the Development Program, was .3%. It's now zero'" (72).

Identifying Davidson with the industrialists of late-nineteenth-century America, Hovanec writes, "In his desire to destroy the forest and convert it to products useful for Terran, he also resembles the deterministic industrialists who saw the environment as an expendable commodity" (88). The concept of the expendability of nonhuman nature is a central, though as we have seen contradictory, justification for capitalist production and, as Le Guin's novel demonstrates, the focus of its rhetoric. And with the mindset that the interests of markets take precedence over a feared and disposable nonhuman nature comes the outlook that everything in this nature must make way for the development that capital brings. Just as Davidson represents the attitude of capitalist agents toward an expendable nonhuman nature, he also represents their feelings about those who dwell in the places they desire to exploit. Davidson remarks about the native Athsheans, "'They're going to get rubbed out sooner or later, and it might as well be sooner. It's just how things happen to be. Primitive races always have to give way to civilized ones. Or be assimilated. But we sure as hell can't assimilate a lot of green monkeys'" (12).

Labeling the Athsheans as inevitable victims of colonialism, as premodern, and as inferior, Davidson validates capitalist activities that threaten a native culture whose lives are interconnected with the living forests and with each other, or in Davidson's estimation, a substandard herd of "creechies" whose wild life ways attest to their baseness. Once "Perfectly integrated into the natural ecology of their planet," the Athsheans are so dislocated as a result of Terran activity that they sacrifice their pacifism to engage in their own fierce project to end Terran exploitation (Yanarella 100–101). Also a culturally critical voice in *The Word for World Is Forest*, Lyubov speculates on the Athsheans' recent violence toward the Terran occupiers:

> "I wonder if they're not proving their adaptability, now. By adapting their behavior to us. To the Earth Colony. For four years they've behaved to us as they do to one another. Despite the physical differences, they recognized us as members of their species, as men. However, we have not responded as members of their species should respond. We have ignored the responses, the rights and obligations of non-violence. We have killed, raped, dispersed, and enslaved the native humans, destroyed their communities, and cut down their forests." (62)

A postcolonial analysis of Le Guin's novel might examine the cultural ramifications of the Terrans' introduction of violence into Athshean civilization, particularly how that civilization is in effect erased as a consequence of the erasure of one of its key defining characteristics: nonviolence. Selver, the Athshean who leads the successful revolution to defeat Terran conquest, even laments to one Terran, "'Maybe after I die people will be as they were before I was born, and before you came. But I do not think they will'" (169).

With the Athsheans' new knowledge of how to kill, their ecological consciousness might forever be changed as well. Though this claim is speculative (Selver's statement ends the novel and we never find out if his prediction comes true, or to what end), it follows that such a drastic mutation of a nonviolent, embedded culture could dissolve any sense of ecological connectedness that the culture has. If the people "they were before" were seamlessly integrated into the ecology of Athshe and had developed their nonviolent, cooperative social tendencies as a result of this integration, then the introduction of social violence is also the introduction of an idea and a state of being that could separate the Athsheans from the nonhuman nature that made them as they were before. Speaking on this point in a different, real-life context, the Okanagan Native activist Jeannette Armstrong writes, "Indigenous people, not long removed from our cooperative self-sustaining life-styles on our lands, do not survive well in this atmosphere of aggression and dispassion" (467). Asserting the idea that Le Guin's book also asserts—that "We are our land/place"—Armstrong recognizes how capitalist violence and its inherent deficit of cooperation and lived embeddedness severs native people from their traditional ways of life (466). Armstrong shares with Le Guin an uneasiness about the effects of capitalism on nonhuman places and on the cultures that dwell in them. Ultimately, Le Guin's tale calls for something to be done about the exploitation of people and place executed in the name of economic growth and the perpetuation of the capitalist mode of production.

Robinson's *Mars* trilogy is especially successful at imagining an economic system that fundamentally rejects the types of capitalist obfuscations, oppressions, and assaults that are underlined in *The Space Merchants* and *The Word for World Is Forest*. Set on Mars, a "blank red slate" of social, economic, political, and environmental historical possibility, the entire trilogy illustrates the challenges of moving beyond the blemished Terran past and toward a utopian Martian future (*Red Mars* 85). Early in *Red Mars* the group of one hundred first settlers who are chosen to establish a Martian colony look forward to beginning a small scientific research station on the planet. Back on Earth capitalism's second contradiction has played out fully and the resulting shortages of exploitable resources encourage mining and oil drilling on the protected continent of Antarctica, "'the last clean place on Earth'" (251). As a result, like Venus in *The Space Merchants* Mars becomes the next site of growth, the latest economic venture necessitated by capital's destruction of its own conditions of production, which is in this case Earth's nonhuman nature.

Capitalist intentions take precedence over the scientific motives of the first settlers, and the subsequent intrusion of transnational corporate interests instigates many of these settlers toward revolt later in *Red Mars*. The first sign of this intrusion is when the millionaire and UN Office for Martian Affairs bureaucrat Helmut Bronski violates a Mars treaty by allowing the Armscor corporation to begin prospecting on Mars. As John Boone, the settlement's symbolic father, observes the mining operations at Bradbury Point his thoughts suggest an environmentalist's distress over the effects of capital's productivist activities:

> John shook his head. That afternoon they drove for an hour back to the habitat, past raw pits and slag heaps, toward the distant plume of the refineries on the other sides of the habitat mesa. He was used to seeing the land torn up for building purposes, but this . . . It was amazing what

a few hundred people could do. . . . wreaking such havoc just to strip
away metals, destined for Earth's insatiable demand. . . . (276–77)

Though at this point in the book Mars has just been settled, the land is
quickly becoming marred by the same industrial overdevelopment that initially compelled the economic exploitation of yet another planet.

Robinson's reflections on the insatiable demands of capitalist production do not end with the mention of Antarctica and the Armscor "gold
rush," as John later calls it (284). One of the most awful (in both senses of
the word) technologies in *Red Mars* is the space elevator, a twenty-three-
thousand-mile-high traversable cable that allows the various ores being
mined on Mars to be shipped efficiently to Earth. Phyllis Boyle, the primary visionary of the space elevator, explains,

> "It will . . . be possible to use the cable's rotation as a slingshot; objects
> released from the ballast asteroid toward Earth will be using the power
> of Mars's rotation as their push, and will have an energy-free high-speed
> takeoff. It's a clean, efficient, extraordinarily cheap method, both for
> lifting bulk into space and for accelerating it towards Earth. And given
> the recent discoveries of strategic metals, which are becoming ever more
> scarce on Earth, a cheap lift and push like this is literally invaluable. It
> creates the possibility of an exchange that wasn't economically viable
> before; it will be a critical component of the Martian economy, the key-
> stone of its industry." (306–7)

Though Phyllis promotes the elevator's clean operation and efficient energy
use, her seemingly environmentally conscious assurances conflict starkly
with John's observation earlier of the "raw pits," "slag heaps," and "distant plume[s]" that litter the Martian landscape and that are the results of
the mining that Phyllis understands to be essential for developing a Martian economy. Phyllis also perceives the scarcity crisis in the availability of
ores back on Earth, yet her attitude toward the very mode of production
that enabled such a crisis goes unchanged.

As a set of economically critical environmentalist texts, *The Space
Merchants*, *The Word for World Is Forest*, and the *Mars* trilogy argue the
same general point: capitalism is ecologically destructive. Pohl and Kornbluth's book looks at the ways capital's symbolic apparatus masks bleak
environmental realities that should signal the need for other economic
paths; Le Guin's book narrates the host of social and ecological abuses
and attitudes that capitalist production requires; and Robinson's books

continue Le Guin's observations of capitalist avarice. But out of these three works, Robinson's trilogy also theorizes an alternative economic system. Against the growth-centered mode of production practiced back on Earth and now being imported onto the newly settled Mars, the *Mars* trilogy presents a counter model of economics: eco-economics. Thought up by two of the trilogy's biologists, Vladimir Taneev and Marina Tokareva, eco-economics places value on individuals and institutions according to their material affects on ecosystems: "'Everyone should make their living, so to speak, based on a calculation of their real contribution to the human ecology'" (*Red Mars* 298). Detailing the eco-economy further in a rousing speech in *Red Mars,* John declares, "'what you take from the system has to be balanced by what you give in to it, balanced or exceeded to create that anti-entropic surge which characterizes all creative life'" (378).

In their related assertions, Vlad, Marina, and John realize collectively that a living, ecologically defined, is determined by one's production of use values with respect to ecosystemic integrity, with respect to safeguarding and contributing to the processes of interrelated, flourishing human and nonhuman life. Kovel writes, "The work of life, and the intricate dance of energy and form that goes into it, are essential enterprises to stave off and reverse the Second Law [of Thermodynamics]," which says that entropy—the loss of energy we know as death—increases over time (95). Individuals of any species cannot succeed alone in the struggle to resist entropy; "each creature is insufficient in-itself," because "life must exist in relation to other life and to nature as a whole if it is to contend with the Second Law" (Kovel 95). Blind to this fundamental ecological phenomenon, and in fact having no "internal (or external) regulatory mechanism that causes it to reorganize" in response to biological and/or ethical imperatives to preserve life-sustaining ecological integrity, capitalism functions under the principle that only rate of return on financial investment determines the success or failure of an economic venture (Foster, "Capitalism" par. 14). Under an eco-economy, though, the success or failure of an economic project is determined by the degree to which it can be continued across generations without threatening the ecosystemic relationships that facilitate the anti-entropic surge.

Having finally gained independence from Earth's political and economic institutions, the leaders of Mars in *Blue Mars* organize a congress to establish an official Martian government. As Marxist literary scholar William J. Burling notes, "At the constitutional congress the 'economic problem' looms over the entire process, and not until the matter is resolved by active debate and democratic political process is a peculiarly Martian

system of 'eco-economics' given birth" (160). During this congress one
character debates that the eco-economic model of the Martian economy
"'is a radical and unprecedented intrusion of government into business'"
(*Blue Mars* 141). Vlad counters by pointing out the inherent problem
of such an attitude: business relations are hierarchical, contradicting the
democratic values that have guided the new Martian civilization since its
earliest days. He then outlines the eco-economic system, which socially
provides the equal rights and self-rule that the hierarchical structure of
capitalism cannot, and which philosophically challenges capitalist conceptions of nonhuman nature. As Vlad states, "'the world is something
we all steward together'" rather than exploit privately (144). Important
in eco-economics is its synthesis of socialist elements—workers owning
the means of production and "'hiring capital rather than the other way
around,'" for example—with environmentalist elements (147). Nonviolent stewardship becomes everyone's responsibility, and environmental
courts "'estimate the real and complete environmental costs of economic
activities, and help to coordinate plans that impact the environment'"
(146). Ultimately, the eco-economic model is voted in and the Martian
civilization becomes a more embedded citizenry through a new economic
paradigm that values ecosystemic integrity.

Burling draws attention to the democratic political process of the
Martian congress and its outcomes to emphasize a key departure of the
Mars trilogy from traditional socialist theory. In such theory, as already
noted, capitalism is predicted to give way to socialism as a result of con-
tradictions *within* the economic system. O'Connor summarizes this "first
contradiction": "capitalist production is not only production of commodities but also production of surplus value, that is, capitalist exploitation
of labor. The exploitation of labor means simply that class struggle and
economic crisis are inherent in capitalism" (127). But as Burling observes
of the Martian congress, "capitalism did not in any sense collapse due to
economic dynamics but was replaced via the *political process*," an observation that allows us to shift our attention from the content of the congress—namely, the details of the eco-economy—to its political form, one
of a radical democratic participation foreign to, and even threatening to,
capitalist social relations (160). This shift in turn allows us to dwell for
a bit on a complementary analysis of this radical political form from the
specifically *ecosocialist* literature: Kovel's discussion of differentiation and
dialectics.

As Kovel notes, ecological integrity is dependent upon differentiation,
"a state of being that preserves both individuality and connectedness"

(106). "Elements of living ecosystems do not exist as separable parts," Kovel writes, "they also exist in relation to the Whole, which is non-reducible to any of its parts, which plays a role in determining them, and cannot exist without them" (105). But "capital is riddled with the sequelae of splitting" (Kovel 139); capitalism disintegrates ecosystemic integrity through its quantification and extraction of exploitable resources from, for example, an ocean ecosystem that is not simply a temporary holding area for marketable seafood but a complex totality of interdependent living and nonliving parts, most of which have no economic value. If we are ethically interested in ecological integrity for the sake of humanity and otherkind, then we need to rise above such splitting with a noncapitalist practice of recognized ecosystemic differentiation. But for this to happen requires a fundamental change from a decidedly nondemocratic economic mode that is deaf to the people who speak for ecosystemic integrity, to a democratic, dialectical communal mode that is always open to the voices of its stakeholders, many of whom for various reasons constitute the new ecological movements that O'Connor sees emerging as a result of the second contradiction of capitalism. In other words, a viable ecopolitics must be modeled on ecological differentiation; it must operate as a dialectical process that brings together individuals "in a dialogical spirit of open discourse—a process the fulfilment of which requires a free society of associated producers, that is, a society beyond all forms of splitting, in particular those imposed by class and gender or racial domination" (Kovel 140).

Critic William Dynes writes,

> Read as a whole, the *Mars* series evokes a utopian call for community: of wholeness within the self, within interpersonal relationships, within political and economic entities, within the species itself. This unity, however, comes not through a creation of shared identity, nor through a hierarchical subordination of the many to the few. Rather, true community is realized in syncretism—messy, complicated, frustrating, but in the end enriching and fruitful. (151)

This "syncretism" reaches its high point in the Martian congress, when twenty-one political parties and other organizations come together with the shared goal to create a Martian government. It is in this congress that those who favor the capitalist mode of production cannot make a good case for private business interests against collective responsibility for the commons, the reuniting of workers with the means of production, and a legal system that oversees and regulates the impact of economic activity on the Martian environment. The genuine democratic political process of the congress becomes, in the end, the key to defeating capital and ushering in the new economic mode.

●

For Burling democratic political process finally enables the supersession of capital. For O'Connor capitalism falls, or at least takes on more transparent forms, as a result of the new social movements that come into being as individuals and communities start to see and feel the environmental and social costs of doing business in the capitalist economic mode. There is a complementary relationship between these two theories, and we can see this relationship in the *Mars* trilogy. In *Green Mars* the democratic congress at Dorsa Brevia generates seven work points, the last of which reads, "'The habitation of Mars is a unique historical process, as it is the first inhabitation of another planet by humanity. As such it should be undertaken in a spirit or reverence for this planet and for the *scarcity of life in the universe*'" (390, emphasis added). Given work points three through five—which affirm the collective stewardship of the Martian commons, the personal ownership of one's labor, and thus the complete incompatibility of the economic order currently practiced on Earth with the order desired by most people on Mars—the issue of scarcity stressed in point seven is a direct response to the now "metanational" corporations that are trying to make their move onto Mars. The perception of scarcity requires some kind of understood environmental crisis, whether species extinction, water crisis, or in the case of the *Mars* books, the combination of Earth's various economogenic environmental problems and the visible effects of capitalism on Mars (e.g., "raw pits and slag heaps" and refinery plumes). Work point seven is thus a public response to capital's degradation of the conditions of production, a response that is codified later in the Martian congress when the eco-economy is approved.

It could be said then that the perception and experience of environmental exploitation leads to increased participation in democracy, which in turn leads to increased social pressures on the economic system that according to ecosocialism is responsible for such exploitation. Of course in the economically developed West our perception and experience of ecosystemic degradation is both mediated by capitalism's symbolic apparatus and limited by the economic mode's geopolitical dynamics. As *The Space Merchants* can help us understand, marketing and advertising teach us nothing about the actual origins of products and in fact necessarily promote consumption as the only path to personal satisfaction. And as Slavoj Žižek observes in the film *Examined Life,* it is too easy for us in the West to fall into ideological disavowal when confronted with issues of environmental degradation, to "act as if [we] don't know" about global climate change or biodiversity loss. This is largely because of the way the evidence of capitalism's effects on ecological integrity is mapped geographically, with economically and politically disadvantaged groups carrying the ecological and social burdens of industrial production. For most citizens of the developed North, however, it is hard to believe that environmental crisis is upon us when after reading books and articles about climate change, peak oil, and water wars, we step outside and see, again in Žižek's words, "nice trees, birds singing, and so on."

There are thus at least two major obstacles in the way of communicating the political urgency with which we need to be addressing the very real ecological exploitations inherent in the capitalist economic mode: (1) the broad lack of serious, action-generating public interest in environmental issues due to the counterforce of ever-present advertising messages that advocate a supposedly benign and life-enhancing consumption, and (2) the broad lack of likewise action-generating experience of environmental issues in a Western society that has distanced itself from the places and people whom it exploits to maintain a certain way of life. Indeed, as environmental degradation comes closer to home, as it did in the United States in April of 2010 with the British Petroleum oil gusher in the Gulf of Mexico, perhaps more and more citizens of the North will enter into fruitful democratic political process. But we do not have to wait for oil spills, water crises, species extinctions, and more to heighten our perception of local and global environmental problems and to generate our concern and action. Among a host of available resources, we have transformative environmentalism and we have environmental science fiction to direct our attention toward what we are doing and what we need to be doing. In the case of the works reviewed in this final chapter, *The Space Merchants, The Word for World Is Forest,* and the *Mars* trilogy can help us overcome the obstacles to our full understanding of capital's role in environmental crisis, as well as lead us to a full appreciation for an as yet unrealized mode of ecologically responsive and democratic economic production.

AFTERWORD

GREEN SPECULATIONS has addressed key works of environmental science fiction ranging from Olaf Stapledon's 1931 *Last and First Men* through Kim Stanley Robinson's 2005 *Fifty Degrees Below.* I want to end this book with a brief look at one of the most recently published works of environmental science fiction, not to activate a new line of inquiry, but instead to look forward to the future of environmental science fiction and its continued engagement with transformative movements. If Paolo Bacigalupi's award-winning *The Windup Girl* (2009) is any indication, the subgenre will continue to bring to the forefront of our consciousness the various issues that have instigated transformative environmentalist critique for at least the past fifty years. Among the several interrelated plotlines of Bacigalupi's ecodystopia is the story of Anderson Lake, an employee of the Des Moines, Iowa–based biotechnology company AgriGen. Anderson runs a factory in Bangkok, Thailand that produces kink-springs, which store energy and make it available for any number of uses in the novel's post-oil future. But the factory is a cover for Anderson's real reason for being in Thailand: to work his way into Thai politics and then to get access to the nation's seedbank for AgriGen scientists.

Along with PurCal and Total Nutrient Holdings, AgriGen is a "calorie company" that secures its global food markets by selling patented seeds engineered to produce edible but sterile crops, preventing seed saving by farmers (2–3). In the book, Thailand's near neighbors India, Burma, and Vietnam—all "starving and begging for the scientific advances of the calorie monopolies" to provide food amidst waves of crop plagues—have already been subsumed into the schemes of the calorie companies (3). But Thailand has remained fiercely protectionist in not allowing calorie company seeds to cross its borders and in employing the former AgriGen genetic engineer Gibbons to help the country stay ahead of new plagues, which Gibbons suggests are actually intentional attacks of corporate sabotage on Thai croplands. It is this protectionist policy that Anderson and representatives of other global corporations want to change in Thai politics. Due to corruption in the powerful Thai Environment Ministry, the outside pressures of business interests such as AgriGen, and other influencing factors, a Thai Trade Ministry once vehemently opposed to doing business with the calorie companies, but no longer so, ascends to power and ushers in a new era of commerce for Thailand—at least until the end of the novel.

The Windup Girl can be used effectively to sustain conversations from the perspectives of all of the environmental philosophies outlined in the previous chapters. This is not to suggest that the other works of environmental science fiction examined in this study cannot be successfully explored from a multitude of transformative environmentalist points of view, but instead to give readers a concise sense of the ways in which decades of carefully debated and formulated environmentalist philosophies continue to find their way into science fiction. Bacigalupi's entire book is persistent in fleshing out the ecodystopian implications of Val Plumwood's Illusion of Disembeddedness—my focus in chapter 1—and Gibbons provides the most succinct admission about the resulting new world of genetic manipulation: "Nature has become something new. It is ours now, truly" (247). But for us, today, nonhuman nature is not something entirely new, yet. It is not yet "ours now, truly" despite the decidedly second nature within which we live. The collective goal of environmental science fiction, and of our ecocritical analysis of it, is to contribute to a host of cultural efforts that aim to prevent the total realization of what Gibbons observes. Indeed, the very focus of ecocritical literary study is extratextual, challenging us "to bring to consciousness [our] views about the world, [our] sense of personal responsibility in that world, and to consider the impact of contemporary society on the environments in which everyone lives and dies" (Murphy, *Ecocritical* 6).

From the perspective of deep ecology *The Windup Girl* offers an interesting and complicating extratextual discourse about the transformative movement's ecosystemic protectionism, bringing to consciousness an understanding both of ecological and community vulnerability and of the challenges that come along with efforts to liberate ecologies and communities from the less-than-ecological trajectory of modern history. Chapter 2 reviewed Arne Naess's principle of ecosystemic vulnerability to outside influences and later examined the wats in John Brunner's *The Sheep Look Up*—utopian enclaves trying unsuccessfully to fend off the dystopian intrusions of the external world. Ecotopian deep ecology admirably wants to maintain a strong localism in self-sufficient communities, and ecodystopian fiction raises important questions for deep ecology about the possibilities of doing so when the borders separating such ecologies and communities can only be imaginary. The corrupted outside world cannot be held at bay, to be sure. But what about the world inside the separatist ecotopia? For Bacigalupi this world is likewise corrupted. Together with being easily bribed, the Thai Environment Ministry's "white shirts" are brutally nationalistic, and along with their laudable policies against calorie company foods comes their unethical stance against Others, whether genetically modified Japanese "windup girls" or Chinese immigrants. In no way does *The Windup Girl* come across as a conservative cry of ecofascism against preservationist efforts, though. Instead the novel imagines a future when, due to a combination of global poverty and hunger, the private control of biology, risen seas, geopolitical strife, intranational political infighting—in short, the phenomena whose seeds are germinating in the modern world today—the deepest ecology might regrettably turn out to be the most vicious.

An ecofeminist look at *The Windup Girl* also produces valuable extratextual observations and critical commentary. The nonfictional, near-future equivalent of the book's AgriGen is the St. Louis, Missouri–based agricultural biotechnology corporation Monsanto, "the Big Brother of the new world agricultural order" (Robin 2). As Marie-Monique Robin details in her book *The World According to Monsanto,* by 2007 Monsanto legally possessed patented genetic material in the crops growing on about 225 million acres of farmland around the world (4). Further, with its 2006 acquisition of the cottonseed supplier Delta and Pine Land Company, Monsanto now holds the patent on the control of plant gene expression technology, otherwise known as Terminator technology, which makes it possible to alter a plant's genetics so it produces sterile seeds.[1] For Vandana Shiva these legal and biotechnological apparatuses, which are employed by AgriGen in Bacigalupi's novel and also receive critical treatment in his short story "The Calorie Man," epitomize the patriarchal colonization of biological regeneration. In *Biopiracy* Shiva replicates the cultural ecofeminist argument, reviewed in chapter 3 above, by asserting that "The continuity between regeneration in human and nonhuman nature" was "the basis of all ancient worldviews" (43). The emergence of patriarchal dualism and its association of women with a passive nonhuman nature severed this continuity, leading to a devaluing of biological regeneration without which, Shiva argues, "there can be no sustainability" (43). About seed technologies, Shiva continues, they "reproduce the old patriarchal divisions of activity/passivity, culture/nature. These dichotomies are then used as instruments of capitalist patriarchy to colonize the regeneration of plants" (45).[2] Shiva's hope is that ecofeminist analysis will lead to the decolonization of regeneration and the reclaiming of a "nonpatriarchal mold" (45).

Finally, while AgriGen's (Monsanto's) presence in *The Windup Girl* provides a clear opportunity for an ecosocialist critique of particular capitalist strategies of global conquest, in this case its agricultural sector's biotechnological, legal, and political tactics, the novel also encourages two related but more general economic criticisms. The first of these is of capital's tendency to turn ecological, social, and political traumas—many of which the economic system directly or indirectly begets, often with state support—into economic opportunities. We have seen this issue foregrounded in Brunner's novels, in *The Space Merchants,* in *The Word for World Is Forest,* and in the *Mars* trilogy, and real life has its examples, too. Referencing the most recent U.S. war with Iraq, Bill McKibben highlights a case in point: "In Iraq, one of the first laws adopted by the U.S.-led transition government in 2003 protected the patenting of plants and seeds, even though 97 percent of Iraqi farmers used seeds saved from their own crops or from local markets to grow their own food" (*Deep* 193). While Iraqi farmers can still save traditional seeds, the postinvasion law "'facilitate[s] the penetration of Iraqi agriculture by the likes of Monsanto, Syngenta, Bayer, and Dow Chemical'" (quoted in McKibben, *Deep* 193). This capitalist propensity to provoke and then take advantage of distress is highlighted in *The Windup Girl* with both AgriGen's and the global shipping company CARLYLE & SONS' involvement in fomenting the civil war that ultimately topples the Environment Ministry. Tellingly, at the very moment of the latter's surrender, AgriGen ships arrive in Bangkok to unload the corporation's rice and soy products, as well as the team of AgriGen employees who will be exploiting the seedbank.

To contextualize another one of *The Windup Girl*'s economic criticisms we can turn to Slavoj Žižek, who counters the common myth that capitalism is sustained by the greed of the owner class, observing instead that greed is "subordinated to the impersonal striving of capital to reproduce and expand" (*Living* 132). Rather than serving his or her own self-interest, the individual capitalist has an ethical responsibility to serve "the capitalist drive," "to put everything, including the survival of humanity, at stake . . . simply for the sake of the reproduction of the system as an end-in-itself" (*Living* 335). While in *The Windup Girl* one character *does* read greed in the eyes of AgriGen's recently arrived employees, and while Anderson *does* promise his colluders on several occasions that a new era of trade will change their fortunes, in its entirety the book supports Žižek's assertion. The world of the novel is suffering through a post-oil "Contraction" (62) and all of the postapocalyptic repercussions of such an end to what Imre Szeman deems our history and our ontology: oil (Szeman 34). But rather than striving to reactivate the era of "Expansion" for his own selfish interests, Anderson does so to keep Des Moines "alive a little longer," as he admits to himself (86). A most frightening prospect is that capitalism is *not* motivated by the greed of the owner class but by an absolute duty to perpetuate the reproduction of the economic mode indefinitely, even—or especially—in the face of overwhelming evidence that capitalism is unequivocally incapable of surviving forever.

With its multifaceted environmentalist critiques, *The Windup Girl* is one of the latest works in a history of involved environmental science fiction texts, a handful of which have made up the analytical emphases of the foregoing chapters. I do not suppose that the subgenre itself will change the world. Yet, if students, teachers, and scholars of (inter)disciplines such as ecocritical literary studies, science fiction and utopian studies, environmental humanities, environmental studies, and more begin—or in some cases continue—to read, teach, and write about environmental science fiction and the value of its cultural commentary, then we can at least expect that the subgenre will become firmly embedded in the canon of fiction and nonfiction environmental writing. It is this canon, made stronger by science fiction's presence, that provides the tools for thinking and building a new way forward.

NOTES

INTRODUCTION

1. For this definition of nonfiction environmental writing I am drawing from Murphy's *Farther Afield in the Study of Nature-Oriented Literature* (11).

2. See Shklovsky, "Art as Technique." Spiegel provides a concise discussion of Shklovsky's *ostranenie* in "Things Made Strange" (369–70).

3. Osborn observes, "the impulse to dominate as well as to destroy . . . is proving continuously disastrous not only in the political and social sense but in the physical sense. . . . man's destructiveness has turned not only upon himself but upon his own good earth—the wellspring of his life" (11). As a result of this destructiveness, he concludes, twentieth-century humans have become for the first time in human history "a *large-scale geological force*" (29).

4. On Carson's apocalyptic strategy, M. Jimmie Killingsworth and Jacqueline S. Palmer write, "In trying to extract a warning with the apocalyptic narrative . . . Carson was courting a number of potential difficulties" (178). These difficulties include the "perverse comfort" and escapism of end-times reading as well as the seeming inescapability of the end times that apocalyptic texts portray, both of which, the authors argue, limit the rhetorical effect of "A Fable for Tomorrow" (179). Recently, though, Amy M. Patrick has defended Carson's narrative choice as precautionary, arguing, "Carson did something important beyond writing a shocking fable: she empowered her audiences with knowledge to make informed decisions, by conveying scientific information about the environment and exposing the uncertainty in which decisions about the environment and human health are often made" (142).

5. The source for this paraphrase in Istvan Csicsery-Roney, Jr., who writes, "Science-fictional estrangement works like scientific modeling: the familiar (that is,

naturalized) situation is either rationally extrapolated to reveal its hidden norms and premises . . . , or it is analogically displaced on to something unfamiliar in which the invisible (because too-familiar) elements are seen freshly as alien phenomena" (118).

6. This definition of sustainability, forwarded by the World Commission on Environment and Development in its 1987 book *Our Common Future,* remains the most widely cited definition for all movements interested in intergenerational ecological and social equity.

7. Suvin wished for the retirement of sense of wonder as a definitional characteristic of science fiction in 1979 (*Metamorphoses* 83), Brooks Landon deems it the "least rigorous of all critical concepts brought to bear on the discussion of science fiction" (19), and Peter Nicholls and Cornel Robu note that the concept reflects a rather adolescent attention to feeling and emotion as literary criteria (1084).

CHAPTER ONE

1. As for Aldo Leopold, his most famous subversion is his "land ethic," which expands traditional, human-centered ethical systems to include as right or wrong our actions upon ecosystems. He writes against economic self-interest in the posthumously published *A Sand County Almanac,* declaring, "a land ethic changes the role of *Homo sapiens* from conqueror of the land-community to plain member and citizen of it" (204).

2. See Lynn White, Jr., "The Historical Roots of Our Ecological Crisis."

3. On the ideological roots of ecological crisis, see also Don D. Elgin's *The Comedy of the Fantastic.* Elgin narrows these roots to attitudes about human separateness from nature. For Elgin, these attitudes grow out of Western Christianity, the movement from hunting and gathering culture to agricultural civilization, and the French and Industrial Revolutions (4–10).

4. Writing about Nazi ideology and its "laws," for example, philosopher Michael E. Zimmerman notes,

> In 1939, [the German philosopher] Alfred Baeumler praised the view that man "must be understood *as a part of Nature.*" As a part of nature, people had to follow its laws in order to survive. For the Nazis, such "laws" included the necessity of racial "purity." As is well known, the Nazis practiced infanticide, euthanasia, genocide, and similar practices to [*sic*] in order to purge "racial parasites," degenerates, and others who posed a threat to the health of the *Volk.* (73)

5. Fred Waage attributes the italicized passages in *Earth Abides,* "which repeatedly ecologize the immediate dramatic situation," to a "Universal Narrator" (284–85). I am borrowing his term.

6. The publication date for Rachel Carson's *Silent Spring,* 1962, is frequently cited as the birth year of environmentalism, and by the first Earth Day on April 22, 1970, environmentalism was firmly established as a social and political movement.

7. When the Duke's son and heir to the Atreides throne, Paul, cries over the death of a Fremen man he killed in a ritual battle, the Fremen appreciate his gift of "moisture to the dead" rather than despise him in his victory (306).

8. For Wildcat, "indigenous realism" comprises a "respect for the relationships and relatives that constitute the complex web of life" (9).

9. When Paul admits he has been studying the great storms of Arrakis, Hawat again prevents him from developing a connection to the planet, but this time scaring him: "'Those storms build up across six or seven thousand kilometers of flatlands, feed on anything that can give them a push—coriolis force, other storms, anything that has an ounce of energy in it. They can blow up to seven hundred kilometers an hour, loaded with everything loose that's in their way—sand, dust, everything. They can eat flesh off bones and etch the bones to slivers'" (28).

10. The Fremen have mastered a style of rhythmless walking that prevents the sand-worms from recognizing their presence in the desert. They also use "thumpers," which are devices that pound the sand to imitate regular walking patterns, attracting sand-worms and thus drawing them away from Fremen who are walking in otherwise dangerous territory.

11. On Ciceronian second nature, landscape historian John Dixon Hunt writes,

> The Roman writer Cicero termed what we would call the cultural landscape a second nature (*alteram naturam*). This was a landscape of bridges, roads, harbors, fields—in short, all of the elements which men and women introduce into the physical world to make it more habitable, to make it serve their purposes. Cicero's phrase "a second nature" of course implies a first; though he does not specify this, we may take it that he implies a primal nature, an unmediated world before humans invaded, altered, and augmented it. A world without any roads, ports, paths, ter-raced vineyards, etc. Today we might call it the wilderness. (131–32)

12. "Third nature" has been used to describe sixteenth-century Italian gardens, "worlds where the pursuits of pleasure probably outweighed the need for utility and accordingly where the utmost resources of human intelligence and technological skill were invoked to fabricate an environment where nature and art collaborated" (Hunt 132). Social ecologist Murray Bookchin has also proposed a third nature in which "the human species actively participates in the differentiation and evolution of life" and real-izes its "potential as 'nature rendered self-conscious'" (Huston 232). My use of the des-ignation is to be taken in all of its apocalyptic meanings, not as fully aestheticized or socialized nature, but as second nature in its utmost exacerbation.

CHAPTER TWO

1. In their introduction to *Beneath the Surface*, an anthology about the philosophy of deep ecology, Eric Katz, Andrew Light, and David Rothenberg define instrumental rationality as "the mode of thinking that makes efficiency and quantifiable results the goal of all human activity" (xiii). Deep ecology, on the other hand, "emphasizes alter-native modes of thinking, such as spiritual enlightenment or artistic expression, that emphasize life-enhancing qualitative values" (xiii).

2. For Devall, this "basic culture" is supported by "myths of economic growth, progress, belief that technology will save us from environmental problems, and human-ism" ("Deep Ecology" 52).

3. As Ursula K. Heise notes, "Dominant terms of the 1960s and 1970s such as 'overpopulation' and 'carrying capacity' have receded in importance, giving way to dis-cussions focused more centrally on issues of distributive justice, gender inequality, and uneven resource consumption patterns" (*Sense of Place*, 69).

4. Of these writers, biologist Paul Ehrlich is most known for his 1968 study *The Population Bomb*. As Brian Stableford notes, Ehrlich's fears were prefigured in fiction with Harry Harrison's *Make Room! Make Room!* (1966) and sustained by such books as Brunner's *The Sheep Look Up*, Philip Wylie's *The End of the Dream* (1972), and Kurt Vonnegut's *Ecodeath* (1972) (138).

5. Statement four of the deep ecology platform reads, "The flourishing of human life and cultures is compatible with a substantially smaller human population. The flourishing of non-human life *requires* a smaller human population" (Naess, "The Deep" 68).

6. As Barbara Drake summarizes, "What Piercy substitutes for the paired father and mother is a cooperative of three 'Mothers' for each child. They may be male or female. They volunteer to 'Mother.' . . . With the mothers, the child becomes part of a loose familial group, co-mothers and others" (114).

7. The educational complement to this spirituality in Mattapoisett is its rite-of-passage ceremony. For children to become full members of the community, they must spend one week in the woods by themselves in a naming ceremony. The ecotopian society thus views wilderness as essential to human formative experience. Another example is less pedagogical, but does demonstrate Mattapoisett's ecological literacy: the town's community gardens follow the principles of organic gardening—"tomato plants growing with rose bushes and onions, pansies and bean plants" (122).

8. We have already seen *Dune*'s assessment of the limited rhetorical and practical possibilities of this kind of thinking about "ecological equilibrium"—or, a nonexistent first nature—in a contemporary world where we can only encounter a second nature. In the interest of highlighting ecotopian fiction as a narrative space for deep ecological fantasies, I will bypass applying this critique again and instead flesh out some other problems with deep ecology in the next section of this chapter.

9. We can see in these words from Naess and Snyder the potential for fueling anti-immigration and racist sentiments. Such sentiments have unfortunately been voiced in ecology and environmentalism, but they are not endemic to them. See Jake Kosek's "Purity and Pollution" (142–44) and Britt M. Rusert's "Black Nature."

10. Wallace Stegner argues, "a place is not a place until people have been born in it, have grown up in it, lived in it, known it, died in it—have both experienced and shaped it, as individuals, families, neighborhoods, and communities, over more than one generation" (201). For Stegner, writing in the mid-1980s, the modern American is displaced—hasty, shallow, restless, rootless—seemingly as a psychological consequence of a cultural history that has privileged motion over settling down.

11. The idea of Earth as mother and conceptual dualisms as patriarchal, as related in the previous two quotations, will be taken up in chapter 3.

12. In *Ecological Utopias,* de Geus discusses several common metaphors for utopian narrative, two of which are the "blueprint" and the "navigational compass" (238). Focusing in a late chapter more on the way we read ecotopian narratives than on the narratives themselves, de Geus challenges the idea of ecotopia-as-blueprint in particular, because if we approach ecotopias as offering completed schematics for the ideal society then we will fall short in locating practical methods of implementation. "In contrast to this blueprinting approach, 'the utopia as the perfect building plan' and as an ideal that can be achieved in reality," de Geus writes, "I would like to propose a more modest model of 'the utopia as navigational compass.' In this model the genre of the ecological utopia is primarily interpreted as an instrument that serves to guide society's general direction" (238).

13. The book's title "is based on a belief that about the time of World War I you could stand the entire human race on the 147-square-mile Isle of Wight, elbow to elbow and face to face. In the 1960's the figuring went that it would take the 221 square mile of the Isle of Man to pack us all in like sardines. By 2100, says John Brunner, you'd need the 640 square miles of Zanzibar to do it" (Wollheim 56).

14. This turn away from neo-Malthusian population fears is best demonstrated today in ecosocialism, my focus in chapter 4. As one ecosocialist writes, not specifically targeting deep ecology, "While it is possible to blame 'greed,' rising population, or the inevitable desire to have more things, economic growth is first and foremost a product of an economic system that dominates our planet: capitalism" (Wall 8). Foster, Clark, and York likewise argue,

> Within capitalist society, there has always been a tendency to blame any-
> thing but the economic system itself for ecological overshoot. Yet if the
> developing ecological crisis has taught us anything, it is that even though
> population growth and inappropriate technologies have played impor-
> tant roles in accelerating environmental degradation, the ecological rift
> we are now facing has its principle source in the economy. (377)

15. Earth First! and the Earth Liberation Front are the most well-known activist organizations, as Bron Taylor notes, "officially devoted to civil disobedience and sabo-tage as means of environmental resistance" (*Dark* 74).

CHAPTER THREE

1. The poststructuralist theorists who inform Armbruster's discussion are Teresa de Lauretis and Donna Haraway, who both declare identity as the always-shifting product of "multiple axes of difference," rather than as the static product of nature or other singular or ranked factors (105).

2. On the connections between cultural ecofeminism and deep ecology, Mary Mellor writes, "Cultural ecofeminists and deep ecologists share a strategy of reversing valuations in the classic culture (man)/nature (woman) dualism: deep ecologists urge humans to subordinate themselves to nature (biocentrism), and cultural ecofeminists celebrate women's connections to nature and many traditionally feminine characteris-tics" (208).

3. Even Prentice admits that (cultural) ecofeminism "reminds all people of the frag-ile, endangered, and inextricable inter-dependence of all life—including human life—and the planet" (9).

4. With respect to the critical possibilities of cultural ecofeminist essentialism, Alaimo also warns against rationalist feminism's "hasty dismissal" of ecofeminist argu-ments that are labeled "essentialist" (8). She references Noël Sturgeon, who writes in *Ecofeminist Natures,* "essentialist moments in ecofeminism, given particular histori-cal conditions, are part of creating a shifting and strategic identification of the relation between 'women' and 'nature' that has political purposes" (11).

5. On King's dialectical ecofeminism, Sandilands notes, "King's project was to tran-scend the 'either/or' assumptions inherent in the debate between rationalist-materialist humanism and metaphysical-feminist naturalism, to create a dialectical feminism that incorporates the best insights of both traditions" (18).

6. Spinel's moment of transformation is cited in the introduction of this book.

CHAPTER FOUR

1. Though sympathetic with deep ecology's "emphasis on the subtle interconnections and complexity of nature, its distaste for human arrogance, [and] its argument for the ethical importance of recognizing that humans are but one among millions of species on earth and not the divinely (or self-) appointed masters of Creation," ecosocialist scholars Foster, Clark, and York argue,

> Deep ecology is based on an anti-materialist theory of causality—one that posits that our value system, particularly the one emerging with the birth of modernity and a scientific worldview, is, at base, the cause of environmental crisis. Rather than a discussion of the social forces that drive social-production, a critique of the dominant worldview—divorced from its social-material influences—becomes paramount. Change becomes a matter of adjusting values and developing the proper eco-ethics, and from there, it is assumed, changes in the social structure will follow. (260–61)

For these authors, deep ecology's philosophical idealism leads it away from what ecosocialists determine to be the ultimate target of criticism: not merely values, in the end, but the social, material processes that drive ecosystemic degradation.

2. On the effects of capitalist productive activity, Merchant notes,

> Examples include the destruction of the environment from the uses of military production (such as oil spills and air pollution during the 1991 Gulf War or the predicted nuclear winter from nuclear war); global warming from industrial emissions of carbon dioxide; acid rain from industrial uses of chlorofluorocarbons; the pollution of oceans and soils from the dumping of industrial wastes; and industrial extractions from forests and oceans for commodity production. (*Radical* 9–10)

3. The challenge of adopting such criticism of capitalist ideology is also demonstrated in William's and Connie's initial reactions to the radically new economic ideas of the respective ecotopias they experience in *Ecotopia* and *Woman on the Edge of Time*.

4. I am reminded of the environmental writer Scott Russell Sanders—an author not only of nonfiction but also of the 1985 environmental science fiction novel *Terrarium*—who worries in his essay "Mountain Music" that his son will deem him "deluded, perhaps even mad" for countering the "chorus of voices telling [his son] that the universe was made for us, that the Earth is an inexhaustible warehouse, that consumption is the goal of life, that money is the road to delight" (104).

5. It is appropriate here to reference a recent cinematic representation of capitalist exploitation and its real-life occurrence: James Cameron's *Avatar* (2009). A Terran mining company and its private military threaten the aboriginal land of the Na'vi people on the planet Pandora. Efforts to educate the Na'vi away from their indigenous ways have not produced the speedy results demanded by capitalist investment, so the mining effort takes a militaristic, genocidal turn. The Na'vi succeed in their revolt against capitalist exploitation, but as Slavoj Žižek writes, "At the same time this film was taking in money all around the world . . . something strangely resembling its plot was taking place in the real world. The hills in the south of the Indian state of Orissa, inhabited by the Kondh tribe, were sold to mining companies who plan to exploit their immense

reserves of bauxite" (*Living* 394). The animistic and subsistence agriculturalist Kondh have appealed to Cameron for help (see Hopkins, "Indian Tribe").

AFTERWORD

1. In a letter on its company website, Monsanto reiterates its 1999 commitment "not to commercialize sterile seed technology in food crops" (par. 3). Beyond overtly not committing to abstain from commercializing this technology in *nonfood* crops, Monsanto leaves open the possibility of its eventual introduction of gene-use restriction by highlighting the technology's potential benefits.

2. The full quotation reads, "The new biotechnologies reproduce the old patriarchal divisions of activity/passivity, culture/nature. These dichotomies are then used as instruments of capitalist patriarchy to colonize the regeneration of plants *and human beings*" (emphasis added). The latter part of this quotation is also played out in *The Windup Girl*, with the novel's title character being a genetically modified human female created to serve and not question her original Japanese master as an office manager and companion, and then forced to withstand the brutal implications of this unquestioning servility when abandoned in Thailand. Thus, with *The Windup Girl*'s dual attention to the biological colonization of both nonhuman nature (in seeds) and human nature (in women) it affords further opportunity for ecofeminist analysis, especially since the windup girl, Emiko, is herself sterile.

BIBLIOGRAPHY

Abbey, Edward. *Desert Solitaire: A Season in the Wilderness.* New York: Ballantine, 1968.

Alaimo, Stacy. *Undomesticated Ground: Recasting Nature as Feminist Space.* Ithaca: Cornell University Press, 2000.

Armbruster, Karla. "'Buffalo Gals, Won't You Come Out Tonight': A Call for Boundary-Crossing in Ecofeminist Literary Criticism." *Ecofeminist Literary Criticism: Theory, Interpretation, Pedagogy.* Ed. Greta Gaard and Patrick D. Murphy. Urbana: University of Illinois Press, 1998. 97–122.

Armstrong, Jeanette. "'Sharing One Skin': Okanagan Community." Mander and Goldsmith 460–70.

Avatar. Dir. James Cameron. Perf. Sam Worthington, Zoe Saldana, Sigourney Weaver, and Stephen Lang. Twentieth Century Fox, 2009. Film.

Bacigalupi, Paolo. "The Calorie Man." 2005. *Pump Six and Other Stories.* San Francisco: Night Shade, 2008. 93–121.

———. "The People of Sand and Slag." 2004. *Pump Six and Other Stories.* San Francisco: Night Shade, 2008. 49–67.

———. *The Windup Girl.* San Francisco: Night Shade, 2009.

Baker, Susan. *Sustainable Development.* New York: Routledge, 2006.

Barnhill, David Landis, and Roger S. Gottlieb. Introduction. *Deep Ecology and World Religions: New Essays on Sacred Grounds.* Ed. David Landis Barnhill and Roger S. Gottlieb. Albany: State University of New York Press, 2001. 1–15.

Baxter, Brian. *A Theory of Ecological Justice.* London: Routledge, 2005.

Biehl, Janet. *Finding Our Way: Rethinking Ecofeminist Politics.* Montreal: Black Rose, 1991.

Birkeland, Janis. "Ecofeminism: Linking Theory and Practice." Gaard 13–59.

Bookchin, Murray. "The Population Myth: Part II." *Anarchy Archives*. Green Perspectives: Newsletter of the Green Program Project, Apr. 1989. Web. 1 June 2010.

———. "Social Ecology versus Deep Ecology: A Challenge for the Ecology Movement." *Anarchy Archives*. Green Perspectives: Newsletter of the Green Program Project, Summer 1987. Web. 1 June 2010.

Booker, M. Keith, and Anne-Marie Thomas. *The Science Fiction Handbook*. Oxford: Wiley-Blackwell, 2009.

Borlik, Todd A. *Ecocriticism and Early Modern Literature: Green Pastures*. New York: Routledge, 2010.

Bowers, C. A. *Education, Cultural Myths, and the Ecological Crisis: Toward Deep Changes*. Albany: State University of New York Press, 1993.

Brown, Lester R. *Eco-Economy: Building an Economy for the Earth*. New York: Norton, 2001.

Brunner, John. *The Sheep Look Up*. Dallas: BenBella, 1972.

———. *Stand on Zanzibar*. London: Gollancz, 1968.

Buell, Lawrence. *The Future of Environmental Criticism: Environmental Crisis and Literary Imagination*. Malden, MA: Blackwell, 2005.

Bukeavich, Neal. "'Are We Adopting the Right Measures to Cope?': Ecocrisis in John Brunner's *Stand on Zanzibar*." *Science Fiction Studies* 29.1 (2002): 53–70.

Burling, William J. "The Theoretical Foundation of Utopian Radical Democracy in *Blue Mars*." *Kim Stanley Robinson Maps the Unimaginable: Critical Essays*. Ed. William J. Burling. Jefferson, NC: McFarland, 2009. 157–69.

Byrd, David G. "George R. Stewart." *Dictionary of Literary Biography, Volume 8: Twentieth-Century American Science Fiction Writers*. Ed. David Cowart and Thomas L. Wyner. 1981. The Gale Group. 26 Nov. 2004.

Callenbach, Ernest. *Ecotopia*. 1975. Berkeley: Heyday, 2004.

Capra, Fritjof. *The Web of Life: A New Scientific Understanding of Living Systems*. New York: Anchor, 1996.

Carlassare, Elizabeth. "Essentialism in Ecofeminist Discourse." Merchant 220–34.

Carson, Rachel. "Help Your Child to Wonder." *Woman's Home Companion* (July 1956): 24–27, 46–48.

———. "The Pollution of Our Environment." *Lost Woods: The Discovered Writing of Rachel Carson*. Ed. Linda Bear. Boston: Beacon, 1998. 227–45.

———. *Silent Spring*. Boston: Houghton, 1962.

Catton, William R., Jr., and Riley E. Dunlap. "A New Ecological Paradigm for Post-Exuberant Sociology." *The American Behavioral Scientist* 24.1 (1980): 15–47.

Clarke, Tony. "Mechanisms of Corporate Rule." Mander and Goldsmith 297–308.

Cokinos, Christopher. "Instead of Suns, the Earth." *orionmagazine.org*. The Orion Grassroots Network, July/Aug. 2010. Web. 17 Aug. 2010.

Collard, Andrée. *Rape of the Wild: Man's Violence Against Animals and the Earth*. Bloomington: Indiana University Press, 1989.

Cooper, David E. "Arne Naess." *Fifty Key Thinkers on the Environment*. Ed. Joy A. Palmer, David E. Cooper, and Peter Blaze Corcoran. London: Routledge, 2001. 211–16.

Cravens, Hamilton. Introduction. *Descent of Man and Selection in Relation to Sex*. By Charles Darwin. New York: Barnes & Noble, 2004. ix–xv.

Creed, Barbara. *Darwin's Screens: Evolutionary Aesthetics, Time and Sexual Display in the Cinema*. Victoria: Melbourne University Press, 2009.

Csicsery-Ronay, Istvan, Jr. "Marxist Theory and Science Fiction." *The Cambridge Com-*

panion to Science Fiction. Ed. Edward James and Farah Mendlesohn. Cambridge: Cambridge University Press, 2003. 113–24.

de Geus, Marius. *Ecological Utopias: Envisioning the Sustainable Society*. Utrecht: International, 1999.

Devall, Bill. "Deep Ecology and Radical Environmentalism." *American Environmentalism: The U.S. Environmental Movement, 1970–1990*. Ed. Riley E. Dunlap and Angela G. Mertig. New York: Taylor and Francis, 1992. 51–62.

———. "The Deep Ecology Movement." Merchant 125–39.

Devall, Bill, and George Sessions. *Deep Ecology: Living as if Nature Mattered*. Salt Lake City: Gibbs Smith, 1985.

Diamond, Irene, and Gloria Feman Orenstein, eds. *Reweaving the World: The Emergence of Ecofeminism*. San Francisco: Sierra Club, 1990.

Dobrin, Sidney I., and Christian R. Weisser. *Natural Discourse: Toward Ecocomposition*. Albany: State University of New York Press, 2002.

Drake, Barbara. "Two Utopias: Marge Piercy's *Woman on the Edge of Time* and Ursula Le Guin's *The Dispossessed*." *Still the Frame Holds: Essays on Women Poets and Writers*. Ed. Sheila Roberts and Yvonne Pacheco Tevis. San Bernardino: Borgo, 1993. 109–27.

Duraiappah, Anantha Kumar et al. *Ecosystems and Human Well-Being: Biodiversity Synthesis: A Report of the Millennium Ecosystem Assessment*. Washington, DC: World Resources Institute, 2005.

Dwyer, Jim. "Ecotopia." Taylor, *Encyclopedia* 564–66.

Dynes, William. "Multiple Perspectives in Kim Stanley Robinson's *Mars* Series." *Extrapolation* 42.2 (2001): 150–64.

Eisler, Riane. "The Gaia Tradition and the Partnership Future: An Ecofeminist Manifesto." Diamond and Orenstein 23–35.

Elgin, Don D. *The Comedy of the Fantastic: Ecological Perspectives on the Fantasy Novel*. Westport, CT: Greenwood, 1985.

Errington, Paul L. "Of Man and Lower Animals." Shepard and McKinley 179–90.

Examined Life. Dir. Astra Taylor. Zeitgeist, 2008.

Foster, John Bellamy. "Capitalism and Ecology: The Nature of the Contradiction." *Monthly Review* 54.4 (2002): n p. Web. 21 July 2010.

———. *Ecology Against Capitalism*. New York: Monthly Review, 2002.

Foster, John Bellamy, Brett Clark, and Richard York. *The Ecological Rift: Capitalism's War on the Earth*. New York: Monthly Review, 2010.

Freedman, Carl. *Critical Theory and Science Fiction*. Hanover: Wesleyan University Press, 2000.

Gaard, Greta, ed. *Ecofeminism: Women, Animals, Nature*. Philadelphia: Temple University Press, 1993.

———. *Ecological Politics: Ecofeminism and the Greens*. Philadelphia: Temple University Press, 1998.

———. "Living Interconnections with Animals and Nature." Gaard 1–12.

Gearhart, Sally Miller. *The Wanderground: Stories of the Hill Women*. Watertown, MA: Persephone, 1979.

Gore, Al. Introduction. *Silent Spring*. By Rachel Carson. Boston: Houghton, 1994. xv–xxvi.

Gough, Noel. "Neuromancing the Stones: Experience, Intertextuality, and Cyberpunk Science Fiction." *Journal of Experiential Education* 16.3 (1993): n.p. Web. 3 July 2009.

———. "Playing with Wor(l)ds: Science Fiction as Environmental Literature." *Literature of Nature: An International Sourcebook*. Ed. Patrick D. Murphy. Chicago: Fitzroy, 1998. 409–14.

Gruen, Lori. "Oppression: An Analysis of the Connection Between Women and Animals." Gaard 60–90.

Harvey, K. J., Britton, D. R., and Minchinton, T. E. "Insect Diversity and Trophic Structure Differ on Native and Non-Indigenous Congeneric Rushes in Coastal Salt Marshes." *Austral Ecology* 35 (2010): 522–34.

Heinzerling, Lisa. "Pragmatists and Environmentalists." *Harvard Law Review* 113.6 (2000): 1421–47.

Heise, Ursula K. *Sense of Place and Sense of Planet: The Environmental Imagination of the Global*. New York: Oxford University Press, 2008.

———. "Letter." *PMLA* 114.5 (1999): 1096–97.

Herbert, Frank. *Children of Dune*. New York: Ace, 1981.

———. *Dune*. New York: Ace, 1965.

———. *Dune Messiah*. New York: Ace, 1975.

Hopkins, Kathryn. "Indian Tribe Appeals for Avatar Director's Help to Stop Vedanta." *guardian.co.uk*. Guardian News and Media, 8 Feb. 2010. Web. 28 May 2010.

Hovanec, Carol P. "Visions of Nature in *The Word for World Is Forest*: A Mirror of the American Consciousness." *Extrapolation* 30.1 (1989): 84–92.

Howard, June. "Widening the Dialogue on Feminist Science Fiction." *Feminist Re-Visions: What Has Been and Might Be*. Ed. Vivian Patraka and Louise A. Tilly. Ann Arbor: University of Michigan Press, 1983. 64–96.

Hudson, William Henry. *A Crystal Age*. 1887. New York: E. P. Dutton, 1906.

Hunt, John Dixon. "Reading and Writing the Site (1992)." *Theory in Landscape Architecture: A Reader*. Ed. Simon Swaffield. Philadelphia: University of Pennsylvania Press, 2002. 131–36.

Huston, Shaun. "Murray Bookchin on Mars! The Production of Nature in the *Mars Trilogy*." *Kim Stanley Robinson Maps the Unimaginable: Critical Essays*. Ed. William J. Burling. Jefferson, NC: McFarland, 2009. 231–41.

Irigaray, Luce. *An Ethics of Sexual Difference*. London: Continuum, 1984.

"Is Monsanto Going to Develop or Sell 'Terminator' Seeds?" monsanto.com. Monsanto, 16 July 2009. Web. 5 Aug. 2010.

Jameson, Fredric. *Archaeologies of the Future: The Desire Called Utopia and Other Science Fictions*. London: Verso, 2005.

Jamison, Andrew, and Ron Eyerman. *Seeds of the Sixties*. Berkeley: University of California Press, 1994.

Katz, Eric, Andrew Light, and David Rothenberg. "Introduction: Deep Ecology as Philosophy." *Beneath the Surface: Critical Essays in the Philosophy of Deep Ecology*. Ed. Eric Katz, Andrew Light, and David Rothenberg. Cambridge: MIT Press, 2000. ix–xxiv.

Killingsworth, M. Jimmie, and Jacqueline S. Palmer. "*Silent Spring* and Science Fiction: As Essay in the History and Rhetoric of Narrative." *And No Birds Sing: Rhetorical Analyses of Rachel Carson's* Silent Spring. Ed. Craig Waddell. Carbondale: Southern Illinois University Press, 2000. 174–204.

King, Ynestra. "The Ecology of Feminism and the Feminism of Ecology." Plant 18–28.

Kosek, Jake. "Purity and Pollution: Racial Degradation and Environmental Anxieties." *Liberation Ecologies: Environment, Development, Social Movements*. Ed. Richard Peet and Michael Watts. New York: Routledge, 1996. 115–52.

Kovel, Joel. *The Enemy of Nature: The End of Capitalism or the End of the World?*
London: Zed, 2002.

LaChapelle, Dolores. "Ritual Is Essential." Devall and Sessions 247–50.

Landon, Brooks. *Science Fiction After 1900: From Steam Man to the Stars.* New York:
Twayne, 1997.

Lahar, Stephanie. "Roots: Rejoining Natural and Social History." Gaard 91–117.

Latham, Rob. "Biotic Invasions: Ecological Imperialism in New Wave Science Fiction."
The Yearbook of English Studies 37.2 (2007): 103–19.

Leach, Melissa. *Rainforest Relations: Gender and Resource Use among the Mende of
Gola, Sierra Leone.* London: Edinburgh University Press, 1994.

Lebow, Victor. "Price Competition in 1955." *Journal of Retailing* 31.1 (1955): 5–10,
42.

Lee, Richard B., and Irven DeVore. Introduction. *Man the Hunter.* Ed. Richard B. Lee
and Irven DeVore. Hawthorne, NY: Aldine de Gruyter, 1968. 3–12.

Le Guin, Ursula K. *Always Coming Home.* Berkeley: University of California Press,
1985.

———. Introduction. *The Left Hand of Darkness.* New York: Ace, 1969.

———. "Introduction to *The Word for World Is Forest.*" 1977. *The Language of the
Night: Essays on Fantasy and Science Fiction.* Ed. Susan Wood. New York: G. P.
Putnam's Sons, 1979. 149–54.

———. *The Word for World Is Forest.* New York: Berkley, 1972.

Leopold, Aldo. *A Sand County Almanac and Sketches Here and There.* New York:
Oxford University Press, 1949.

Love, Glen A. *Practical Ecocriticism: Literature, Biology, and the Environment.* Charlottesville: University of Virginia Press, 2003.

Löwy, Michael. "What Is Ecosocialism?" *Ecosocialism or Barbarism.* Ed. Jane Kelly
and Sheila Malone. London: Socialist Resistance, 2006. 1–12.

Luckhurst, Roger. *Science Fiction.* Cambridge: Polity, 2005.

Maciunas, Billie. "Feminist Epistemology in Piercy's *Woman on the Edge of Time.*"
Women's Studies 20 (1992): 249–58.

Mander, Jerry, and Edward Goldsmith, eds. *The Case Against the Global Economy and
for a Turn Toward the Local.* San Francisco: Sierra Club, 1996.

———. "Engines of Globalization." Mander and Goldsmith 295–96.

Marber, Peter. *Money Change Everything: How Global Prosperity Is Reshaping Our
Needs, Values, and Lifestyles.* Upper Saddle River, NJ: Pearson, 2003.

McKibben, Bill. *Deep Economy: The Wealth of Communities and the Durable Future.*
New York: Holt, 2007.

———. *The End of Nature.* New York: Anchor, 1989.

Meadows, Donella H. et al., eds. *The Limits to Growth: A Report for the Club of
Rome's Project on the Predicament of Mankind.* New York: Universe, 1972.

Mellor, Mary. *Feminism & Ecology.* New York: New York University Press, 1997.

Merchant, Carolyn, ed. *Ecology.* Amherst, NY: Humanity, 1999.

———. *Radical Ecology: The Search for a Livable World.* New York: Routledge, 1992.

Mogen, David. *Wilderness Visions: The Western Theme in Science Fiction.* San Bernardino: Borgo, 1993.

Mohr, Dunja M. *Worlds Apart?: Dualism and Transgression in Contemporary Female
Dystopias.* Jefferson, NC: McFarland, 2005.

Moore, Kathleen Dean. "The Truth of the Barnacles: Rachel Carson and the Moral
Significance of Wonder." *Rachel Carson: Legacy and Challenge.* Ed. Lisa H. Sid-

eris and Kathleen Dean Moore. Albany: State University of New York Press, 2008. 267–80.

Morton, Timothy. *Ecology Without Nature: Rethinking Environmental Aesthetics.* Cambridge: Harvard University Press, 2007.

Moylan, Tom. *Demand the Impossible: Science Fiction and the Utopian Imagination.* New York: Methuen, 1986.

———. *Scraps of the Untainted Sky: Science Fiction, Utopia, Dystopia.* Boulder: Westview, 2000.

Murphy, Patrick D. *Ecocritical Explorations in Literary and Cultural Studies: Fences, Boundaries, and Fields.* Lanham, MD: Lexington, 2009. ρ · 6

———. *Farther Afield in the Study of Nature-Oriented Literature.* Charlottesville: University Press of Virginia, 2000.

———. "The Non-Alibi of Alien Scapes: SF and Ecocriticism." *Beyond Nature Writing: Expanding the Boundaries of Ecocriticism.* Ed. Karla Armbruster and Kathleen R. Wallace. Charlottesville: University Press of Virginia, 2001. 263–78.

Naess, Arne. "The Deep Ecology Movement." Sessions 64–84.

———. "Deep Ecology and Lifestyle." Sessions 259–61.

———. *Ecology, Community, and Lifestyle: Outline of an Ecosophy.* Ed. David Rothenberg. New York: Cambridge University Press, 1989.

———. "The Shallow and the Deep, Long-Range Ecology Movements: A Summary." Sessions 151–55.

Nicholls, Peter, and Cornel Robu. "Sense of Wonder." *The Encyclopedia of Science Fiction.* Ed. John Clute and Peter Nicholls. New York: St. Martin's, 1995. 1083–85.

Nijhuis, Michelle. "A Sci-Fi Writer and an Environmental Journalist Explore Their Overlapping Worlds." *Grist.org.* Grist, 21 Feb. 2008. Web. 9 Oct. 2009.

O'Connor, James. *Natural Causes: Essays in Ecological Marxism.* New York: Guilford, 1998.

O'Reilly, Timothy. *Frank Herbert.* New York: Frederick Unger, 1981.

Orr, David W. *Ecological Literacy: Education and the Transition to a Postmodern World.* Albany: State University of New York Press, 1992.

Ortner, Sherry B. "Is Female to Male as Nature Is to Culture?" *Readings in Ecology and Feminist Theology.* Ed. Mary Heather MacKinnon and Moni McIntyre. Kansas City: Sheed & Ward, 1995. 36–55.

Osborn, Fairfield. *Our Plundered Planet.* Boston: Little, Brown and Company, 1948.

Patrick, Amy M. "Apocalyptic of Precautionary? Revisioning Texts in Environmental Literature." *Coming Into Contact: Explorations in Ecocritical Theory and Practice.* Ed. Annie Merrill Ingram, Ian Marshall, Daniel J. Philippon, and Adam W. Sweeting. Athens: University of Georgia Press, 2007. 141–53.

Pepper, David. *Modern Environmentalism: An Introduction.* London: Routledge, 1996.

———. "Utopianism and Environmentalism." *Environmental Politics* 14.1 (2005): 3–22.

Phillips, Dana. *The Truth of Ecology: Nature, Culture, and Literature in America.* Oxford: Oxford University Press, 2003.

Piercy, Marge. *Woman on the Edge of Time.* New York: Fawcett, 1976.

Plant, Judith, ed. *Healing the Wounds: The Promise of Ecofeminism.* Philadelphia: New Society, 1989.

———. "Searching for Common Ground: Ecofeminism and Bioregionalism." Diamond and Orenstein 155–61.

Plumwood, Val. *Environmental Culture: The Ecological Crisis of Reason.* London: Routledge, 2002.

———. *Feminism and the Mastery of Nature.* London: Routledge, 1993.

Pohl, Frederik, and C. M. Kornbluth. *The Space Merchants.* New York: St. Martin's, 1952.

Prentice, Susan. "Taking Sides: What's Wrong with Eco-Feminism?" *Women and Environments* 10 (1988): 9–10.

Quinby, Lee. "Ecofeminism and the Politics of Resistance." Diamond and Orenstein 122–27.

Robin, Marie-Monique. *The World According to Monsanto: Pollution, Corruption, and the Control of the World's Food Supply.* New York: The New Press, 2010.

Robinson, Frank M. *Science Fiction of the 20th Century: An Illustrated History. Art of Imagination: 20th Century Visions of Science Fiction, Horror, and Fantasy.* Ed. Frank M. Robinson, Robert Weinberg, and Randy Broecker. Portland, OR: Collector's, 2002. 13–262.

Robinson, Kim Stanley. *Blue Mars.* New York: Bantam, 1996.

———. *Fifty Degrees Below.* New York: Bantam, 2005.

———, ed. *Future Primitive: The New Ecotopias.* New York: Tor, 1994.

———. *Green Mars.* New York: Bantam, 1994.

———. *Red Mars.* New York: Bantam, 1993.

Rockström, Johan et al. "A Safe Operating Space for Humanity." *Nature* 461 (2009): 472–75.

Rusert, Britt M. "Black Nature: The Question of Race in the Age of Ecology." *Polygraph* 22 (2010): 149–66.

Sanders, Scott Russell. "Mountain Music." *The Impossible Will Take a Little While: A Citizen's Guide to Hope in a Time of Fear.* Ed. Paul Rogat Loeb. New York: Basic, 2004. 99–105.

Sandilands, Catriona. *The Good-Natured Feminist: Ecofeminism and the Quest for Democracy.* Minneapolis: University of Minnesota Press, 1999.

Sandner, David. "'Habituated to the Vast': Ecocriticism, the Sense of Wonder, and the Wilderness of Stars." *Extrapolation* 41.3 (2000): 283–97.

Sargent, Lyman Tower. "The Three Faces of Utopianism Revisited." *Utopian Studies* 5.1 (1994): 1–37.

Scigaj, Leonard M. "*Prana* and the Presbyterian Fixation: Ecology and Technology in Frank Herbert's *Dune* Tetralogy." *Extrapolation* 24.4 (1983): 340–55.

Sears, Paul B. "Ecology—A Subversive Subject." *BioScience* 14.7 (1964): 11–13.

Sessions, George, ed. *Deep Ecology for the 21st Century: Readings on the Philosophy and Practice of the New Environmentalism.* Boston: Shambala, 1995.

———. "Deep Ecology as Worldview." *Worldviews and Ecology: Religion, Philosophy, and the Environment.* Ed. Mary Evelyn Tucker and John A. Grimm. New York: Orbis, 1994. 207–27.

———. "Ecocentrism and the Anthropocentric Detour." Sessions 156–83.

Shepard, Paul. "Ecology and man—A Viewpoint." Shepard and McKinley 1–10.

Shepard, Paul, and Daniel McKinley, eds. *The Subversive Science: Essays Toward an Ecology of Man.* Boston: Houghton, 1969.

Shiva, Vandana. *Biopiracy: The Plunder of Nature and Knowledge.* Boston: South End, 1997. p 43

Shklovsky, Viktor. "Art as Technique." *Russian Formalist Criticism: Four Essays.* Ed. Lee T. Lemon and Marion J. Reis. Lincoln: University of Nebraska Press, 1965. 3–24.

Slonczewski, Joan. *A Door Into Ocean*. New York: Orb, 1986.

———. "A Door Into Ocean: Study Guide." Kenyon U, 4 Jan. 2001. Web. 13 May 2005.

Snyder, Gary. "Four Changes." Sessions 141–50.

Sobchack, Vivian. *Screening Space: The American Science Fiction Film*. New Brunswick: Rutgers University Press, 1998.

Spiegel, Simon. "Things Made Strange: On the Concept of 'Estrangement' in Science Fiction Theory." *Science Fiction Studies* 35.3 (2008): 369–85.

Spretnak, Charlene. "Ecofeminism: Our Roots and Flowering." Diamond and Orenstein 3–14.

Stableford, Brian. "Science Fiction and Ecology." *A Companion to Science Fiction*. Ed. David Seed. Malden, MA: Blackwell, 2005. 127–41.

Stapledon, Olaf. *Last and First Men: A Story of the Near and Far Future*. 1931. New York: Dover, 1968.

Starhawk. "Feminist, Earth-Based Spirituality and Ecofeminism." Plant 174–85.

Stegner, Wallace Earle. *Where the Bluebird Sings to the Lemonade Springs: Living and Writing in the West*. New York: Modern Library, 1992.

Stewart, George R. *Earth Abides*. New York: Ballantine, 1949.

Stratton, Susan. "Intersubjectivity and Difference in Feminist Ecotopias." *FEMSPEC* 3.1 (2001): n.p. Web. 12 July 2005.

———. "The Messiah and the Greens: The Shape of Environmental Action in *Dune* and *Pacific Edge*." *Extrapolation* 42.4 (2001): 303–16.

Sturgeon, Noël. *Ecofeminist Natures: Race, Gender, Feminist Theory, and Political Action*. New York: Routledge, 1997.

Sussman, Herbert. "Victorian Science Fiction." Rev. of *Victorian Science Fiction in the UK: The Discourses of Knowledge and of Power*. *Science Fiction Studies* 11.3 (1984): 324–28.

Suvin, Darko. *Metamorphoses of Science Fiction: On the Poetics and History of a Literary Genre*. New Haven: Yale University Press, 1979.

———. *Victorian Science Fiction in the UK: The Discourses of Knowledge and of Power*. Boston: G. K. Hall, 1983.

Szeman, Imre. "The Cultural Politics of Oil: On *Lessons of Darkness* and *Black Sea Files*." *Polygraph* 22 (2010): 33–45.

Taylor, Bron. *Dark Green Religion: Nature Spirituality and the Planetary Future*. Berkeley: University of California Press, 2010.

———, ed. *The Encyclopedia of Religion and Nature*. 2 vols. London: Thoemmes, 2005.

———. "Snyder, Gary (1930–) - and the Invention of Bioregional Spirituality and Politics." Taylor, *Encyclopedia* 1562–67.

Taylor, Bron R., and Michael Zimmerman. "Deep Ecology." Taylor, *Encyclopedia*, 456–60.

Tokar, Brian. *Earth for Sale: Reclaiming Ecology in the Age of Corporate Greenwash*. Cambridge: South End, 1997.

Twitchell, James B. *Living It Up: America's Love Affair with Luxury*. New York: Simon & Schuster, 2002.

van der Bogert, Frans. "Nature through Science Fiction." *The Intersection of Science Fiction and Philosophy*. Ed. Robert E. Myers. Westport, CT: Greenwood, 1983. 57–69.

Vincenzi, S., Crivelli, A. J., Jesensek, D., and De Leo, G. A. "Detection of Density-

Dependent Growth at Two Spatial Scales in Marble Trout (Salmo Marmoratus) Populations." *Ecology of Freshwater Fish* 19 (2010): 338–47.

Waage, Fred. *The Crucial Role of the Environment in the Writings of George Stewart (1895–1980): A Life of America's Literary Ecologist.* Lewiston, NY: Edwin Mellen, 2006.

Wall, Derek. *The Rise of the Green Left: Inside the Worldwide Ecosocialist Movement.* New York: Pluto, 2010.

Warren, Karen J. *Ecofeminist Philosophy: A Western Perspective on What It Is and Why It Matters.* Lanham, MD: Rowman, 2000.

Wegner, Phillip E. *Imaginary Communities: Utopia, the Nation, and the Spatial Histories of Modernity.* Berkeley: University of California Press, 2002.

Wells, H.G. *The Island of Dr. Moreau.* 1896. New York: Tor, 1996.

Westoby, Mark. "What Does 'Ecology' Mean?" *TREE* 12.4 (1997): 166.

White, Lynn, Jr. "The Historical Roots of Our Ecological Crisis." *Science* 155 (1967): 1203–7.

Wildcat, Daniel R. *Red Alert!: Saving the Planet with Indigenous Knowledge.* Golden, CO: Fulcrum, 2009.

Wilkinson, Jessica, Sara Vickerman, and Jeff Lerner. "Conserving Biodiversity Through State and Regional Planning." *Nature in Fragments: The Legacy of Sprawl.* Ed. Elizabeth Ann Johnson and Michael W. Klemens. New York: Columbia University Press, 2005. 284–312.

Wollheim, Donald A. *The Universe Makers: Science Fiction Today.* New York: Harper, 1971.

Wolmark, Jenny. *Aliens and Others: Science Fiction, Feminism and Postmodernism.* Iowa City: University of Iowa Press, 1994.

World Commission on Environment and Development. *Our Common Future.* Oxford: Oxford University Press, 1987.

Worster, Donald. *Nature's Economy: A History of Ecological Ideas.* 2nd ed. Cambridge: Cambridge University Press, 1994.

Yanarella, Ernest J. *The Cross, the Plow, and the Skyline: Contemporary Science Fiction and the Ecological Imagination.* Parkland, FL: Brown Walker, 2001.

Zimmerman, Michael E. "Martin Heidegger: Antinaturalist Critic of Technological Modernity." *Minding Nature: The Philosophers of Ecology.* Ed. David Macauley. New York: Guilford, 1996. 59–81.

 Žižek, Slavoj. *In Defense of Lost Causes.* London: Verso, 2008.

———. *Living in the End Times.* London: Verso, 2010.

INDEX

Abbey, Edward, 12–14, 70
Abrahamic religion, 31, 39, 58
advertising, 101, 103, 105–7, 109, 120, 121
agriculture, 4, 5, 34, 40, 125
Alaimo, Stacy, 77, 82, 131n4
Always Coming Home (Le Guin), 6, 75, 87–93, 99–100
American Romanticism, 47
American West, the, 105; and frontiersmanship, 107
androcentrism, 19, 74, 111
animal liberation, 4
Animism, 57, 133n5
anothers, 88, 90
anthropocentrism, 5, 19, 25, 34, 45, 52, 72, 75, 96–97, 111
anthropology, 34, 76–77, 81, 112
apocalypse, 3, 8, 30–31, 33–34, 46, 126n12; in *Silent Spring* (Carson), 125n4
April Fool's Day, 34
Armbruster, Karla, 75, 131n1
Armstrong, Jeanette, 114–15
astonishment: and sense of wonder, 13–14

Atlantic Ocean, 13
atomic weapons, 28, 71, 94, 109
automobiles, 33, 68
Avatar (Cameron), 132n5
awe: and sense of wonder, 13, 116. See also marvels; wonder

Bacigalupi, Paolo, 10–11, 15–16, 122–25
Baconian science, 24
Baker, Susan, 67
Barnhill, David Landis, 25
Baxter, Brian, 14
Bellamy, Edward, 48
Biehl, Janet, 80, 85, 92, 96
biodiversity, 16, 25, 45, 67; loss of, 68, 121. See also species extinction
biology, 21, 27, 80, 95, 124; Darwinian, 5, 23, 27, 29
bioregionalism, 4, 59, 72–73, 78
biosphere, 29, 32, 66, 72
Birkeland, Janis, 98
Blue Mars (Robinson), 117–18
Bookchin, Murray, 65, 72, 96, 129n12
Booker, M. Keith, 105

Borlik, Todd A., 29
Bowers, C. A., 58
Brin, David, 3
British Petroleum, 121
British Romanticism, 47
Brown, Lester R., 54–55
Brunner, John, 3, 5–6, 11, 47, 50, 61–72, 73, 100, 124–25, 130n4, 131n13
Buddhism, 57
Buell, Lawrence, 3
Bukeavich, Neal, 62
Burling, William J., 117–18, 120
Byrd, David G., 30

Callenbach, Ernest, 5, 6, 40, 45–47, 52–53, 57, 59, 61, 67–68, 71, 73, 100
"Calorie Man, The" (Bacigalupi), 10, 125
Cameron, James, 132n5
capitalism: and dissatisfaction, 103; and erosion of tradition, 106, 115; global, 19, 47, 54, 62, 65, 101–2, 104–10; and greed, 126, 131n14; and growth imperative, 5, 80, 103; and profit motive, 68, 80, 103. See also ecosocialism; socialism
Capra, Fritjof, 48
carbon dioxide, 2, 132n2. See also climate change
care, 78, 88
Carlassare, Elizabeth, 81
carrying capacity, 129n3
Carson, Rachel, 1, 5, 8, 9, 11, 68, 74, 127n4, 128n6; and part-of-nature thinking, 23–24, 40; and sense of wonder, 12–15
Cartesianism, 29, 32
Catton, William R., Jr., 24
Children of Dune (Herbert), 39
Christ, Carol P., 79
Christianity, 3, 33; and dominion, 24; Franciscan, 47; Western, 128n3. See also Abrahamic religion
Christmas, 34, 63
Cicero, 129n11; and second nature, 40, 129n11
Clark, Brett, 17, 20, 131n14, 132n1

Clarke, Tony, 106
class, 37, 43, 75, 102–4, 111, 118–19, 126
classism, 35, 37
climate change, 2, 22, 121. See also carbon dioxide
climate science, 2; denial of, 17, 121
Club of Rome, 11
coal, 27–28, 104
cognitive estrangement, 8–10, 49. See also defamiliarization; diegetic estrangement; estrangement; ostranenie
Cokinos, Christopher, 4
Coleridge, Samuel Taylor, 12
Collard, Andrée, 78–79, 92
colonialism, 5, 37, 43, 92, 95–96, 102, 113–14, 125, 133n2
commons, the, 119–20
conditions of production, 104, 115, 120
consumerism, 5–6, 9, 54–55, 59–60, 62, 64–65, 105, 108, 110
contraception, 53
convenience, 29, 32
Cooper, David E., 45
Cravens, Hamilton, 27
Creed, Barbara, 26–27
critical dystopia, 50–51, 71
Crystal Age, A (Hudson), 27
Csicsery-Ronay, Istvan, Jr., 127n5
cultural homogenization, 63, 73, 81, 106

Darwin, Charles, 5, 23, 26–27, 29
DDT, 68
de Beauvoir, Simone, 76
deep ecology, 4, 5, 6, 19, 25, 45, 47–49, 52, 54–62, 64–73, 74, 75, 77, 96, 102–3, 110–11, 124, 129n1, 129n2, 130n5, 130n8, 131n14, 131n2, 132n1; and anti-immigration, 130n9; and community, 53–54, 58–59; idealism of, 132n1; and overpopulation, 5, 50, 52–54, 56, 60–62, 64, 65; and spirituality, 25, 48, 57, 75, 84, 88
defamiliarization, 7, 50. See also cognitive estrangement; diegetic estrangement; estrangement; ostranenie

deforestation, 46, 112
de Geus, Marius, 61, 130n12
de Lauretis, Teresa, 131n1
Delicate Arch, 12
democracy, 102, 120
Descent of Man, The (Darwin), 26
Devall, Bill, 46, 47–49, 58, 129n2
DeVore, Irven, 34
Diamond, Irene, 78
diegetic estrangement, 10. *See also* cognitive estrangement; defamiliarization; estrangement; *ostranenie*
difference: cultural, 73, 75, 106; ecological, 12, 14; gender, 12, 85–86, 99
discourse: and place, 32–33
disembeddedness, 20, 21, 24, 29, 31, 34–35, 39, 60, 71, 123. *See also* Illusion of Disembeddedness
Dispossessed, The (Le Guin), 48
Dobrin, Sidney I., 32
domestication, 22, 67
dominion, 24, 27
Door Into Ocean, A (Slonczewski), 6, 15, 75, 91–92, 94–99
Drake, Barbara, 130n6
drought, 2, 25
dualism, 19, 21, 26, 33, 60, 75, 87, 92–94, 97, 125, 130n11, 131n2
Dune (Herbert), 5, 6, 16, 20–21, 35–44, 51, 100, 130n8
Dune Messiah (Herbert), 42–43
Dunlap, Riley E., 24
Duraiappah, Anantha Kumar, 2
Dwyer, Jim, 58
Dynes, William, 119
dystopia, 5, 6, 8, 9, 47, 49–50, 61–64, 66, 68, 84, 85, 100, 124. *See also* ecodystopia; ecotopia; utopia

Earth Abides (Stewart), 6, 20–21, 26, 29–36, 39, 44, 100, 128n5
Earth (Brin), 3
Earth Day, 128n6
Earth First!, 70, 131n15
Earth Liberation Front, 70, 131n15
Earth Policy Institute, 54
Eastern spiritual traditions, 47

ecocentrism, 21, 30, 39, 40, 52, 56–58, 60, 69, 70, 78, 91, 96
ecocriticism, 3, 18, 123, 126
Ecodeath (Vonnegut), 130n4
ecodystopia, 5, 9, 10, 44, 49, 50, 61, 66, 71–73, 122, 124. *See also* dystopia; ecotopia; utopia
eco-economics, 117–18, 120
ecofascism, 124
ecofeminism: affinity, 75–76; constructionist, 75–76, 92–93, 98; cultural, 6, 57, 76–83, 84, 86–88, 91–93, 95–97, 99, 125, 131n2, 131n3, 131n4; dialectical, 6, 92, 93, 96, 131n5; and essentialism, 6, 83, 87, 131n4; social, 96. *See also* feminism
ecofiction, 18
ecological ethics, 3, 7, 12–16, 18, 19, 56, 80. *See also* environmental ethics; ethics of sexual difference
ecological footprint, 60, 72
ecological literacy, 22, 41, 58, 130n7
ecology, 3, 21, 36–38, 40–41, 54, 58, 72, 91, 98, 106, 112, 114, 117; as language of the house, 78; as subversive science, 22–25
economic growth, 5, 11, 45–46, 54–55, 64–66, 72, 101, 109–10, 115, 129n2, 131n14
ecopolitics, 119
ecosocialism, 5, 6, 7, 19, 25–26, 101–2, 104, 111, 118, 120, 125; and class, 102; and deep ecology, 131n14, 132n1; and democracy, 102, 120; and socialism, 102, 118. *See also* capitalism; socialism
ecospirituality, 57, 58, 60, 75–76, 79, 84, 88, 91, 93
ecotage, 50
ecoterrorism, 5
ecotopia, 5, 9, 40, 47–50, 52, 55, 60–62, 64, 67, 69–70, 72–73, 95, 99, 100, 105, 124, 130n8, 130n12. *See also* dystopia; ecodystopia; utopia
Ecotopia (Callenbach), 5, 40, 45–61, 69, 71, 132n3
education, 22, 49, 57–58, 60, 130n7; conservative models of, 57–58; liberal models of, 58

egalitarianism, 52, 79
egotism, 12
Ehrlich, Paul, 61, 130n4
Eisler, Riane, 79, 84
Elgin, Don D., 128n3
embeddedness, 18, 20, 21, 24, 26, 29, 31–33, 35, 37, 39, 41, 43, 48–49, 58, 63, 82, 88, 94, 98, 106, 114–15, 118. *See also* disembeddedness; Illusion of Disembeddedness
Emerson, Ralph Waldo, 13
emotion, 12–13, 60, 92, 98, 128n7
empathy, 78
End of the Dream, The (Wylie), 130n4
Enlightenment, the, 41
entropy, 117
environmental degradation, 1–2, 4, 6, 7, 17, 46, 59, 63, 65, 68, 71, 73, 101, 104, 120–21, 131n14, 132n1
environmental ethics, 3, 7, 13–15, 18, 80; and ecological difference, 12, 14; and sense of wonder, 12, 14–16. *See also* ecological ethics; ethics of sexual difference
environmental humanities, 126
environmentalism, 1, 3, 5, 11, 17, 23, 26, 28, 35, 46, 74–75, 78, 128n6, 130n9; strategies for activism, 71. *See also* transformative environmentalism
environmental literature, 2, 4
environmental nonfiction, 7, 9–11, 16
environmental policy, 1, 46
environmental science fiction, 4–7, 10, 11, 14–16, 18, 30, 38, 40, 100–101, 103, 111–13, 121
environmental studies, 4, 126
Errington, Paul L., 30–31
essentialism, 6, 83, 87, 97, 131n4
estrangement, 7–11, 17, 31, 127n5. *See also* cognitive estrangement; defamiliarization; diegetic estrangement; *ostranenie*
ethics of sexual difference, 12. *See also* ecological ethics; environmental ethics
ethnicity, 75
evolution, 18, 23, 26, 27, 53, 72,129n12

exchange value, 102
expansionism, 26
expediency, 42
extinction, 2, 22; of humans, 20, 29, 34; of nonhuman animals, 2, 22, 41, 46, 50, 120, 121
extrapolation, 3, 7, 10–11, 17, 49, 112; as global awareness, 11
Eyerman, Ron, 7

family: alternative models of, 53, 54, 88; nuclear, 88; patriarchal, 89, 97
fantastic, the, 12
fantasy, 8, 17, 82
far-future history, 20
farms, 9, 104, 107, 123, 125
faucet, 10, 31–32, 43
feminine, the, 6, 76, 82, 84, 85, 95, 98, 131n2
feminism, 17, 47, 54, 74–75, 77–78, 87, 131n5; liberal, 78; radical, 77, 85; rationalist, 80, 92, 93, 96, 131n4. *See also* ecofeminism
Fifty Degrees Below (Robinson), 13, 122
fire, 25
first nations, 88
first nature, 40, 130n8. *See also* nature; second nature; third nature
fisheries, 55, 119
flood, 25
food, 9, 11, 22, 32, 40, 51, 59, 66, 68, 69, 105, 119, 123–25, 133n1
forests, 16, 43, 46, 55, 58, 65, 101, 110–13, 132n2
Foster, John Bellamy, 17, 20, 26, 104, 117, 131n14, 132n1
Freedman, Carl, 8
freedom, 30
French Revolution, 128n3
freshwater use, 2, 104
future, the, 2, 3, 4, 7, 10, 16, 28, 34, 50, 113. *See also* extrapolation

Gaard, Greta, 74, 96
Gaia, 79, 82, 84

Gearhart, Sally Miller, 6, 75, 76, 81–86, 91–93, 95, 99–100
gender, 6, 19, 26, 75, 80–81, 84–85, 88, 91, 93, 96–99, 119, 129n3
Gimbutas, Marija, 79
glacial melting, 13. *See also* climate change
Glen Canyon Dam, 14
globalism: contrast with localism, 3
globalization, 105, 106
GMOs, 10, 43, 123, 133n2; and Monsanto, 124–25, 133n1
GNP, 56, 101
goddess-worship, 79–80
Golden Age science fiction, 17
Goldsmith, Edward, 106
Gore, Al, 24
Gottlieb, Roger S., 25
Gough, Noel, 1, 2, 36
Green Mars (Robinson), 120
green politics, 4, 104
grocery store, 9, 31–32
Groundhog Day, 34
Gruen, Lori, 77
Gulf of Mexico, 121
Gulf Stream, 13
Gulf War (1991), 132n2

Halloween, 34
handicrafts, 55, 69
Haraway, Donna, 131n1
Harrison, Harry, 130n4
Heinzerling, Lisa, 1
Heise, Ursula K., 2–3, 129n3
"Help Your Child to Wonder" (Carson), 12
Herbert, Frank, 5, 6, 16, 20, 35, 40–41, 44
hierarchy, 52, 73, 75, 77–78, 82, 89–91, 94, 97–98, 103, 111, 118–19; and social ecology, 96–97
historical materialism, 19
holidays, 34; Abrahamic, 31, 34; national, 31, 34; seasonal, 33
Hopkins, Kathryn, 132n5
Hovanec, Carol P., 113
Howard, June, 85

Hudson, William Henry, 27
human health, 46, 127n4
human–nonhuman relationships, 6, 59, 75, 111
hunger, 124
hunting and gathering, 34, 40, 128n3
Hunt, John Dixon, 129n11, 129n12
Huston, Shaun, 129n12
Huxley, T. H., 27

idealism: of cultural ecofeminism, 79; of deep ecology, 132n1
identity: and commodities, 106; in deep ecology, 60, 68; and gender, 75, 85, 131n1
ideology: capitalist, 9, 35, 37, 55, 63, 64, 107–11, 132n3; Nazi, 128n4; patriarchal, 84, 97, 99
Illusion of Disembeddedness, 20–21, 24, 27, 29, 34–35, 39, 123. *See also* disembeddedness; embeddedness
imagination, 12–13, 103; utopian, 48
imperialism, 7, 35, 62, 100
indigenous peoples, 5, 36–38, 47, 67, 102, 106, 114, 128n8, 132n5. *See also* native societies
individualism, 5, 25, 58
Industrial Age, 88, 91, 95
Industrial Revolution, 128n3
insecticides, 9, 23, 66, 94. *See also* pesticides
instrumental rationality, 45, 71, 129n1
interdependence, 40, 47, 77, 83, 92, 119
intergenerational responsibility, 41, 128n6
intrinsic value: of nonhuman nature, 37, 48, 102
intuition, 92
Iraq, 125
Irigaray, Luce, 12
Island of Dr. Moreau, The (Wells), 27

Jameson, Fredric, 100, 109, 110
Jamison, Andrew, 7
Judeo-Christian theology: and apocalypse, 3; and human dominion, 24

Katz, Eric, 129n1
Killingsworth, M. Jimmie, 127n4
King, Ynestra, 92–93, 96, 131n5
kinship, 25, 53, 75, 79, 84, 88
Kornbluth, C. M., 7, 101, 106–7, 109, 116
Kosek, Jake, 130n9
Kovel, Joel, 101, 103, 117–19

LaChapelle, Dolores, 33
lactation, 76
land ethic, 4, 60, 128n1
Landon, Brooks, 128n7
landscapes, 12, 22, 57, 67, 116; alien, 12; cultural, 129n11; restoration of, 4
land use, 2, 59, 102
language, 25, 32–33, 38, 77; capitalist, 56, 107, 110; in ecofeminism, 78, 85, 89–91
Lahar, Stephanie, 98
Last and First Men (Stapledon), 20–21, 26–29, 35, 39, 44, 100, 122
late capitalism, 109
Latham, Rob, 17
Lathe of Heaven, The (Le Guin), 3
Leach, Melissa, 77
Lebow, Victor, 101
Lee, Richard B., 34
Le Guin, Ursula K., 3, 6–7, 48, 75–76, 87, 89, 91–93, 95, 99, 100–101, 110–17
Leopold, Aldo, 23, 68; and land ethic, 60, 128n1
Lerner, Jeff, 67
life sciences, 1, 22, 24, 38–39
Light, Andrew, 129n1
Limits to Growth, The (Meadows), 11
localism, 3, 124
logic of domination, 74, 82, 95
Looking Backward (Bellamy), 48
Love, Glen A., 22–23
Löwy, Michael, 103
Luckhurst, Roger, 101

Maciunas, Billie, 71
Macy, Joanna, 79

Make Room! Make Room! (Harrison), 130n4
Malthusianism, 46, 65, 131n14
Mandel, Ernest, 109
Mander, Jerry, 106
Marber, Peter, 106
marriage, 53
Mars: terraforming of, 15–16
Mars trilogy (Robinson), 7, 15–16, 101, 104, 115–21, 125
marvels, 7, 11–15. See also awe; sense of wonder; wonder
Marxism, 9, 104, 117
Marx, Karl, 19, 104
masculinity, 77, 88–90, 93, 97–98
matriarchy, 79, 88
McKibben, Bill, 16, 65, 68, 125
McKinley, Daniel, 30
Meadows, Donella H. See Limits to Growth, The
means of production, 102–3, 118, 119
Mellor, Mary, 96, 131n2
menstruation, 76
Merchant, Carolyn, 101, 104, 132n2
militarism, 22, 81, 89, 92, 94, 96, 98, 132n2, 132n5
Minoan Crete, 79–80
misogyny, 83, 85, 111
modernity, 82, 132n1; absence of, 32–33; and disembeddedness, 35; and economy, 44, 55; and ideology, 52; and industry, 89; and nonhuman nature, 68, 82, 110; and part-of-nature thinking, 40, 43
Mogen, David, 105, 109
Mohr, Dunja M., 49, 61
Monkey Wrench Gang, The (Abbey), 70
monoculture agriculture, 5, 34, 40, 102
monotheism, 90. See also Abrahamic religion
Monsanto, 124–25; and Terminator technology, 124, 133n1. See also GMOs
Moore, Kathleen Dean, 12, 14–15
More, Thomas, 48
Morton, Timothy, 40
Moylan, Tom, 48–50, 61, 63
Muir, John, 4
Murphy, Patrick D., 3, 10, 88, 90, 124, 127n1

mythology: capitalist, 112; Christian, 33; Norse, 13

Naess, Arne, 45, 52–53, 55–57, 59, 69, 71, 124, 130n5, 130n9
national parks, 16
native societies, 33, 114–15. *See also* indigenous peoples
Natural Resources Defense Council, 46
nature: as concept, 35, 37–40, 73, 100, 118, 123; and culture, 74, 87, 92–93, 125, 129n11, 133n2; end of, 65; human dependence on, 1, 18–21, 23–27, 29, 37, 48, 63, 117, 125; human exploitation of, 14, 23–24, 27, 38, 62, 64, 85, 97, 100, 104, 109–11, 113, 115; human separation from, 19, 21, 24, 26–27, 29, 32, 34, 44, 48, 58, 102–3, 128n3; and marvels, 12–13, 98; and modernity, 68; and science fiction, 101; self-realization in, 59–60; simulation of, 63–64; and spirituality, 58; value of, 48, 102; and the wild, 57, 67–68, 82, 110, 112; and women, 6, 75–81, 83, 93, 131n4. *See also* disembeddedness; embeddedness; first nature; Illusion of Disembeddedness; intrinsic value; modernity; part-of-nature thinking; second nature; sense of wonder; third nature
Nazi ideology, 128n4
Neolithic culture, 80
Neolithic Revolution, 40
New Wave science fiction, 17
New Years [*sic*] Day, 34
Nicholls, Peter, 128n7
Nijhuis, Michelle, 10
nonviolence, 47, 69, 71, 95, 98, 114, 118
normative ecology, 22–23, 30, 111
novum, 8–10, 54, 82. *See also* cognitive estrangement
nuclear weapons, 94
nurturance, 54, 77, 79, 84, 92, 95

ocean acidification, 2

O'Connor, James, 101–2, 104, 118–20
oil, 10, 43, 65, 115, 121–22, 126, 132n2
Old Europe, 79
O'Reilly, Timothy, 36
Orenstein, Gloria Feman, 78
organic gardening, 9, 130n7
Origin of Species, The (Darwin), 26
Orr, David W., 21–22, 24, 30, 43
Ortner, Sherry B., 76–77, 81
Osborn, Fairfield, 7–8, 11, 127n3
ostranenie, 7, 127n2. *See also* cognitive estrangement; defamiliarization; diegetic estrangement; estrangement
Our Plundered Planet (Osborn), 7
overpopulation, 5, 30–32, 46–47, 50, 52–54, 56, 60–62, 64–66, 72, 129n3

pacifism, 85, 95, 114
Palmer, Jacqueline S., 127n4
partnership 58, 84
part-of-nature thinking, 5, 21, 25, 35, 38–41, 43, 57, 110
passivity, 92, 125, 133n2
pastoral, 3, 8
patenting, 40, 123–25
patriarchy, 5, 6, 52, 60, 76–83, 85, 88–89, 100, 125, 130n11, 133n2
Patrick, Amy M., 127n4
peace, 30, 62, 79, 80, 86, 101
peak oil, 121
"People of Sand and Slag, The" (Bacigalupi), 15
Pepper, David, 19, 72
pesticides, 22, 104. *See also* insecticides
Phillips, Dana, 23
phosphorus, 2
physics, 47
Piercy, Marge, 5, 6, 9, 11, 40, 45–47, 51, 54, 56, 58, 61, 67–68, 71–73, 100, 130n6
place: and discourse, 32–33. *See also* sense of place
Plant, Judith, 78, 92
plumbing, 32, 39, 40
Plumwood, Val, 19–20, 24, 29, 77, 123
Pohl, Frederik, 7, 101, 106–7, 109, 116

politics, 22–25, 37, 41–44, 80, 95, 122–23; and boundaries, 59; colonial, 35, 91; emancipatory, 75, 93, 95; environmental, 4, 62, 75, 119; and oppression, 71, 79, 95; and power, 6, 21, 38, 74; process of, 86, 95, 117–21; and utopia, 49–50, 60, 72

pollution, 2, 46, 50, 52, 68, 103, 109, 132n2

Population Bomb, The (Ehrlich), 61, 130n4

population growth, 64, 131n14. *See also* overpopulation

postapocalyptic fiction, 4, 20

postindustrial age, 109

postnatural, 16, 30, 40, 68

poststructuralism, 75, 131n1

poverty, 62, 107, 124

predation, 22, 68

pregnancy, 76, 79

Prentice, Susan, 79–80, 85, 92, 96, 131n3

profit, 68, 80, 101–3, 106, 108–9

pulp science fiction, 17

Quinby, Lee, 99

race, 75, 97, 103, 111

racism, 35, 37, 80, 96, 111, 130n9

radical ecology, 21. *See also* transformative environmentalism

radioactivity, 22

Reagan, Ronald, 101

realist fiction, 2, 26

Red Mars (Robinson), 15, 115–17

religion, 34, 58, 79, 90. *See also* Abrahamic religion

reproductive technology, 54

ritual, 33

Robin, Marie-Monique, 124

Robinson, Frank M., 112

Robinson, Kim Stanley, 4, 7, 13–16, 101, 115–17, 122

Robu, Cornel, 128n7

Rockström, Johan, 2

Rothenberg, David, 129n1

Rusert, Britt M., 130n9

Sanders, Scott Russell, 132n4

Sandilands, Catriona, 54, 92, 131n5

Sandner, David, 12–13

Sargent, Lyman Tower, 48–49, 50

scarcity, 11, 24, 109, 116, 120

science, 2, 7, 10, 21–25, 27, 38–39, 47, 93, 95, 103; denial of, 17, 42

science fiction: and the frontier, 105; role in environmentalism, 17–18, 100, 112–13; and technophilia, 20; Victorian, 26–27. *See also* cognitive estrangement; defamiliarization; diegetic estrangement; estrangement; extrapolation; Golden Age science fiction; New Wave science fiction; pulp science fiction; sense of wonder

Science in the Capital trilogy (Robinson), 13

science journalism, 10

scientific revolution, 24

Scigaj, Leonard M., 42

Sears, Paul B., 22, 24

self-realization, 59–60, 99

self-sufficiency, 59, 124

sense of place, 3, 59, 84, 91, 98, 130n10

sense of wonder, 11–17, 65, 69, 98, 128n7. *See also* awe; marvels; wonder

Sessions, George, 34, 47–49, 54, 60

sexism, 80, 96

Sheep Look Up, The (Brunner), 5, 11, 47, 61, 65–71, 73, 108, 124, 130n4

Shepard, Paul, 22–24, 30

Shiva, Vandana, 106, 125

Shklovsky, Viktor, 7, 127n2

Sierra Club, 46

Silent Spring (Carson), 1, 8, 23, 68, 128n6

simulation technologies, 63

Slonczewski, Joan, 6, 15, 75–76, 91–99, 100

Snyder, Gary, 52–57, 59, 69, 130n9

Sobchack, Vivian, 109

social ecology, 4, 72, 96

socialism, 102, 118. *See also* capitalism; ecosocialism

social justice, 41, 42, 101, 106, 129n3

sociobiology, 4

soil, 46, 104, 112

something: concept of, 15–16
Soylent Green (Fleischer), 10
Space Merchants, The (Pohl and Korn-
    bluth), 7, 111, 114–17, 121, 125,
    126, 130, 131, 135
species extinction, 2, 32, 51, 56, 60,
    130, 131. *See also* extinction
Spiegel, Simon, 9–10, 127n2
spirituality, 25, 48, 57, 58, 75, 81, 84,
    88, 91, 92, 130n7. *See also* ecospiri-
    tuality
Spretnak, Charlene, 79
Stableford, Brian, 18, 130n4
stable-state economy, 6, 55–56
standard of living, 30, 55, 56, 101
Stand on Zanzibar (Brunner), 3, 5, 47,
    61–65, 68
Stapledon, Olaf, 20, 27–29, 100, 122
Starhawk, 79
state, the, 80
steady-state economics, 4. *See also*
    stable-state economy
Stegner, Wallace, 59, 130n10
sterilization: of humans, 53; of seeds,
    123, 125, 133n1, 133n2
stewardship, 53, 118, 120
Stewart, George R., 6, 20, 29–32,
    34–35, 100
Stratton, Susan, 38, 97
Sturgeon, Noël, 83, 131n4
sulfur, 2
Sussman, Herbert, 26–27
sustainability, 2, 11, 125, 128n6
sustainable agriculture, 4
Suvin, Darko, 8–9, 26–27, 128n7
Szeman, Imre, 126

Taylor, Bron, 57, 60, 131n15
technocentrism, 3, 5, 17, 49
technology, 9, 16, 17, 24, 25, 34, 36,
    39, 63, 73, 77, 84–85, 122, 124,
    129n2, 133n1; end of, 30; reproduc-
    tive, 54
technophilia, 17, 20
terraforming, 15, 38, 41–43
third nature, 44, 63, 68, 129n12. *See
    also* first nature; nature; second
    nature

Thomas, Anne-Marie, 104
Through the Arc of the Rain Forest
    (Yamashita), 3
Tokar, Brian, 106
transformative environmentalism, 1,
    4–6, 16, 18, 19, 21, 24, 25, 38, 39,
    41, 45, 48, 61, 74, 76, 101, 121,
    122–123
Twitchell, James B., 112

use value, 102, 103, 117
utopia, 9, 45, 48–50, 60–61, 63–64,
    69–72, 115, 119, 124, 130n12. *See
    also* dystopia; ecodystopia; ecotopia
Utopia (More), 48
utopian studies, 5, 126

van der Bogert, Frans, 18
Vickerman, Sara, 67
Victorian culture: and Darwinism, 23,
    26–27; and science fiction, 26–27
Vietnam War, 69, 101, 110
violence: and culture, 114–15; and envi-
    ronmentalism, 66, 71–72; as libera-
    tory strategy, 46–47, 72; and sex,
    98. *See also* nonviolence
vivisection, 27
Vonnegut, Kurt, 130n4

Waage, Fred, 128n5
wage labor, 102–3
Wall, Derek, 104, 131n14
Wanderground, The (Gearhart), 6, 75,
    81–87, 90, 91–93, 99
Warren, Karen J., 74
water, 10, 22, 31–32, 36–37, 39, 40–43,
    46, 50, 58, 66, 68, 70, 88, 91, 102,
    110, 120, 121
weapons, 9, 71, 89
weeds, 33
Wegner, Phillip E., 48, 72
Weisser, Christian R., 32
Wells, H. G., 27
Western worldview, 24, 49, 71
Westoby, Mark, 21
White, Lynn, Jr., 24, 33, 128n2

Wildcat, Daniel R., 37, 106, 128n8
wilderness, 12, 13, 33, 36, 44, 54, 57,
    68, 81–82, 89, 91, 129n11, 130n7;
    defense of, 7; domestication of, 22,
    67
wildness, 33
Wilkinson, Jessica, 67
Windup Girl, The (Bacigalupi), 122–26,
    133n2
winter solstice, 34
Wollheim, Donald A., 131n13
Wolmark, Jenny, 84
woman–nature link, 6, 77–79, 93. See
    also ecofeminism
Woman on the Edge of Time (Piercy), 5,
    9, 40, 45–47, 51, 54, 58, 60–61, 69,
    71, 132n3
wonder, 11–17, 65, 69, 98; artifactual,
    14–16; nonhuman, 14–16. See also
    awe; marvels; sense of wonder
Word for World Is Forest, The (Le
    Guin), 7, 101, 110–11, 114–16,
    121, 125
World Commission on Environment and
    Development, 11, 128n6
Worster, Donald, 21
Wylie, Philip, 130n4

Yanarella, Ernest J., 3, 41, 114
York, Richard, 17, 20, 131n14, 132n1

Zimmerman, Michael E., 57, 60, 128n4
Žižek, Slavoj, 40, 43, 44, 121, 126,
    132n5